HEARTS STRANGE AND DREADFUL

TIM MCGREGOR

OFF LIMITS
PRESS

For the bright lights in my constellation; Monique, Ginger, and Ruby.

Rhode Island
April 1821

1

THE LAMB HAD been slaughtered, but the butchering had yet to begin. Neither brother Samuel nor brother Jacob were up for the task, and the two of them stood quarreling about whose role it was to eviscerate our Sunday feast.

"I did the killing," Samuel said, the ax still red in his hand. "And that is the hard part. That leaves you to do the butchering, Jacob."

"And a fine job you did," rebuffed his brother, who, at thirteen years old, considered himself a man. Samuel was seventeen. As was I. My name is Hester Ervin Stokely.

"You bludgeoned the poor thing," Jacob complained. He was right. The lamb's head lay cleaved open in a clumsy manner upon the spring clover. Poor aim and shoddy work on Samuel's part. "Father wanted the brains, but he won't get his head cheese now, will he? Smeared all over the ground like that."

Samuel unsheathed the large carving knife from his belt and thrust the haft into his brother's hands. It was an immense instrument, more than a foot in length. More of a cutlass than a knife really. "Don't shirk your role now, Jacob. Slit the belly and remove the victuals. Daylight is wasting."

More bickering ensued. Jacob and Sam often quarreled, the way brothers do. Sometimes it was good-naturedly and sometimes it grew hot and the two fell to blows until their father, Pardon Stokely, stormed in and tossed each to a corner of the room like pugilists awaiting the bell. Boys will be boys, but they will also be brutes when they want to be. They were not all bad.

I should clarify a few points here. Samuel and Jacob Stokely were not my brothers in the true sense. They were my cousins, but I think of them as brothers as I have been sheltered in their home since the age of twelve when my own parents passed. My uncle, Pardon Stokely, father to Sam and Jacob, took me in and he and his wife Katherine raised me as their own. Or, almost as their own.

The quarreling grew tiresome. I stood waiting with my baskets and bowls to collect the offal and the head cheese, which was now spoiled. Piqued, young Jacob finally took the great knife and bent to the task, but despite his puffed-up bravado, he had no stomach for it. He made one pass with the blade and when the gore rumbled out onto his scuffed shoes, he paled and retreated.

"I can't," he said, wiping the sweat from his brow. With defeated eyes, he looked to his brother, but Samuel shook his head. Then, as was often the way, the brother-cousins turned to me.

"Hester? Please."

So it went. The lowlier the task, the more it fell into my lap. Pardon, my uncle and head of our household, was fond of saying that God molded all men from the same clay and were thus equal in all things. But this was not equivocally so, as the weaker sex were remaindered from that equation. And for the orphaned cousin in a busy household of siblings, there was a caste rank in place, although no one would admit to it. We all choose our own blinders.

The lamb lay in the clover, its skull broken and the blowflies already gathering over the dashed brains. I took the leather apron from Jacob and cinched it tight round my waist. Butchering was a messy business and I worried over ruining my boots; hand-me-downs from my sister-cousin, Prudence, they were the only pair I owned. I unlaced them and kicked them off, along with the stockings, which were also secondhand and mended many times with course thread. The blood I could wash from my feet later.

Taking the large knife from Jacob, I completed the incision he had started, opening the belly all the way to the groin. The steaming intestines were set aside in the basket, to be cleaned and used. The other victuals, like the heart, liver, and spleen I separated and placed in a ceramic bowl. The sweetbreads were trimmed out and placed in another receptacle. My cousins looked on, sometimes turning their heads from the smell of the gore. The inside of an animal is often more pungent than its hide. Butchering was not a new task to my hands, calloused and rough as they are. My mother taught me the skill at an early age, as that task fell to her to perform as my father disliked it so. This was the way of it, and who was I to question its practice? Still, I often wondered in my own impertinent way if perhaps there was something a touch too frail about the Stokely men that they shied from tasks such as butchering an animal. They had their other qualities.

With the offal collected and removed from the hot sun, Samuel and Jacob stepped forward to lash the hind legs of the lamb and hoist it up in the block tackle. I cut through the hide to open the jugular and a geyser of blood ran forth onto the milkweed below. We waited as the carcass swayed on its hemp and fountained its life force onto the earth. Within a week's time, the ground where the blood had spilled would turn lush and verdant with new growth, as nothing revives like blood. I reflected on Abraham and his offering, and of the ancient Hebrews pouring blood onto their altar before the Romans destroyed their temple. I thought also of the blood of our Lord and Savior splashed onto the dusty rock of Golgotha, spilled for our sins and the Redemption thereof. I felt unworthy.

It was impossible not to step onto the blood-slaked ground as I began trimming the hide away. My mother was a deft hand at this, carving through the layer of fat without ruining the meat. I was clumsier but got the job done. With the hide peeled back like some strange garment, I looked down at my blood-stained feet. My toes were crimson, not unlike the manner in which the trollops of Paris are said to wear them. I disliked it and felt ashamed. My hands were slathered to the elbows with scarlet gloves. Red is not a color to be worn lightly and it unsettled me to be stained thus. My skirts and petticoats are gray or a dull brown. Color does not suit me, I have been told.

The hide was folded away to be delivered to the tannery

later. Samuel and Jacob ferried the carcass to the barn where it would hang to age for a few days before further trimming. By then the blowflies were boiling around it in a buzzing, vile mass. I took the basket to the pump and washed my hands and feet before settling down to the noxious business of squeezing the unguents from the intestines and washing the casings in clean, cold water. The sun was going down and Mother Stokely would soon be calling her brood in for the supper hour. I was famished.

2

THE KITCHEN IN my uncle's house was a chaotic place, especially in the early evening, but it was not without warmth and sometimes laughter. Mother Stokely hovered over the large hearth, feeding another birch log onto the flames or stirring the cauldron. She was my aunt, as I have said, but she wished me to call her mother just as her own children did. For reasons that are difficult to articulate, I found this presumptuous, so I met her halfway and called her Mother Stokely or, in intimate moments, Mother Katherine. Mother Stokely was a handsome woman with a kind heart although I have heard others refer to her as stony. Gossips are so tiresome. I have had more than my fair share of tittering, given the scar that mars my face. Mother Stokely bore a few scars herself in the pitted aftermath of smallpox that had left a smattering of divots on an otherwise flawless brow. Her eyes were gray and they sparkled when she laughed, which was not often. She was mindful and judicious in the upbringing of her children; myself included. She had strong hands.

"Do you have the victuals?" she asked, her eyes dropping to the bowl I carried into the kitchen.

I handed it to her. "A smallish amount of it. The lamb

seemed underfed to my eye."

Mother Stokely picked through the soft flesh of the tenders. "And the sweetbreads? They need a delicate hand to extract."

"The pancreas is there, the throat gland also. The casings I wrapped in muslin and put in the icehouse."

A smile eased the puckered stitching around her mouth. "Then our Lord's bounty shall enliven this night's supper," she said. Mother Stokely and her husband shared a fondness for the sweetbreads. I did not.

I scratched a curlicue of dried blood from under a fingernail and moved to the sideboard where the pail of beer sat. I ladled a cup's worth, and a cup only as Samuel and Jacob would want their share when they came in from the day's toil. Gluttons were not tolerated under this roof. Prudence stood at the table kneading dough, although it wasn't baking day. Her slender hands were chalked with flour and more of it dabbed the pert end of her pretty nose. Prudence was the eldest of the Stokely children and my sister-cousin. She had a knack for baking bread that I envied, for my own attempts produced loaves that were either too hard or prone to falling. Pru was two years older and more experienced in her hands, and I took pleasure in watching her pound and roll the dough on the wooden board. She was graceful even in this, but she talked overly much. Her singing was lovely.

Slapping the mound to the wood again, Prudence looked up and saw me observing her. The smile on her pretty face dimmed when she looked down at my feet.

"Hester," she said, rubbing her forearm against her nose, "do put your boots on before entering the kitchen. It's so unladylike."

I had forgotten the boots and stockings in the yard. One of my failings, this absentmindedness. "Glory be," I said, too tired to think of any other response.

Prudence's demeanor shifted immediately, flitting about like a bee from petal to petal. "Do you know who I saw at the merchant's today?"

I knew, of course. As did Mother Stokely. And Pardon, Samuel, Jacob, Hiram and little Polly. His name was James Corwin, and he was Prudence's sweetheart. Nothing had been stated formally, but it was certain that Pru and James were to be wed at some future point. She spoke of little else these days, which led me to believe that a formal announcement was imminent. My sister-cousin was nineteen years old, a grown woman, and too old to be living under her mother's wing. High time to fly from the nest as Mother Katherine whispered to me once as we sat darning at the end of a long day.

"Was it the ghost of Cotton Mather?" I replied. Mother Stokely aimed a withering eye in my direction.

"James, silly," announced Prudence. The apples of her cheeks bloomed. "He's escorting me to the meetinghouse this coming Saturday. Isn't that wonderful?"

"Hallelujah," I replied, too exhausted to elide the sarcasm from my tone. That earned a second harsh look from Mother Stokely.

"Prudence," my aunt said to her eldest daughter, "lay the dough to rise already and gather the younger ones for supper."

My cousin protested. "It's not ready to rise yet, mother. Send Hester."

Mother Stokely puffed out her cheeks. She disliked back talk, but she settled her gaze on me. "Hester, would you? There's a dear."

I looked down into my empty tin cup. I wanted more but did not want to steal any from the shares of my brother-cousins. I rose and padded back out the low-framed door, remembering to collect my boots from the yard as I did so. There was a drop of blood, baked black from the sun, on the toe of one of them.

My uncle's property was goodly sized and as prosperous as he could render it. Our veranda faced the main road into town, but the property widened behind it to include the barn, a paddock, an orchard, and the fields beyond. A small creek formed the western border and when the weather warmed up, we would bathe in its cold water and enjoy a picnic on the bank. It was a fine place to explore and daydream and skip stones when time allowed, which was not often.

I found the remaining cousins situated under the shade of an apple tree. The youngest of Pardon and Katherine's brood were Hiram and Polly. Polly was nine and as sweet as a blind kitten. Hiram was a year younger and also sweet, but sulky and occasionally destructive. Boys can be savages. Both of them sat quiet as their older sister read to them from the Bible.

Faith was a curious one. Studious and literate, Faith Stokely was also very pious. She spent hours in prayer or reading about the lives of the saints. Her parents must have had some inclination to her character as her name attested, but I sometimes wonder if one grows to become the name we are given. I do not know the meaning behind my own name. I don't know if I wish to know it. I dislike the fact that Hester rhymes with pester, which Jacob often teases me with. Hiram will follow suit, which I will not tolerate. It is meant in good fun, I know, but I get enough teasing and tattling as it is on account of my deformity.

Faith was sixteen, three years younger than Prudence and forever stranded in the shadow of her older sister. Where Prudence was comely, Faith was plain. Where Pru could be haughty and quick to argue, Faith could be sullen to the point of morose. She held grudges. I don't mean to paint a poor picture of my sister-cousin. Faith was generous in all things, often foregoing her own happiness to please others. Coupled with her piety, I often thought Faith would do well in a convent but, of course, our sort held no truck with the rustic Catholics. Faith was also a capable teacher, which came in handy as our village was often without a schoolmaster. Faith was teaching Hiram and Polly at the moment, and her lessons usually ended with a reading from the Bible. Or, if the children had done well with their lessons, Faith would read from *The Sketch Book of Geoffrey Crayon*, which had quickly become a favorite in our household.

With the Bible balanced on her knees, Faith placed a finger to a certain verse on the page and held aloft the opposite hand as if to testify before the smaller children. "When Lot entered into Zoar," she recited, her voice solemn and terrible, "the Lord rained upon Sodom and Gomorrah brimstone and fire out of Heaven. And he overthrew those cities and all the plain and all the inhabitants of the cities."

I stood listening for a moment, curious to what lesson my sister-cousin was teaching the babes. Faith's fondness for biblical tales often ran to the harrowing or inexplicable aspects of the holy book. This afternoon was no different.

"Time to wash up for supper," I said, startling young Polly who sat enraptured. Her gray eyes, inherited from her mother, flashed at me before returning to her older sister.

Faith disliked being interrupted. "One moment, Hester," she said, and resumed her lesson. "But his wife looked back and became a pillar of salt. And Abraham got—"

"Salt?" Hiram piped up, his mouth gaping open.

"Hush, Hiram."

Faith rumbled along. "Abraham got up in the morning and went to the place where he stood before the Lord. And he looked toward Sodom and Gomorrah, and to all the land in the plain, and beheld, and lo, the smoke of the country went up as the smoke of a furnace."

Questions were lobbed from the children at her feet.

"Why did she turn into salt?"

"Because she disobeyed. She looked back when she was told not to."

"Did the Lord burn up the whole city?"

"Every house, every stone."

"But why?"

Here, Faith closed the book, ending the lessons. "Because the people were mired in sin and horrors and filth of all kind. Their nature brought about their own destruction. That is clear enough if you'd been paying attention."

Hiram raised his hand. "How tall was the pillar of salt?"

"Come along," I interjected, returning a harsh eye to Faith. I never understood some of her teachings. They seemed designed to frighten rather than instruct. "Mother will have our hides if we're not at the table in time for grace."

The children bolted away chattering as they raced to the pump. Faith brushed the chaff from her hem and came alongside me as we stepped out into the waning rays of the sun.

"Why do you frighten them with these stories, Faith?"

My sister-cousin held the good book to her chest as if to protect it from the elements. "To guide them morally," she said. "Otherwise they will turn into little beasts."

It wasn't my place to question my cousin's instruction. Or to question any of them if I were to be honest. I had shelter. I should be grateful. Still. "Aren't you worried they'll have night terrors? You know how skittish they can be. Hiram, especially so."

Faith slid her hand through my arm, linking us at the elbows as we walked. "There are two kinds of fear, Hester. Childish fears of the thing under the bed and the goblin at the window. And there is true fear of damnation and the ruination of our souls through our own ignorance. Fearing God is not only the right frame of mind, it is the only way to conduct one's self in the day-to-day. Don't you agree?"

I stated that I did, but that was an untruth. Where Faith's instruction frightened the children, it left me baffled. My own failings, really, in not having the brains to understand. I would try harder.

3

SUPPER WAS LAID on the long table with all of us seated at our places, hands in our laps. The chair at the head of the table sat unoccupied. There was a banging at the door as my uncle knocked his boots against the frame before entering. Scooping his pewter stein into the pail of beer, he settled into his place and looked out at the faces of his assembled family.

Pardon Stokely was a tall man with long arms on a stout frame. Dressed in black as he always was, he could be mistaken for a well-fed pastor or, worse, a Jesuit, but there was often a smile on his face, which ran counter to most men of the cloth that I knew. There was a strong resemblance between my uncle and my father, God rest his soul, as the two were brothers. The long face, the protruding ears, and the dimpled chin, but it was the smile that was mostly the trait they shared. Pardon told me once that they both inherited that from their mother, and each counted it as a blessing. Their father, according to Pardon, never smiled. If that was true, then I am not sorry to have never met the man. But that smile of Pardon's was something I cherished, for it reminded me so much of my Papa. His name was Steadfast.

Pardon and Steadfast. Irregular names, I know, but the

Stokely men were originally of Puritan stock and the tradition of virtuous names was stamped on them although they had long fled that pack of rigid religionists. Pardon had maintained the tradition with Prudence and Faith, but I suppose Mother Stokely had had enough when their sons were born, electing to christen them with the regular nomenclature of Samuel, Jacob, and Hiram. Polly's true name was Margaret, but no one called her by it. Hester, as far as I know, has no meaning to it.

Pardon bowed his head. Around the table, hands were clasped in fellowship and thanksgiving. His voice rumbled, deep and rocky. "For the tender mercies of our Lord and Father, let us be truly grateful. Amen." He looked up and added: "Now pass the head cheese, if you will."

Silence around the table. I saw Samuel and Jacob both stiffen in their seats. I'll admit, my stomach dropped a notch when I recalled the image of the lamb's brains spilled in the clover.

Samuel cleared his throat. "I'm sorry, father. It was lost."

"Lost how? Did the crows snatch it away?"

Samuel let his gaze fall to his untouched plate. "An errant blow with the ax. My blunder."

"Mine also," said Jacob. "We both misjudged the thing's skull."

The look on my uncle's face turned tart. "Both of you took a whack at it? And what about you, Hester? Did you all take turns cudgeling the poor beast?"

"No, sir," I said. "But the thing was skittish, which made a killing blow difficult."

Pardon laid his large hand flat on the table. "I had so looked forward to having head cheese."

"As did I," spoke Mother Stokely. She slid the platter of tenders to her husband. "There are the sweetbreads, though. We shall content ourselves with these."

His mood shifted instantly, and he pilfered a portion of the seared pancreas onto his plate. "Ah! Glory be, the tenders escaped the savagery." His focus darted from one boy to the next and back again. "Did you hang the carcass like I told you?"

"Yes, father," Samuel replied, eager to redeem himself. "The lamb was butchered and dressed correctly. It's suspended in the barn."

No mention was made of the fact that neither lad wanted to eviscerate the thing, nor was my involvement in it brought to light. I said nothing but Jacob and I shared a glance, him offering a sly wink. I had no wish to embarrass either of them. Their father's disappointment was enough.

All tucked into their meal. The sliver of lamb's heart that graced my plate was chewy, but under-salted to my taste. I devoured it.

Prudence straightened up, dabbing her cloth to her lips. "I saw James today. He had news."

Faith rolled her eyes. Jacob sneered. "Here we go about James again."

"Don't be crude, Jacob," Prudence scolded.

Little Polly looked confused. "But Pru loves Master Corwin." She always defended her big sister.

"And he loves her," added Hiram. The two of them were like a chorus, often stating the obvious in our domestic catastrophe.

The bickering started, followed by the teasing. Prudence spoke constantly of James Corwin, but who could blame her? An announcement was expected any day now. Or at least the request from James to Pardon for his daughter's hand. It was her favorite topic of conversation and sometimes it grated on her siblings.

Mine also, I confess. Love can be quiet, too, can't it? It doesn't have to be cried out from every watchtower. It can run silent and unobserved by all but the two people concerned. That was my assumption at any rate. I knew little of the subject.

Mother Stokely silenced the teasing and addressed her eldest child. "James had news?"

"From a traveler. His horse had thrown a shoe," Prudence confirmed. James was apprentice to his blacksmith father. "There was a rash of cholera in Boston, resulting in a number of deaths. Over a hundred by this traveler's count."

"That's dreadful," declared her mother, waving a hand before her face as if to ward off a miasma.

"According to this man, it's made its way to Providence also."

My uncle's brow furrowed into deep trench lines. "That is too close for comfort. I'll speak to the selectmen, see if anyone else has news of this."

Prudence perked up in her chair. "We could pay the Corwins a visit? You could speak to James directly."

Jacob laid a cruel glance at his sister. "And you could see young James and bat your eyes, all kissey-kissey!"

"Manners, Jacob," scolded Mother Stokely. "Leave the vulgar talk in the barn where it belongs."

"Yes, mother."

Cholera. The mere word conjured terror. My own mother called it the night thief, for it would steal inside the house under invisible means to poison one's home. Plague and illness were something we lived in constant fear of. The camp fever after the war, the waves of cholera and fevers both yellow and scarlet. The mysterious consumption and the constant dread of smallpox, which Katherine Stokely herself bore witness to in the scars on her face.

Mother Stokely bore her deformities with dignity, paying them no fuss if anyone was impolite enough to mention them. Polly had once asked her about them. Not with malice but with the simple curiosity of a child. Katherine made light of the question at the time, dismissing them as the puckered scars left by a ticklish rose bush, but later that evening I observed my aunt pondering her reflection in the glass in her room. Tipping a cloth against a bottle, she dabbed at the scars with what I came to learn later was a tincture of mercury. By morning it had blazoned her skin to an angry rash, and she shelved the ampule forever. Alone before the glass, I saw her head drop in frustration but never did a tear fall for her misfortune. She has, through her conduct, acted as a guide and teacher for dealing with my own disfigurement. Shed no tear on how the Almighty has destined for you to appear and carry on.

I try. I often fail.

While I woolgathered, the conversation continued to churn around the table. The topic had spun back around to Prudence and her beau, the handsome James Corwin. Jacob, as usual, was trying to take his big sister down a peg or two, but Prudence was having none of it.

"Scoff away," Prudence rebuffed. "Scorn is the tool of the ignorant, especially in matters of the heart. Or is there a mistress in your wings that you haven't told of yet?" Jacob's face flushed red, called out as he was. Pru put a pin through it, adding: "I thought not."

Young Polly piped up, always defending her sisters against her brothers. "You're just being cruel, Jacob. Everyone will find their sweetheart, just as mother and father have. And as Pru has done with master James. Even you, Jacob, will find someone to love you."

"I don't want a sweetheart," Jacob gruffed, sawing angrily at his dinner.

"But you will," Polly said. She was all of nine years old, yet absurdly rigid in her convictions. Puritan roots, I suppose. "Everyone will find their mate."

Hiram was a year younger than Polly, and in many ways he was a toddler. As the baby of the family, he was Katherine's favorite. Unswayed by the argument, he shot a glance in my direction before replying to his sister.

"Even Hester?"

Pardon and Katherine turned to stone; forks frozen halfway to their open mouths. Prudence and Samuel reached for a cloth and Faith kept her head bowed, eyes fixed on her plate. Even Jacob seemed at a loss for words.

Mother Stokely spoke, breaking the spell. "Polly, will you pass the turnips? There's a dear."

My gaze floated down onto my plate. It was half finished but my appetite had fled.

~

My uncle's house was modestly attired and befitting a man of his stature, if at times cramped for a family of nine. Especially in winter when the frigid winds trapped us indoors for too long. The house was not the largest in Wickstead, but nor was it the cottage or sod hut that some of our townsfolk dwelt in. Our home had a dining hall and a parlor with an enormous hearth and a kitchen that took up the rear half of the ground floor. There was a proper foyer and even a study for Pardon with French doors that he could use to shut out the ever-present clamor of his large family. He often complained of young Jacob who seemed unable to speak in a volume below a roar and stomped the floorboards like some great ape. There was an icehouse in the yard next to the coop, steps from the rear kitchen door and a root cellar stocked with hanging vegetables and preserves that were accessible through a trapdoor.

The second floor held four bedrooms along with a small sewing nook under the south gable end. The largest bedroom was situated at the back of the house where its mullioned windows overlooked the glen and the creek. This bed chamber belonged to the patriarch and his wife. The boys were situated in the west bedroom and the two older girls and myself occupied the smaller eastern bedroom. Prudence often argued with her father for the girls to switch rooms with the boys, but to no avail. Having made the poor decision to be born female, the girls were told to be content with their lot and not to grouse so. When the room became too cramped, I often slept on the floor of the nursery with Polly and Hiram. Faith, who was silent much of the time, snored like a drunken bear.

Bedtime was often chaotic for the daughters of the house. Being not of the inner familial circle, it was my duty to help the others unlace their corsets and free themselves of shifts and crinolines. The girls all braided their hair before bed, but Faith chose to do it herself where Prudence preferred to be pampered. We all took turns combing and plaiting Polly's long tresses. Reading bedtime tales often fell to me, with little Polly curling up in my lap as I read by the tallow light. Prudence was a chatterbox and would prattle on about her dear James Corwin or her plans for a wedding and a home of her own. She could be a silly girl, but she was not brainless. Prudence was well read, and the most educated of all the children, even more than Samuel, and Pru would sometimes read poems to us or speak of faraway places such as London or Paris or Vienna. Faith preferred to study her Bible or to pray in silent meditation. I would often catch Faith glowering at her older sister for chattering on so. Faith and Pru shared the one proper bedstead in the room, a four-poster with a headboard and generous mattress of horsehair. I reposed on a cot under the eave. It was comfortable enough, cushioned on a mattress of dry corn husks and straw.

When my head met the pillow, my hand involuntarily found its way to the scar on my face. This happened when I was tired or careless. It is a rivulet of twisted flesh that extends from the corner of my mouth and across the left cheek to the ear. In appearance it resembles molten wax, pitted and lumpen in spots with variations of crimson and pink. My left ear is practically gone, leaving only a twisted nub of flesh in its place. Although it is unsightly for a woman to let her hair down in disarray, I often leave the tresses loose on that side in a vain attempt to cover the unsightly business.

The burned flesh was the result of a fire that had consumed my childhood home. I know not what started the blaze, for I was asleep at the time. I woke to the sound of screaming and saw the room was rippling with flame and heat. I heard the cries of my mother and the shrieks of my father in another part of the house. I ran for the door, but a sprite of flame knocked me down and I felt the fire eat at my face and hair. After that, darkness. I awoke a day later in the most excruciating torment I had ever known. I was told that my home was burned to cinders and both my parents lost in the fire. I was twelve years old. I shrieked and thrashed about, from both the pain and the tragic news until someone forced a spoonful of laudanum down my throat and oblivion came on.

This was the root of the abrupt cessation of conversation at the dinner table. Polly, in her guileless way, had simply stated aloud a topic that was best kept shushed. The pain in my aunt's eyes was as clear as the moon on a cloudless night. My prospects, you see, were scant to none because of my facial deformity. Like any mother, she wished for all of her daughters, by blood and by misfortune, to be suitably married off and squared away with a family of their own. Prudence was already halfway there and Polly, with her sweet nature, would have no trouble finding a suitor when her time came. Faith may have to be pushed from the nest, but she too will become someone's bride. Mother Stokely will be stuck with one ugly duckling in her nest and it breaks her heart to contemplate that future. Bless her.

I snuffed the candle and pushed away these thoughts as they are unproductive to dwell on. Sleep was taking its sweet time and after turning this way and that, I became aware of a dull noise inside the house. A rhythmic tapping as if a piece of furniture was knocking against a wall, and suddenly I was blushing even though it was dark as pitch in the room. The sound was coming from the grand bedroom and growing louder and, sure enough, there came Katherine's whisper trying to hush her husband. After a while the sound ended and my cheeks cooled, the house quiet again. Bullfrogs croaked out in the creek. To my dismay, a face bloomed in my mind's eye, and that face belonged to a young man named

Henry Beecham. Henry lived in town where his family owned Wickstead's only inn. My cheeks began to burn again. Or the right cheek did as the scarred one had no sensation. Idle hands indeed become the Devil's playthings. Afterward, my thoughts cooled, and I was left mortified and ashamed, promising God that I would not sin like that again. The spirit is willing, as Faith often reminded me, but the flesh is weak. I feared mine was weaker than most.

4

THE SABBATH DAY. We walked to church on the muddy lane that cut through Wickstead to the town green where the meetinghouse stood. All of us were turned out in our Sunday best, evading the puddles and the manure in the roadway as we greeted the tinsmith and the barber and the men outside the cooperage. When we passed Beecham's Landing, the inn, I discreetly scanned the tavern's veranda for Henry, but I saw no sign of him. As usual, Peg-Leg Wilkins sat tilting a chair, doffing his hat to every young lady that passed by. Contrary to his name, Peg-Leg sported no ivory stump in place of a foot. His Christian name was Peleg, but all had resorted to addressing him by his nickname. He was a drunkard and a lout and, as far as I knew, had never once stepped foot inside church, thus blindly forsaking his immortal soul. He was cordial in his greetings.

The village green was a half-acre of verdant bluegrass in the center of our town, hemmed on all sides with rows of willow, and black oak which provided shade during the summer months. On the southern end of the green stood the pillory and whipping post used for capital punishments. We had to pass by these on our way to the church and all within our little party averted their eyes from the gruesome sight. Young Jacob looked. Jacob always looked, and Pardon scolded him to keep his eyes on the path.

The last time the pillory was employed was the previous October when a local man was punished for setting fire to his own house. The man was in debt to his neighbors and most of the merchants in town and had schemed to have his arrears waived in sympathy for the misfortune of having lost his home. The fool had boasted of his wicked plan to his fellows at the tavern, including the aforementioned Peg-Leg Wilkins, who reported it to the selectmen after the watchmen put out the cry of a fire on the high street and half the town hurried out in bedclothes to fetch water buckets. Fire was a terror that we lived with daily, one that spreads frighteningly fast if not contained immediately. I have already related mine own experience with it. At any rate, the foolish man was tried, sentenced, and punished by the council with three days in the pillory to be followed by expulsion from the boundaries of Wickstead forever.

During his public humiliation in the device, a placard was hung about his neck bearing the word "Arson," the nature of his crime. But during his three-day penance, the placard kept changing, being replaced with different crimes and sins. Arsonist was swapped with Thief, and then Drunkard, Liar, Fornicator, Heretic, and finally Traitor. The man had become like the fabled scapegoat of the ancient Hebrews, bearing the collective sins of the community around his neck. At the end of the three days, the man, crazed with exhaustion and torment, was driven from the town by a mob of women and children, never to be seen again. An impromptu celebration occurred that evening with citizens carousing in the street and letting off rockets into the sky as if the community itself breathed some sigh of relief for the expulsion of its collective sins. I suppose some truly believed it had.

I have resided in Wickstead for five years with my uncle and aunt, but still this village is strange and unfamiliar, its customs foreign and often bewildering. I fear that I shall forever be the outsider to this arcane mix of Quakers and Baptists, Unitarians and Methodists. We have a handful of Jews within our midst, but thankfully no Catholics nor any of Puritan stock. No one can abide their absurd notions here. Faith was fond of repeating a familiar credo of our community. "First," she declared, "that we love our neighbors as ourselves. Second, that we hate the

Puritans of Massachusetts with a perfect hatred. Third, that we hold the Presbyterians of Connecticut in like contempt."

Church service was, well, serviceable. Our rector, the Reverend Tobias Crane, was a pleasant man who enjoyed dropping in for tea with his flock, but he was not the most gifted orator. His tone was flat and somewhat droning, never rising in passion or lowering in sadness, but always keeping to a steady hum that made it difficult to focus one's attention. It may seem ungracious to speak of, but the truth was evident in the number of heads nodding and bobbing in the pews around us. One parishioner began snoring, and another passed wind loudly, which caused a muffled snickering and all the while Reverend Crane droned on as if nothing happened. I believe his sermon was about the grace of forgiveness. Or was it the sin of pride? Nonetheless, the sermon ended, and all rose, eager for the truly happy part of every Sunday, which is the socializing on the lawn outside the meeting-house. News was shared, well wishes were given, and gossip was passed in whispers. After the dour penance of the service, the congregation became gay and lively as they greeted one another.

The heavens were much changed when we emerged from the church doors. They were bright and clear when we entered, but now all was overcast and a strong wind had picked up, tossing hats from heads and ruffling skirts.

"I fear there is rain in the offing," said Reverend Crane as he stepped forward to shake hands with Pardon. "Blessing to you, Pardon and Mrs. Stokely. Children."

"And to you," replied my uncle, greeting the clergyman. "Wonderful sermon today. Grave but pertinent as always."

The reverend almost blushed. "Bless you, Pardon. That is too kind."

Mother Stokely shook the pastor's hand. "I do hope we'll see you this Wednesday, Reverend?"

The clergyman assured Mother Stokely that he was looking forward to his usual tea. Like most households, ours was regimented into tasks for the week. Mondays were for the washing, Tuesdays were for baking, and so on. Reverend Crane scheduled his visits for tea on Wednesdays, the day after baking day. He had a fondness for Mother's tipsy cake.

Faith spoke up to ask the Reverend to clarify an ecclesiastical point of his sermon. Of course, she had paid full attention to the rector's words. Fortunately we were all spared when young James Corwin stepped in to greet the family. Prudence beamed hotter than a lamp wick in the presence of her beau. And no wonder, really. James was a very handsome man and cordial as well, having won favor with Pardon and Katherine with his easy grace.

The sky continued to darken over us, but no one wished to leave yet, hungry as everyone was for the fellowship of kith and kin. I froze when a certain voice rose up behind me and when I turned, sure enough he was there. Henry Beecham stood talking to Samuel, as the two were friends, and were discussing the possibility of an early morning turkey shoot in the fen beyond the marsh. Even under a gloomy sky, something seemed to shine within young Henry Beecham that is difficult for me to put into words. It wasn't just his features (he was beyond comely), nor was it his warm voice (smooth though it was), or even his easy charm (which earned friends wherever he went). It was all of those elements and yet some other, intangible quality that made me clumsy and awkward in his presence. It felt like his very proximity caused my brains to drop from my head and roll away like an errant pumpkin.

I dared not turn all the way around, for that would give me away and I could feel little Polly watching me. With a pretense of adjusting my bonnet, I let a lock of my dark hair tumble down to drape my disfigurement and left it there, graceless as it may have appeared. Only then did I turn and act surprised to see him there speaking to my brother-cousin.

"Good morning, Henry," I said, as casually as could be. "How did you like this morning's service?"

"Enlightening as always," Henry replied with a smile that prompted my brains to drop a second time. Then he nudged Samuel in the ribs and added: "Especially the part when old Turnbecker broke wind."

The two of them laughed, and I blushed from my one good cheek. Boys. I moved the conversation along before either of them tried to repeat the incident.

"And how is the tavern?" I asked. Did I mention that Henry's family operated the inn? "I heard Captain Shelby passed away in his sleep."

Henry nodded. "He did. With a grand amount still owing

on his tab."

Sam returned the nudge to Henry's ribs. "Did you go through his trunks? Was the gold there?"

"Empty. Just his moth-eaten uniform and a broken pistol."

A footnote of a tale there regarding Captain Shelby. He arrived in Wickstead shortly after the repulsion of the British at Fort Erie on his way home to Exeter where he was to wed his betrothed. He took a room at the Beecham's inn, as his horse had failed him and he had walked the last ten miles into town. He had intended to stay only a few days to rest and procure another mount, but he never left, maintaining a room permanently at the inn. Rumor had it that he had received word that his fiancée had wed another while he was away at war and now, lost and heartbroken, he never went home. A second rumor began circulating after the Captain had been at the inn for a year with no visible means of employment. Whispers went round that he had a sack of gold in his sea chest, spoils of war as it were, that he had intended to establish himself and his new bride when he returned home. There was much speculation about this mythical trove and over the years, the Captain's room had been broken into and burgled, but no secret cache was ever recovered. Speculation then turned to the notion that the Captain had buried the gold in some secret location or hid it in the hollow of a tree. Townspeople had been scouring the outlying woods for years searching for it. Samuel and Henry both used to scavenge the forest for it when they were younger. But now poor Captain Shelby was dead, and the mystery of his secret treasure would never be known. If indeed, there ever was one.

"I was sad to hear of his passing," I said. "Is there to be a burial soon?"

"In the potter's field if my father has anything to say about it." Henry beamed his smile at me again, but I saw his eyes flicker momentarily to my ruined cheek. My tresses must not have hidden it properly, and I felt another bloom of heat on my face.

When I first arrived in Wickstead, Henry Beecham was kind to me. We attended school together briefly, in a tiny house with a stern schoolmaster who had a fondness for the switch. In the yard outside of the schoolmaster's house, a brutish little girl had mocked me for my scar, which was still red and raw to look at. She hooted at me, calling me a goblin and an ogre. Or was it a witch? I don't recall. But I do remember Henry coming to my defense and upbraiding the girl for being cruel. He gave me his kerchief to dry my eyes. I have never forgotten the incident.

Samuel, pest that he was, nudged Henry a second time and wagged his chin in the other direction. "The young sprite is about and free from her parents, Henry," he said. "Best to take your chance now."

Henry and I both turned in the direction that Samuel indicated. Across the church lawn was Miss Elizabeth Wickes, resplendent in a fine dress and proper lady gloves over her delicate hands. Her father was a friend of Pardon's and the two of them served as selectmen together. Elizabeth was a pretty girl, considered by many to be a catch. Apparently Henry agreed as he tipped his hat to us and set out across the lawn to speak to her before she was whisked home by her parents.

I frowned at my cousin. "You are such a boor, Sam."

"You've got some competition there, Hester," he said with a laugh. "Our Elizabeth catches hearts left and right and presses them into a book like flower petals."

"Don't be ridiculous—"

A great thunderclap stole the remainder of my reply, booming across the green with a great rippling crack that startled man and beast alike. And then something smacked my wrist with such force that it stung. Samuel cursed as something pelted the crown of his head.

"Hail!"

I don't know who had cried out, but all were running for cover. The lawn was now bedlam as hailstones as big as walnuts rained down, pummeling everyone. Children cried out in pain and the men cursed and the women gathered their youngest into their skirts to shield them. People scrambled for the church doors while others sought protection under the oak trees. A few crawled under a chaise. I saw Mr. Hendershot prone on the ground as if knocked senseless by the punishing ice pellets. The youngest in our family were taken up and shielded by their parents while the rest of us covered our heads as best we could to avoid the same fate as poor Mr. Hendershot.

It stopped as suddenly and harshly as it had come on. The cowering congregation looked up uneasily to see the ground bestrewn with hailstones that now steamed the air with an eerie mist. The village green was utterly silent as all held their breath, fearing another torrent of ice from the heavens.

The first sound we heard was a dull clopping of a horse. Coming north on the main road into town, we all looked up in stunned silence to see a bedraggled horse wandering into town with a rider lying slumped over the horn as if dead.

The stranger arrived that day, and, like the horseman in Revelations, death followed him, although none of us knew it at the time.

5

A FOREBODING SIGHT as ever I saw, this pale rider ambling into town on a rough-looking mount. I couldn't see his face as the figure was doubled over the saddle horn with his arms jangling along the withers. A dead man on a horse, with the animal looking not far from that of its master. Stunned as we all were from the hailstorm, none spoke or moved to stop the shambling horse. We gaped as it staggered past us, moving south on the road, crunching the steaming hailstones under its hooves.

Someone cried for help and with that, the spell was broken. Commotion and confusion played out as the parishioners picked themselves from the ground or crawled out from their shelter. People moaned and clutched their heads where they had been struck. Parents checked their little ones for goosebumps while others looked about in a daze as if their wits had been dashed by the pummeling ice. All within our small party were smarting from the hail but none were seriously hurt. Polly and Hiram were both in tears but more from fright than injury. I saw Henry and Samuel lifting Mr. Hendershot from the ground and settling him onto the church steps. The poor man's eyes wheeled about in a darting, confused manner.

Someone called out for a doctor and another cried out in reply that we had none. Doctor McTavish had died this winter, leaving the town scarce of a professional healer. Another call went out for a bonesetter, or even the barber. Among the congregation was a midwife, Mrs. Amblin, who busied herself with tending to the worst injuries. Pardon, after ensuring his own family was seen to, took my arm and asked that I help Mrs. Amblin to treat the injured. I obeyed.

Mr. Hendershot proved to be the worst hurt of the calamity. I gathered up a handful of the very hailstones that had struck him down and wrapped them in a kerchief to ice the swelling goose-bump on his skull. Henry and his father walked the man to the tavern and the rest of us dusted ourselves off and limped home.

"Who was that strange rider?" Faith asked as we made our way across the common. "Where did he come from?"

In the aftermath of the hailstorm, the dead man on horseback had simply been forgotten. No one knew, of course, but then, as if in answer to the query, the horse appeared. Rounding a bend in the road, we saw the animal lying prone in the dust of the street, blowing harshly in pain. Of the strange rider, there was no sign.

The boys ran to it first, bending down to inspect the poor thing. The rest of us limped and bustled along.

"The beast is in sad shape," said Samuel as he ran a palm down the withers. "She's been badly used up."

He spoke the truth. The animal was trembling with sweat and blowing hard as it had been ridden to the point of collapse. Its eyes were wild and crazed, the hooves cracked. Two of its shoes had been thrown.

Pardon knelt and conferred with his sons on the animal's fate. "Will she stand, boys?"

Jacob ran his palm down the horse's nose to comfort it. "She won't budge. I fear she's lost, Father."

Mother Stokely held the younger ones back, clutching them tight to her skirts. I crept forward for a closer look. The saddle was strange to me, the leather fanciful with handworked markings. Odder still were the bits and trinkets pleated into the horse's mane. There were two crosses tangled into the coarse black hair. One was plain and wooden and the other a proper crucifix of brass, the brazen idolatry of the Catholics. There were a few glass beads of royal blue with white dots painted on them, resembling an eye. A small leather pouch was braided there also, its sash cord pleated in horsehair. I wanted to see what it contained when Pardon upbraided me for being too close.

"Stay back, Hester," he warned. "This animal is half-crazed."

"She's too spent to be any threat now," I said. I flattened my palm against the poky ribs. The animal's heart was pounding from exertion, but I could feel it weakening with each pulsation.

Samuel looked up with a great sadness in his brown eyes and he held first my gaze and then my uncle's. "We can't let it suffer."

Pardon rose to his full height. "Jacob, run home and fetch my flintlock. Katherine, take the children home, will you? They don't need to see this."

By now a throng had surrounded the dying horse, neighbors summoned from their stoops or the other parishioners returning from church. Some were still clutching their heads, confused at this new situation before them. Mother Stokely began shooing her brood from the scene.

"Come along, Hester," Katherine said. "Leave the business to the men."

Samuel was in tears by this time. Despite his braggart tongue and constant teasing, Sam was a gentle soul who fawned over animals great and small. That was the true reason for the catastrophe with the slaughtered lamb. He had no wish to hurt any living thing and, although we all knew it was a merciful act, he wanted no part in firing a musket ball into this poor animal's brain. Pardon seemed unaware or unmoved by his son's tears, and I feared that, when Jacob returned with the flintlock, Father Stokely would make Sam pull the trigger.

"Maybe I should stay, uncle," I pleaded. "Sam was knocked rather hard by the hail. I fear his aim may be off."

Suddenly alert to his son's tears, Pardon grimaced in distaste. "Stiffen up, lad. It's an act of mercy. You know this."

Samuel wiped a hand quickly over his face and fought to control himself. Fortunately, a nearby resident had strode forward with an archaic blunderbuss in tow. He was already jamming the ramrod down the barrel to compact the powder.

"Mind your brogans, Mister Stokely," the man said,

motioning for us to step away. "No sense having them spoiled, now is there?"

Jacob appeared out of nowhere, flushed and out of breath. "Father," he panted. "Come quickly!"

"What is it?"

"You better see for yourself," Jacob gasped. "Please come!"

We all rushed for home, catching up to Mother Stokely with the younger children. I was grateful for the neighbor with the blunderbuss in sparing Sam so appalling a task. We were nigh twenty yards on when we heard the thunder of the weapon behind us.

~

The mystery of the pale rider was solved. The man lay collapsed in our very own yard. The picket fence lay broken where the horseman had staggered in before falling to the clover.

"Good gracious," exclaimed my uncle, kneeling to get a better look at the man.

Mother Stokely held the children back just as she had done before the dying horse. Polly and Hiram looked positively terrified. It had been a dreadful day for all of us.

"Is he dead?" Katherine asked.

"Not far off," Pardon replied. "Boys, help me turn him over."

The three of them rolled the man onto his back and we got a look at him. He was a tall fellow, with a barrel chest and a prominent chin underscoring a strong face. His jacket and waistcoat were fine, as that of a gentleman, and the pocket watch that hung from a chain spoke of ample means. His boots also, as these were of burnished leather and English-made by the looks of them. At some interval in the past, the man was of means but he had clearly seen a rough go of it. His clothes were filthy with mud. His face was bruised along the throat and under one eye, the lip split and swollen. The man was also armed. A flintlock pistol was tucked into the belt, along with an enormous dagger with a bronze hilt.

"Is he a soldier?" asked Prudence.

Jacob shrugged. "Maybe he's a brigand?"

Pardon tapped the man's cheek to rouse him. "Or he was set upon by robbers and left senseless."

"That may explain why he'd ridden his horse to the breaking point," added Samuel.

Mother Stokely strode closer. "Will he not wake?" She pinched my arm, pushing me closer, and said: "Go help."

Pardon frowned at my interference but did not order me away. I knelt opposite him and put my ear to the man's lips and listened to his breathing. Dry and ragged. I loosened the collar so he could breathe easier and palmed the flat shelf of his brow. Its heat was troubling.

"The fever has him," I announced, meeting my uncle's gaze. "We need to get him inside."

Each boy took a limb, but Mother Stokely put her foot down. "Not in my house. We don't know what he suffers from. Into the barn."

Pardon nodded for us to comply, so Jacob and I took a leg while Samuel hooked his arms round the stranger's chest, and we ferried him to the barn. The unconscious man was exceedingly heavy and more than once we almost dropped him but with much straining, we settled him onto a bed of dry straw under the greased paper window in the barn. Our horses, Caesar and Phantom, stirred and whinnied. Caesar kicked the stall in fright, jangling my nerves as he always did when he bucked the wood. He was a headstrong animal.

Faith lit the lamp and brought it closer to illuminate the prostrate figure. I turned the man's chin from side to side to inspect the numerous cuts and abrasions that left his face smeared with dried blood. There was more of it on his hands. The man looked as if he'd crawled through brambles.

"Look," said Jacob, pointing at the stranger's left hand.

Another cross appeared; a silver crucifix linked on a chain of rosary bead. Pushing the sleeve up, we could see that the beads were looped tight around the wrist so as to not fall away.

"Why the devil does he have so many crosses?" asked Samuel, who had spotted another one peeking out from the waistcoat pocket. "Is he some fugitive priest, driven mad into the woods?"

"Maybe he was rushing off to church?" Jacob said glibly. "Late for confession or some other Catholic malarkey."

"Looks more like he was running from something," said my uncle.

"But what?"

No one hazarded a guess. Pardon hummed at the puzzle before us. "What do we do with him?"

"Let him rest," Mother Stokely announced, drawing the children away. "Hester, I'll bring you a pan of water and a sop. Clean him up a little if you can. Everyone else, come inside. We've had enough excitement for one day, I think."

Gazing down at the bedraggled stranger on a bed of our straw, I couldn't agree more.

6

THE STRANGER REMAINED senseless for the rest of the day. Occasionally he moaned and whined as if from a bad dream, but he did not wake. Old Caesar continued to kick the stall and snort about until I got Samuel to lead him out to the paddock. I've never liked Caesar; he's a headstrong horse who will brook no rider except the master of the house. Pardon is partial to the animal, claiming Caesar once saved his life in a scrape with a wolf out in the wilds of Vermont. I have no way of knowing if that story is true. What I do know is that the haughty beast caused nothing but trouble for the rest of us. Even Samuel couldn't control him, and Sam was a sturdy horseman. The only person besides my uncle who could nudge the horse into any kind of submission was Will Treves, a brooding young man who worked occasionally for Pardon. Lefty Will, they call him. He has but one hand.

After things had settled within the household, I returned to the barn to do what I could for the unfortunate wretch who had collapsed in our yard. Prudence and Faith brought out a receptacle of clean water and some cloths, and I cleaned the dried blood from the stranger's face. His thick neck bore a deep cut that opened when I washed it and ran red with fresh blood. Prudence squealed and Faith looked near to fainting, both of them fair-natured and delicate as butterflies. I told Faith to gather up every cobweb she could find, which wasn't difficult as barns were always swathed in spider webs, and I asked Pru to cut a small patch of cloth for a dressing. The cobwebs would jelly the blood.

Faith seemed pleased to be helpful, and she watched me patch the wound with interest. She brushed a stray lock of hair from the stranger's brow.

"Do you think he'll revive?"

I rinsed the cloth in the now ruddy water and wrung it dry. "I honestly can't say."

"Who do you suppose he is?" queried Prudence.

"We may never know," Faith said. "Whoever he is, he's clearly run afoul of some bad business."

Pru leaned in closer. "He doesn't look like a wicked man to me."

"And what, pray tell, does a wicked man look like?" Faith scoffed.

"I don't know. This poor creature looks more pathetic than wicked. That's all."

My own mind was not made up. He could have been a knight without armor or a pirate without a ship for all I knew. I went to dab at the scabbed blood on his knuckles when the man jerked in a spasm. His hand snatched my wrist and his eyes opened. I shrieked, as did my cousins. I tried to retrieve my hand from his gasp, but it was like a vise.

His jaw popped up and down with a muttering that I tried to decipher. "Gone," he wheezed. "All gone, all damned."

Prudence clawed at his hand and Faith pushed him down, but his strength was prodigious. The man's eyes rolled back in his head and he collapsed against the straw again, senseless.

"Are you hurt?" Pru asked, scanning my wrist for injury.

"I'm fine."

Faith studied the disheveled man. "What did he say? We are all damned?"

"He's delirious with fever," Prudence replied. "Pay it no mind."

Faith was unconsoled. The man's babbling had unnerved her unreasonably, but I put this down to her religious zeal. Our village, as remote as we were, was no stranger to itinerant preachers who weekly proclaimed that the end of the world had come and deliverance was upon us. I despised their holier-than-Jasper demeanor. Smugness is an ugly quality, even among the pious.

I asked Prudence to take her sister into the house, which she was more than willing to do. The man lay still, and I reset the cobwebbed bandage on his throat as it had been dislodged by his sudden fit. With that accomplished, I decided to ransack his pockets. My uncle had confiscated the man's weapons and rifled the outer pockets of his coat for any clue as to the man's identity, but his search had not been thorough. A gentleman's clothes are riddled with pockets both large and small, some secret and hidden, whereas a woman's garments possess no pockets at all. I often wondered why. Did tailors think we had no need for pockets?

Foraging through the inner lining of the coat, I found one sliver of a pocket containing a fragile piece of paper. I unfolded to find that it was scripture, torn blasphemously from a Bible. A chapter from Psalms that I was not familiar with, nor could make much sense of. I set it aside and continued my search but came away with nothing but a few pennies. My eye went to the pocket watch and chain on the waistcoat. It was a fine piece of silver plate with a ceramic face on a pewter chain.

I pried the lid open with my thumbnail. As I had hoped, an inscription was engraved into the bowl of the inside. However, the scribed words set my brow to a furrow:

From one bruder to another, please welcome a sister.
Bountiful, RI, 1816

The sentiment meant nothing to me. What was a bruder? The initials RI clearly stood for Rhode Island, but the name, Bountiful, struck deep. Bountiful was the village where I was born, two days ride from here, and where I lived until the fire took my parents. Was this stranger from the same village that I was? The year stamped there on the metal held significance also. Who could forget the year of 1816? A summer without sunlight or warmth. I remember a snow squall in July.

I covered the feverish man with a horse blanket, but not one of our good ones. There was no telling what malady inflicted this wanderer, and I had no wish to lace good bedding with pox. I took the articles from his pockets to the house for Pardon to puzzle over. On the way I passed the broken pickets where the stranger had tumbled into our yard and noticed a few spatterings of blood on the clover and made a note to flush it away later with a pan of water.

Mother Stokely was in the kitchen setting out some cheese and cured meats onto a platter. There was a hubbub of noise from the hallway, which could only be visitors.

"Do we have guests?"

My aunt set the cleaver aside and wagged her chin in the direction of the parlor. "The selectmen are here. Pardon wished to discuss our guest out in the barn."

I frowned. "I see. Will he mind if I interrupt them?"

"Knock first." Katherine dabbed at a bead of sweat on her brow. It had been a long day for all of us. "How is he? The stranger?"

"He had some sort of fit a moment ago, but he's settled. His fever worries me."

My aunt did not look pleased. "He'll have to be watched through the night. I dislike the thought of a transient dying in our barn."

I concurred and offered to do the watching.

"We'll take turns," she said. "You, myself and Samuel. No sense one person bearing the burden."

I wondered why Prudence and Faith were left off the duty list. Were they too delicate for such a task or did my aunt disdain the idea of a girl passing the night alone in the barn with a man? She handed me the board she had prepared and shooed me away.

"Take this in with you," she said. "And see if anyone's cider needs refreshing."

Our parlor was not overly grand, but it was spacious enough to host a meeting of the selectmen. Henry's father, Arthur Beecham, stood before the fire alongside Mr. Halton Hazard. George Corwin was the father of Prudence's beau, the handsome James. He stood with his cup of cider, gazing out the mullioned window with a pensive mood. Mr. Ebeneezer Wickes sat opposite Pardon in one of the wicker chairs. The selectmen were the proviso council that oversaw matters civil and martial within our community. This usually consisted of settling disputes between neighbors or planning some public work, like the proposed paving of the main road (all were in favor but none could agree on how to raise the capital to pay for it). Occasionally they came together to deal with more dire issues, like a flood or an outbreak of some pestilence. There were six members of the selectmen, with Mr. Hendershot rounding out their number but he was home recovering from the pummeling of the hailstorm. Service within the council was supposed to be limited to two years only, with new members voted in as another's term was up, but for as long as I have lived in Wickstead, this current assembly of selectmen had never altered. Whether no other gentleman in town wanted the position or the current roster refused to step down, I cannot say.

At the moment, they were debating the stranger in our barn.

"The man is clearly some kind of bandit," stated Halton Hazard in a somewhat imperious tone. "Why else would he be armed thus?" Here he passed a hand over the table where the flintlock and fearsome-looking dagger lay. "I say we run him out of town before he causes trouble."

Arthur Beecham fired back. "We can't just run him off, Halton. We don't know anything about the man."

"We know he is ill with fever," said Mr. Wickes. Even seated as he was, Ebeneezer Wickes presented a towering figure. He was forced to duck before entering almost every doorway. "That is reason enough to send him packing. Or does anyone relish the thought of another wave of pox in our community?"

"Perhaps a pest-tent would be in order," suggested Mr. Corwin, turning away from the window. "We can isolate any potential harm that way. Hire someone to watch over him and carry out his slops."

Halton Hazard sneered at the idea. "And who is paying for this nursemaid, George? You?"

Arthur Beecham stirred the fire in the grate. "If it's all right with you, Pardon, perhaps we should leave him in the barn for the time being."

"Ah! The cheeses!" declared Mister Hazard as he spotted me lingering in the doorway. He rushed forward to take the board from me. Halton, like all the Hazard men, was as lank as a beam but possessed of a powerful appetite. If the other gentlemen didn't act quickly, the delicacies would soon be ravaged.

Arthur Beecham was the only one to say hello to me. The others either nodded or simply paid me no mind. It was clear to see that Henry had inherited proper manners from his father, in whose countenance I could see the semblance of the son. I smiled and dropped a tiny curtsy to him.

Pardon patted my arm. "How is the patient, Hester?"

"Resting, sir."

"No change?"

"He was taken with a fit earlier," I replied. "He babbled something incoherent and then dropped back into oblivion. He's peaceful now."

Arthur Beecham smiled at me again. "What do you make of his illness, Hester? Is it scarlet fever or the yellow variety?"

Halton Hazard choked on a wedge of cheese. "Is the young miss a physician?"

"Miss Stokely has a discerning eye for contagion," Beecham replied. "Far better than you or I."

I blushed and looked at my feet.

"Come, come, girl," insisted Mr. Wickes. "Give us your prognosis."

My feet wanted to run, but I ordered them to stay planted. "There is a rash on his skin that could be pox. And a swelling in his hand that I've seen with dropsy. But I cannot be sure if either is the case. A night's observation may reveal more."

"Then it's settled," declared Mr. Corwin. He drained his cup and set it on the mantelpiece. "The man shall stay here for the night where he can be watched. The morning will offer a new assessment of the danger."

"And," suggested Ebeneezer Wickes, "some of the man's character."

My cue to be dismissed, but I lingered and turned to Pardon.

"There is something else, uncle."

"Yes?"

I brought forth the items. "I found these in his pockets."

My uncle unfolded the torn page and held it to the lamp-light. "Scripture. A chapter from Psalms."

Mr. Wickes noted the ragged edge. "Ripped from the book like it was trash. The man's a heathen as well as a bandit."

"What else, Hester?"

I placed the pocket watch in his palm. He turned it over,

unimpressed. "It's a handsome timepiece, but there's nothing remarkable about that, my dear."

"There's an inscription inside."

Pardon clicked it open and squinted at the engraving. When his features fell, the other men drew closer to peer over his shoulder.

"The man's from Bountiful?" said Arthur Beecham. "He's practically a neighbor."

Halton Hazard examined the watch again. "If it isn't stolen, you mean. This sentiment is strange. 'From one bruder to another, please welcome a sister.' What the devil is a bruder?"

"It's German," announced Ebeneezer. "Means brother."

"You speak Deutsche, Ebeneezer?"

"My wife does," he replied. "Often in her sleep."

Mr. Wickes rose from the chair. His hair lightly brushed against the ceiling beams. "Perhaps we should send someone to Bountiful to enquire if they are missing any of their citizenry. Or bring someone to identify and collect our curious guest."

"A day and a half's ride each way," mused Mr. Corwin. "Who can we spare for those days? Peg-Leg?"

"Peg-Leg wouldn't make it beyond the creek before passing out drunk in a ditch," said Arthur. "I'll send Henry. His horse flies like lightning."

"Then it's settled," Mr. Hazard announced. He scooped up the last morsel of sausage from the board.

George Corwin examined the inscription on the timepiece once more before returning it to my uncle's palm. "1816. Who could forget the year without summer?"

Pardon agreed, laying the watch on the table. "Aye. Or the year of starvation that followed."

It seemed an unfortunate note to end the meeting on as each man recalled those awful times. They filed out the door, shouting their thanks to Katherine in the kitchen. Ebeneezer Wickes stooped to duck the doorway but still managed to knock his crown against the lintel.

7

OUR GUEST WAS peaceful throughout the night with no more fits or babbling. As planned, Mother Stokely, Samuel, and I took turns sleeping in the barn to watch over him, but our rest was not so placid. I don't mind sleeping rough, but the noise of the animals kept me awake. The three of us were a bleary-eyed bunch when the sun rose.

With the scullery fires lit, we sat down to a perfunctory breakfast of porridge with a little treacle and tea. I prepared yesterday's bread soaked with milk for the children, as this was all Hiram and Polly would eat in the morning. Mother Stokely asked if I would help her with a certain task after breakfast. She wished to visit her other children and wanted help making garlands for them. I told her I'd be happy to.

Katherine Stokely was something of a complex creature when viewed at a distance. Of course she was a loving mother and dutiful wife, but she was not "without her warts" as my own mother used to say. Katherine was a deeply felt soul who harbored some terrible storms in her heart. Private ones, as she rarely spoke her innermost thoughts to me. More than once I had found her at her spinning wheel, weeping deeply from some injury that she would not speak of. A past tragedy or some inner conflict, I knew not, but my heart broke when I came upon her with her head low with sobbing. At other times, a great rage would take hold of her, possessing her like one of those dervishes that whirl about. She would lash out, both with cruel words and with the wooden ladle, and God help you if you were within striking distance. Even her husband could not cool her fever in those moments. He would shoo all of us from the room, close the door behind them and wait it out. We would sit in fright listening to her howling with rage or shrieking from anguish. Occasionally there was the crash of a dish hurled against the wall. When things stilled, Pardon would take her for a walk out beyond the paddock to a small clearing near the creek where they would sit quietly. The two of them would return with Katherine much humbled and meek. Only once did I see Pardon strike her during these outrages. He was not a violent man and I know he was ashamed of himself for it afterward.

What am I trying to parlay here? Katherine could be a hard woman to live with, but she was also kind and exceedingly protective of everyone under her wing. I had a rough go of it when I first came to live with them after my parents died. I was prone to brooding or fits of outright catatonia. The memory of the fire and the sound of my parent's cries were always with me and my sullen presence created a great deal of disruption in my uncle's house, but Katherine was patient with me. She seemed to know how to gauge my moods and adjusted her response accordingly. In that first year, she never once scolded my outbursts. There were more times than I can count when she simply held me as I wept or raged like a lunatic. I would have done anything Mother Stokely asked of me. I adored her, warts and all.

We made garlands of wildflowers, whatever was in bloom that we could find. Some cowslip, some jack-in-the-pulpit, and periwinkle. Nothing lavish, but cheerful and fragrant. I checked on our guest in the barn and found him peacefully in oblivion and so we set off, my aunt leading the way into town.

To save time, as there was much to do that day, we took a shortcut through a footpath that bordered the marsh and wound its way into town toward the common. This acreage of our little village was somewhat desolate as it was mostly swampland and there was but one house that persisted there. Its windows were dark, the gables sagging. No one lived there.

"That wretched house," Mother Stokely said as we trod through knee-high timothy. "How I wish your uncle would get shed of such an eyesore."

My uncle owned the property in question. It was once a grand house, complete with high gable ends, two chimneys and a deep veranda that shaded the entrance. It was known as Cogburn Hall, after the man who had built it a generation ago, but among the children in town it was referred to as the ghost hall. The stories vary as to the tragedy that befell it. In some tellings, Mr. Cogburn hanged himself from a ceiling beam when his creditors came for him. Other narratives hold that Cogburn was murdered by his wife with an ax, or sometimes a tomahawk he had acquired in the Indian wars. I know not what tale to be true. I do know that the house has sat abandoned for years and, because of its proximity to the marsh, had fallen into a moldy disrepair. It squatted out there on the edge of the swamp with its sagging beams and rotting clapboard like some forlorn toad. Swamp moss crawled up the veranda and creepers tangled between the posts.

Pardon had purchased the house sometime after the tragedy when it was still fine and one of the more ostentatious homes in town. Surely, he wagered, someone would want to lease the manor and, having secured it at a good price, he looked forward to making it profitable. This was not the case, as no one wished to abide in a house with such recent tragedy, and so it sat rotting and sinking into the marsh. The money spent on it was forfeit and the sight of it bristled Mother Stokely's nerves like a burr under a chemise.

"I've half a mind to tramp over there myself," she huffed, quickening her pace to put the unsightly thing behind us, "with a quart of lamp oil and burn the damned thing down."

By the time we reached the graveyard, Katherine's ire had cooled, and a different mood took her spirit. Winding past the tilting headstones with their crusts of lichen, we stood before her other children. Four small grave markers stood dappled in sunlight under the shade of a hemlock tree. Apart from the six children under her roof, and the adopted one beside her now, Mother Stokely had four other children, silent and still in the peace of the churchyard. Two of the headstones bore only the scribed dates of 1801 and 1799 with a single epitaph of "Known unto God." These children were born blue and, according to Pardon, were not given Christian names since they were not baptized. The other two babies had lived only a few weeks. Strive, a boy in 1800 and Hope, a girl born and died in 1796. These babes, whom Katherine had loved briefly or only in the womb, had never been forgotten.

"To be forgotten," she said in a quiet voice, "is a sad state to bear. If they know that they are loved and are mourned, the happier they will be in Paradise."

Not for the first time was I struck at the largeness of her heart. It sheltered us all, the ones here and the ones who had gone.

Mother Stokely lowered herself to her knees. "Look at this, fiddleheads everywhere. Let's clean this up first."

We plucked the coiled sprigs from around the tombstones, along with clutches of milkweed and thistle.

"Should we keep these fiddleheads?" I asked. "My mother used to like these done with butter in the pan."

Katherine held one up to the light. "These are too long in the stem, dear. Improperly cooked, they can be poisonous. Besides, it's not wise to sup on anything plucked over a grave. The dead might take offense."

That was a new admonition to my ears. Five years among these people and still their ways were strange to me. I wondered if I would ever get used to it. Their manners were pleasant enough.

With the graves tidied, we said a prayer and strung our garlands over each of the headstones. We took the long way home, through town. Mother Stokely had no wish to see the disgraceful Cogburn Hall, and we needed supplies from the mercantile. The weather had been warm and dry after the freak hailstorm and the high road was parched. I would have to beat our cloaks on the line to get the dust out when we got home.

At the merchant's we ordered coffee, sugar, cornmeal, and some paper leaves for Pardon, along with a ragtag list of other sundries. Mrs. Van Tassel, who ran the counter while her husband lugged the requested items, was pleasant enough but professed to be clumsy with figures and was known to lend an errant thumb to the weigh scale. Katherine was annoyed with me for questioning her totals and asking to look over her calculations. My aunt's irritation with my fussiness abated when I relayed a difference of a quarter eagle between Mrs. Van Tassel's maths and my own. A week's wages for a day laborer. The merchant woman laughed it away as pure silliness, but Mother Stokely whispered a thank you to me as we pushed through the saloon doors to the street.

"Oh look," she said, aiming her index finger at the livery stable, "there's master James."

James Corwin stood outside the livery, cinching down the saddle on a fine-looking chestnut. The horse shone in the sunlight from a good grooming, its saddle laden with a bedroll and supply bags. The horse matched the rider; handsome and vital, eager to run a good game.

Next to Prudence's sweetheart stood a second rider with his mount. Henry Beecham was resplendent in tall riding boots and a fine coat that was tailored to his broad shoulders. Leaning into the horse's shoulder, he lifted a foreleg to inspect the shoe. A small knife in hand, he cleaned the frog of the hoof and seemed satisfied with what he saw.

Katherine was already marching across the dusty street to greet the young men. I nipped at her heels with the sack of booty over my shoulder.

"Master James and Master Henry," Mother Stokely hailed them. "How handsome you are turned out today. And with such fine animals."

The two men bowed and doffed their caps. James smiled at us with warmth. "Mrs. Stokely, Hester. Thank you."

Henry smiled at my aunt and nodded to me. I despaired at the state I was in; flushed from the burden and floured with road dust. "I trust the day finds you ladies well," he said.

"Aye," Katherine replied. "Are you two off hunting? I see no muskets on you?"

"We're off to Bountiful," James replied. "To inquire about the stranger in your barn."

"Of course. It looks like you'll have the weather behind you."

Mother Stokely and James fell into conversation about his horse. I let the sack of chattels drop from my shoulder and watched Henry cinch the belt on his saddle. It was English, the leather burnished and hand-tooled. As usual, my tongue was suddenly too big for my mouth.

"That's a fair journey," I said. "Two days ride apiece, there and back?"

The horse whinnied. Henry tied off the leather strap and smoothed a hand down the flank. "Not with these mounts. Grendel here was born to run. We'll be there before nightfall, I wager."

"Of course, there's a wager," I replied. "You and James are always contesting one another. An eagle this time?"

Henry dug a coin from his pocket and spun it in the air. "Half-eagle. James is tired of losing his wages to me."

The grin burning my face would not withdraw. I looked at the ground, at his horse, the stable behind him. Anything but him. My tongue was dry.

"Well, do be careful," I sputtered. "We would hate for anything to happen to you."

"Would you now?"

I met his gaze clean on and held it without stammering or wavering. I wanted my meaning to be clear. "I would."

He did not look away, and he did not dismiss the reply with a joke. But his eyes softened as if genuinely moved. I thought my knees would buckle.

And then James piped up and ruined everything.

"Let's get a move on, Henry. I intend to claim that half-eagle before nightfall!"

The two men hoisted themselves onto their horses, tipped their hats again, and cantered away.

"Be safe!" I called out although they were well out of earshot by then. Katherine relayed a sharp look at me before we strode off for home. I felt as guilty as a burglar with his hand in the honeypot.

We walked on for a moment, listening to the sound of the hooves drift away.

"Master James is quite gallant," Mother Stokely said. "I have to admit, I was initially displeased with Prudence's choice of suitor, but I've since come around. He's a decent young man, don't you think?"

"It's clear he holds Pru in high regard."

We walked on, and then she said, "I do hope he treats her right once they're squared away."

The remark surprised me. "Why wouldn't he?"

"Marriage changes people sometimes. And not always for the better."

I had nothing to add on that subject. Was she speaking of James or Pardon? I switched tactics, perhaps a little too boldly. "And what of Henry Beecham? He cuts a fine figure on horseback, don't you think?"

Mother Stokely seemed perplexed. "Arthur's son? Prudence has no interest in him."

"Of course." How stupid of me. We walked in silence the rest of the way.

Arriving home, we found Jacob and Hiram in the yard with a hammer and some raw-milled boards. Katherine went on into the house, but I stopped to ask what they were doing.

"Mending the fence that man broke," said Hiram proudly. "Jacob's teaching me how."

"Mind you don't hammer your thumb," I said. "Jacob lost a thumbnail doing that once."

Jacob grinned up at me. He stood a fresh picket in place for his brother to hammer. "Don't remind me. I still shudder at how the nail blackened and fell off."

"You were brave about it. How is the fence coming along?"

"We'll have her done in a minute."

Hiram nudged his older brother. "Show Hester the weeds."

"The what?"

Jacob stood upright and nodded at the yard before us. "Strangest thing," he said. "That patch of ground where the stranger collapsed. It's all gone brown."

The clover and timothy in our yard were lush from the spring rains, save for the spot indicated. A swath of it had withered brown, all of it dead in the spot where the man had fallen.

"Curious, isn't it?" Jacob said. "It's as if quicklime was spilled all over it."

Last summer, Jacob had dropped a bucket of the chalky stuff in the garden and the quicklime had killed the carrot patch. His mother was furious. I agreed with him that it did resemble lime poisoning. Had the stranger been carrying a sack of it when he collapsed? The patch of dead vegetation was troubling, but I couldn't account for it. A proper explanation would present itself in time. It always did.

8

I FOUND PARDON sitting on the veranda with his ledger perched on his lap, his brow creased in concentration.

"Hello, uncle," I said, laying aside the sack of provisions. "Have you eaten?"

"Yes," he replied without looking up. "No. I'm not hungry."

He seemed overly distracted by his work and a shadow darkened his features. "Is everything all right?"

"Figures do not always conform to our needs, no matter how we manipulate them." He closed the book with a clap and set it aside. "How was the trip to the churchyard? I trust the children are all still there?"

"We tidied up the stones and lay the garlands. All was in its proper place."

He removed his spectacles and cleaned them with his kerchief. "That's good. It wouldn't do to have one of them go missing, would it?"

That sounded odd to me. "You don't approve of Mother's visits to the graves?"

"I worry she dwells on it too much." My uncle rose and hooked the spectacles back over his ears. "Hester, would you be

46

a dear and run a mug of beer out to Will."

"He's here?"

"I sent for him. Caesar's been acting up. He wouldn't let me saddle him this morning, so I asked Will to have a look at him. I've been so caught up with the accounts that I neglected my manners."

I said I'd be happy to. When the supplies were squared away, I dipped a large tankard into the barrel and tried not to spill any as I went out the back. In the paddock stood the tall silhouette of Caesar and the lank frame of the young man leading him by the halter.

Will Treves was a favorite of Pardon's. He was the only person besides my uncle who could settle that unruly horse. He was a thin fellow and probably underfed as his family was not prosperous. There is talk that Will's father lit out for the Carolinas when the gold rush was on and never returned, but I do not know if this is true. People gossip so. In fact, many people referred to Will as Left-Handed Will or One-Wing Will, on account of his missing his right hand. It had become separated from his wrist in an accident some time ago. The exact nature of the accident varies, according to whom one is speaking to. Some claim it was crushed in an apple-press, others swear that his own father cleaved it with an axe in a drunken rage. Again, one mustn't pay the gossips any mind. I do not know how Will lost his hand, nor have I ever asked. It seemed rude. The courtesy was repaid as he had never asked about the ragged scar on my face.

I waved a hello and the young man led the horse forward to meet me at the fence. The smile on his face was lopsided.

"Afternoon, Hester," he said. "You look well."

"Your flattery is wasted on the deaf, Will. I would have thought you'd reckon that by now."

"But it makes you smile all the same."

I wasn't aware of this. I was sure I always scowled at his sour compliments. Didn't I?

Caesar clopped forward, bent his great neck over the rail and snorted loudly in my face. The horse has never taken a shine to me, nor I to it. I looked at Will.

"How is the ungrateful beast? Pardon thinks he's ill."

Will ran a hand down the shimmering withers. "To be honest, I'm not quite sure. I thought it might be a stray thistle pinching him somewhere, but I can't find anything. He's not himself, that's for sure."

"Perhaps he's just getting old," I suggested. "And cantankerous, as the aged do. He was never mild to begin with."

Will shrugged. "He seems more skittish than cranky. Has he had a fright recently? Did a fox get into the barn again?"

"I don't think he likes the guest convalescing next to his stall. He gave us all a fright, to tell the truth."

"So I hear," he said. "Everyone's been tittering about it. Has he spoken yet?"

"He babbles from time to time, but it's all drivel."

The horse dipped its head to get at the milkweed, knocking Will askew in the process. He leaned his shoulder against it and gently pushed Caesar back. The raw stump of his right wrist poked out of his cuff and it was difficult not to stare at it. Like all of God's creatures, Man is an engine of precise symmetry. Two eyes, two limbs, two wings. When this symmetry is out of balance, it seems to unsettle everything around it. Like a ladder with a broken rung, its absence draws the eye.

The reason for my errand was still in my hand, forgotten. I detested my absentmindedness. I held the tankard out to him. "Pardon thought you might be thirsty."

"That's very kind," he said with delight and took a great swig of it. Wiping the foam from his lips, his gaze went past mine to the barn in the distance. He seemed troubled.

"Are you sure it's safe? Keeping a stranger in the barn like that."

I shrugged this time. "He's harmless."

"For now. But what happens when he recovers? You don't know anything about the man."

"We'll cross that bridge when we come to it, I suppose. Besides, it's not up to me."

Will's brow stitched over. "That's what worries me. I suppose you're the one looking after him, too?"

"Who else is there? Pru is far too delicate for that sort of thing and Faith is preoccupied with becoming a saint." I winced at my own cruelty, but it was too late to take it back.

"That's a bit sharp."

"Too harsh?"

"It was funny." He took another sip from the tankard and

let out a sigh. "Still. If you feel any alarm, I'd be happy to spend the night watching over the poor fellow."

"You'd be happy sleeping in a barn?"

"It'd not be much of a step-down, as you know. All the same, say the word and I'm here."

Will's circumstances were rough. He and his mother and siblings occupied a small cottage out near the tannery. Cottage was putting it nicely. It was a hovel. They were a miserably poor lot.

I thanked him for his offer. "Some of the selectmen are of the same suspicion. They think he's some wicked villain, based on nothing more than his ragged appearance."

"What do you think?"

"There's more to character than appearance." The sun was high, and I shielded my eyes with my hand. "They believe he's from Bountiful. They sent James and Henry off to find out if anyone there is missing him."

"I'm sure those two will have a high time of it," Will replied, with something of a smirk on his face. "Is your sister still keen on marrying Jimmy?"

"She is. He hasn't asked yet, but we expect it any day now." I was annoyed by this. I don't know why. I decided to tweak his nose over it. "Why do you ask? Don't tell me you're in love with Prudence, too? Along with every other man in the county."

He found this amusing. "Your sister's a pretty girl, but she's a bit haughty."

"I agree," I replied. "She does adore James. The sooner they marry, the sooner I won't have to listen to Pru moon over him all day."

"And you'll gain a brother-in-law in the bargain."

"I hadn't thought of it that way."

There was a pause. I kicked at a pine cone in the grass and then blurted out: "Henry looked especially fine this morning. He's a splendid horseman."

"He's a bit enthusiastic with the spurs. He likes the speed, I suppose." He returned the empty tankard to me and took hold of Caesar's halter. "Thank you for the beer, Hester. I should walk Caesar some more, just to be sure."

He touched his cap and led the horse away. I stood watching the two of them for a spell until I heard Mother Stokely's voice calling me inside.

~

When Henry and James rode out for Bountiful, I wished I could have accompanied them, but my wants are plug nickels, useless as currency and an annoyance to others. Katherine could never spare me and there was no practical way a girl my age could ride rough with two young men. Still, I longed to see my hometown again. In all the years since I had been placed with my uncle here in Wickstead, I had not been back to Bountiful. What would have been the point? My parents were dead, the house razed to cinders. There was nothing there for me.

The more time that passes, the more I have difficulty remembering things. Important things, like the way my mother's eyes squinted when she smiled or the pleasant smell of pipe tobacco that hovered around my father like a vapor. Comforts and mementos. There was a day last winter when I found I could not recall my mother's face. It was gone, erased from my memories like it was some unimportant detail. I panicked and shut my eyes fast to conjure the image of her face in my mind. The arc of her squinted eyes or the freckle of her cheek, anything. How could one forget the countenance of their own mother? What monster could do that?

They were slipping away from me with each passing day and week and year. How long before I lost them altogether and their memory was gone, their love and their souls forgotten and unmourned?

That was the reason for wanting to ride off with Henry and James. I'm sure that if I could lay eyes on the village where I was born, other memories would return in a flood. I prayed to the Lord to keep the young men safe and to forgive this wretched child for having such a scatterbrain.

Two days passed quietly. I tried to estimate the return of the reconnaissance party. Bountiful was a day and a half's ride from here, but both Henry and James were quicksilvers in the saddle and their horses were light and fast. They would return in three days. I prayed for their safe journey and busied myself with the laundering, the cooking, gathering herbs, and minding the younger children, among a dozen other tasks. Within all that, I kept a vigil around the stricken outlander in our barn. The fever had broken, but he remained senseless for most of that time. He had visitors though. The brindle barn cat, a vicious one-eyed creature, would often lie on his chest as if it were a roost. I shooed the damn thing away every time. Cats steal breath from babes and from the ill. Other times I found Polly and Hiram spying on the stranger. Like the cat, I hurried them away with a sharp word or snap of my kerchief. Twice I stumbled upon Faith praying over the stricken man's soul.

After supper on that second day, I went out to the barn to check on our guest. Caesar was kept out in the paddock on Will's advice and I was grateful for it. Entering the dark and musty barn with a candle, I lit the wick of the lamp and jumped back in a fright when I saw the stranger sitting up, watching me.

He didn't move or speak, resting with his back against the rough boards and his gaze fixed on me. The horse blanket was drawn around his shoulders and his face was slick with sweat.

I composed myself and spoke in a soft manner. "Hello. How are you feeling?"

He flinched at the sound of my voice. Suspicion and fear passed over his face in alternating waves before he spoke.

"What are you?"

An odd question. Perhaps he could not see me properly. The light of the lamp was watery within the blackness of the barn.

"My name is Hester. You are on the grounds of Pardon Stokely, my uncle."

His hand passed over his nose. "It reeks like a stable in here," he said.

My face reddened. How to explain this? "It is a stable," I said. "I'm sorry about the—"

The man flung the blanket away. "I have to go."

I told him that was impossible, but I did not have to argue. The stranger thrust himself to his feet, staggered to one side and collapsed again.

"You mustn't strain yourself. Sit still while I get my uncle. He will answer your questions."

The poor man buried his head into his hands but did not protest. I dashed back to the house and told Pardon to come quickly. The entire household followed him.

Our guest hadn't run off. He looked barely able to sit up-right, but he stiffened nonetheless when he saw my uncle approach.

Pardon knelt before the stranger. "Sir," he said loudly as if the vagabond was deaf, "I am Pardon Stokely. I apologize for the rough lodging, but I was afeared you were stricken with the cholera or some plague. Do you understand me?"

The man nodded.

My uncle relaxed his stance, setting down onto the hard-packed floor of the barn. "Splendid. Now, to whom am I speaking?"

The man was looking at his hand, clenching a fist and splaying it flat. It trembled. "My name is Ephraim Fiske. Where am I?"

"You are in Wickstead, sir," Pardon informed him. He maintained a gentle tone to avoid spooking the frail-looking man. "You have been with us three days, convalescing. You rode into town in a dreadful state—"

"My horse," interrupted Mr. Ephraim Fiske, looking over the barn. "Is she here?"

"Gone, I'm afraid. There was no way to save the poor animal."

The man took this hard. A little life seemed to drain out of him at the news. "She was a good horse. Loyal." His hands went to his belt. "I had a pistol. And a knife."

"They are safe," my uncle replied. "We didn't want you to injure yourself while recovering. They will be returned to you when you are well. Now, Mister Fiske, can you tell me—"

"Hold!" Again, the stranger spoke over my uncle. He had spotted me hanging back near the door. and startled in fright. "Who is with you?"

"This is my niece, Hester. She's been nursing you the while." Pardon pivoted and waved me forward. "Step out of the shadows, dear, so Mister Fiske can see you better."

I did as I was told and dipped a respectful curtsy. "I am glad you are feeling better, Mr. Fiske."

His eyes narrowed as he scrutinized me. "You looked after me?"

"I did as best as I could," I said. "You were in an awful state when we found you."

"Thank you," he said meekly.

His gratitude made me uncomfortable. I bowed my head and looked away.

Mister Fiske took a breath and tried to stand. "I have to go."

Pardon held him still. "Easy now. You are unwell and I require a few answers from you. Where are you from?"

He was winded. "Bountiful. Not far from here."

"We thought as much. Hester found the inscription on your watch. Now, sir, tell me what happened to you. What brought you to such a hard scrabble state?"

Ephraim Fiske said nothing, but his face darkened as if recalling something tragic.

My uncle continued his questioning. "Perhaps there's someone in Bountiful that we could alert to your stay here? A wife, family?"

"There is no one."

"You have no family, sir?"

Mister Fiske shook his head slowly. "There is no one left in Bountiful. There is no Bountiful at all."

"I'm not sure I understand—"

"It's gone!" the man shot back. "Burned to the ground, all of it. Everyone is dead. Or worse. God help me."

The man buried his face in his hands and sobbed pitifully. It made us all uncomfortable. Mother Stokely and my older cousins were now crowded around me and we all waited in silence for the man to compose himself.

My uncle put a hand on the man's shoulder to steady him. "I am sorry for whatever you have been through, Mr. Fiske. Take it slowly, sir, and tell me what happened. There was a fire?"

"It began with illness. Consumption, the galloping kind. It knocked us down one after another, tick, tick, and tock. But it was much worse than that. The Devil himself had come home to roost. We tried to smoke him out, but the winds changed direction and the fire blazed out of control."

His words were choked off as he began to weep again. We stood there in an awkward silence, more mystified than ever. Had the man's wits been stolen by the fever?

The man pushed my uncle away and leapt to his feet. He demanded the return of his weapons, exclaiming that he had to leave, that it was not safe and other such ravings. Samuel and Jacob rushed the man and brought him down. Pardon barked at me to get a length of hemp to restrain the man, which I did, but it was unnecessary. Mr Fiske succumbed again, fainting dead away from his outburst. Pardon had the boys lash him to a beam nonetheless and ordered everyone out of the barn.

Back inside the house, Katherine ordered all of us to go to bed and reminded us to say our prayers. I let Faith and Prudence take care of the little ones and lingered to eavesdrop on my aunt and uncle in the kitchen.

"What do you make of it?" Mother Stokely asked.

"He's still in a fever, babbling nonsense."

"But, what if it's true? Bountiful gone?"

No reply came. A moment and then she spoke again. "What do we do?"

"We shall deal with him in the morning. Hopefully he'll be in a clearer mind by then, and we can get to the bottom of this."

I could hear my aunt pacing the floor. "Masters Henry and James should be home soon. We'll know more then when they return."

"Go to bed, Katherine," my uncle said. "There is nothing more to do now."

"Where are you going?"

"To the barn. I want to keep an eye on him for a bit, make sure he's bound safe."

I scurried to the stairs and hid behind the post. I watched my uncle go to the hearth where he retrieved the stranger's pistol and powder horn and went back out into the night.

9

"WHAT IF IT'S TRUE?"

I fixed my cousin with a sharp eye. "Prudence, stop," I said. "The man is sick. He doesn't know what he's saying."

Prudence wasn't listening to me. Her eyes had taken on a blasted sheen, imagining the worst. "But what if it is? The whole town gone? And James riding straight into it? I couldn't bear it if something happened to him, Hester. I would die."

She buried her tears in her pillow for the second time this morning. She had stayed in bed when we all rose, claiming she felt unwell. I came back up after breakfast to check on her and found her in a fit. As the firstborn child, Prudence was no stranger to high drama.

After the horrid declaration of the man in the barn, Prudence had fretted the whole night through, imagining some awful fate befalling her beloved James Corwin. I understood her fears. A nagging sense of doom had infested my own thoughts thinking of Henry alongside him, riding into God only knew what danger.

"Steady now, Pru," I said. "Tears won't protect them."

Was Ephraim Fiske telling the truth or was he a liar of the most venal sort? Or was he just a very sick man whose sanity had shattered like an egg fallen to the flagstone?

And here was poor Pru, whipping herself into a lather with each minute, unable to break free from the looping fear in her heart. She would not listen to reason, and I knew not how to help her.

Footsteps rang off the wooden stairs. Faith entered the room and looked down indifferently at her older sister. "What's the matter with her?"

"She's worried about James."

Faith pursed her thin lips. "James, James, James," she uttered with a healthy dollop of scorn. "How I grow tired of hearing that name."

"Go away," Prudence sobbed.

"Dry up, Pru. The stranger's story is naught but lies. Only a ninny would believe them."

All siblings fought, sisters more than most, but even I was taken aback at Faith's unkindness. I called her out. "We don't know that, Faith."

"Do you really think the Lord would let the entire village of Bountiful burn to the ground? Its denizens are hewers of wood and drawers of water, not the rabble of Gomorrah."

"That is not helpful," I replied.

Prudence wept anew. I took her frock from the peg and laid it on her bed. "Get dressed, Pru. Wash your face and meet me downstairs. We're going into town."

Pardon rejected my plan. He and Mother Stokely were on the veranda, he with his ledger and she shelling pecans into a bowl.

"Please, uncle."

"To what end?" he asked. "There's no need for the two of you to go traipsing through town. If there was news, we would have heard."

I tried not to bristle, but judging by the upraised brow of my aunt, I had failed. "The girl's beside herself. The walk will do her some good. And who knows, we may learn something."

"You're both needed here. There's still chores to be done."

Prudence appeared in the doorway, dressed but her face was still puffy. I pressed my cousin's bonnet into her hands and faced my uncle again.

"We are leaving. We won't be long."

He was about to protest when Katherine gripped his arm to stifle him. Pardon grunted and turned his focus back to his ledger. Katherine waved us on.

The open air did her some good, drying her tears and giving her some purpose. The truth of it was that Prudence's fretting had begun to gnaw at my own fears for Henry. The plan was simple. We would walk to Beecham's Landing, the inn owned by Henry's parents to see if they had returned yet. Our pace was marshal and quick.

"But why there?" Pru asked.

"It's the first place they'll go when they return," I replied. "They'll want supper after a long journey."

Prudence brightened at the notion. "And the inn is closer than the Corwin farm. I see your reasoning."

Duly cheered, we marched on to where the road wound through the glen to the outlay of our town. Wickstead is not a large settlement. There are a few houses of brick and stone but most are timber-framed and dressed with clapboard. Cedar shingles on the roof, glazed glass on the windows on the better houses, greased paper on the shabbier. Its people are a hardy stock, but not ostentatious in any way. Gaudiness, or the flaunting of good fortune, was the worst sin.

The inn owned by Henry's family reflected this taciturn outlook. Beecham's Landing was two floors under a low-pitched roof with a beam and mortar exterior. Nothing extravagant by any means but even so, it was rebuked by the more pious of Wickstead as being too gaudy. Ebeneezer Wickes often slandered it as a shelter for gypsies and roustabouts. Despite his lofty vantage point, his view of the world was rather narrow.

Henry's parents, Arthur and Martha Beecham, were good people who ran a respectable public house. They sold drink but did not allow drunkenness. Arthur was known to eject anyone who got too far into his cups. Still, every alehouse has a shadow of disrepute about it and it was not a place for two young women to enter alone without risk of setting tongues wagging. It was midday and we wouldn't tarry long, so through the door we went.

The tap room was large, taking up most of the footage of the first floor with the rooms upstairs and the kitchen in the back. The hearth was spacious and built out of fieldstone with a massive beam for a mantel. The tables and chairs of the saloon were fanned around the fireplace, which was as much for light as for heat since the interior was quite dim. Traversing the threshold from sunny day to the inner tavern was like stepping into a dank burrow. One was blind until the eyes had time to adjust.

The long counter ran the length of the southern wall, its surface polished smooth by countless elbows. Arthur Beecham stood behind it, tall and austere, fixing a tap on a barrel. His wife, Martha, stood on the other side, jotting figures onto a scrap of rough paper. Their daughter, Agnes, swept the floors. Mister Beecham was a very fine-looking gentleman and his wife was comely and, to my mind, almost noble-looking, like the blood of some forgotten aristocracy ran in her veins. With these two as progenitors, it was little wonder that Henry had grown into the handsome lad he was. But I'm forgetting myself.

"Well, hello there, young Stokelys," declared Arthur as we stood blinking in the doorway. "Come in."

Prudence and I doffed a curtsy and crossed to meet them. "Mr. Beecham. How are you, Mrs. Beecham?"

Martha greeted both of us with a kiss. "What brings you girls out today?"

Pru couldn't contain herself. Her eyes had scanned the room twice for any sign of the errant horsemen. "Have James and Henry returned yet?"

"No, miss," replied Arthur. "I don't expect them back till tonight. Maybe tomorrow, if they tarry in town."

"Aren't you worried about them?" Pru stammered. "Should someone go looking for them?"

I gripped my cousin's hand to steady her and addressed the queer look on Martha's face. "We're concerned, that's all," I said. "We thought they might come here to rest after their ride."

"I fully expect them to stop here first," Martha Beecham replied. "I'm looking forward to hearing news from Bountiful. Or any news at all, to be quite honest."

News from the outside world did not travel fast in our remote corner of the map. The broadsheets we received were often days, if not weeks, stale, and the mail regularly delayed. Social news and hearsay trickled in like the wax from a candle, splotchy and unreliable.

Arthur wiped his hands on a rag. "I'm eager to learn about the guest in your barn."

"Such a ruckus he's caused," said Martha. "How is he, by the by? Has he spoken more?"

Prudence's grip squeezed my knuckles. She had begun stammering. "He's woken here and there. Uttered some terrible things—"

"He's still feverish," I interrupted to clam her up. I hewed to Pardon's wisdom on this; there was no sense alarming anyone about the man's strange claims. Especially Henry's parents. "We are hopeful he'll recover soon."

"We're all eager to hear more," Martha said. "You should hear the speculation over the man's origins. The tales spin more fanciful with each pull of the keg."

A curious look passed between the couple, suggesting some prior disagreement between the two. I had observed the same grudging look between Pardon and Katherine in my time with them. Marriage, it seemed, was often a long string of old quarrels and quibbles that never quite died and could, with little provocation, flare up to full heat at a moment's notice. Unwilling to stoke the fire at the moment, Arthur excused himself and withdrew to the scullery.

A noise from behind me drew my attention to the staircase. My eyes had adjusted to the gloomy aspect of the tavern, allowing me to take in the source of the footfalls on the steps. If they had not, I would not have seen the black figure on the stairs, so draped in darkness was she. She stood at the bottom step with one gloved hand on the railing. Her attire was finer and more lavish than what we were used to seeing in our rustic part of the world and every stitch of it was black. Her hat, which was wide brimmed, was also black with a dark veil draped down to cover her face. She stood without uttering a word, waiting for the lady of the house.

"Excuse me, girls," Martha said as she hurried to her guest. The two spoke quietly, their words out of earshot.

Prudence blanched. "Who is that?"

"How should I know?"

"She's not from around here," Pru added. "She's a proper lady if ever I saw one."

I tried to be discreet as I watched Martha conferring to the woman on the stairs. The lady pressed a small envelope in the innkeeper's hand.

"She must be in mourning in all that black," I said to Pru.

"But who is she mourning?" asked Prudence.

Martha bowed, and the woman retreated up the staircase again, the heels of her black brogues ringing smartly on each step. When Mrs. Beecham returned to us, we besieged her with questions.

"Who is that?"

"Where is she from?"

"Who died?"

Martha raised a hand to quell our tittering. "Mind your manners, you nosy parkers. She's a guest, arrived late last night."

"She's quite refined," I remarked. "Who is she?"

Martha held the envelope in her hand. The red sealing wax still glistened. "She gave her name as Lady Szabina. More than that she did not say."

"Szabina?" Pru repeated. "A foreigner?"

"She does speak with an accent. What kind, I do not know. I have no ear for that sort of thing."

"But all that black," I said. "Clearly she's in mourning."

"My guess is that she's a widow. Why else would a woman travel alone?" Martha laid the envelope on the bar and picked up her tray. "As for the veil, well, who hasn't lost someone recently?"

Martha was right. Black crepe was a common enough sight among us. Death was always near and mourning clothes were common. Aside from church and the tavern, the cemetery was the most visited place in town. Every week someone was being buried, it seemed.

Mrs. Beecham resumed her workday, and I didn't want to impose on anymore of her time. I said goodbye.

Prudence bowed and said, "Will you send word when James and Henry return?"

"I promise, you'll be the first to know. Send your mother my regards, girls."

We left, stepping back out into the blinding sun of midday. Prudence's worries about her beau had not been assuaged but the intrigue over the lady mourner gave her something new to prattle about on the way home. My oldest cousin professed to abhor gossip, having been on the receiving end of it over her courtship with James, but in private, Pru loved nothing more than a spicy morsel of hearsay to chew on. In truth, I was no better, with ears like a rabbit, attuned to pick up the slightest hushed whisper in a room. Another black mark on the docket of my sins.

10

WE RETURNED HOME to be duly scolded by Mother Stokely for lollygagging the day away. A fuss was made with much complaining, but dinner was prepared and served with no one injured. Katherine had a penchant for hyperbole that often whipped minor incidents into tragedies of Greek proportion. One would think that the heavens themselves would crash around our ears if supper were served a minute later than the appointed time. Prudence managed to detract my aunt from our rebellion by recounting the sighting of the mysterious widow at the inn. Speculation and imagination ran a bit wild, but I was grateful as the distraction lessened the harsh look in my aunt's eye.

After the dishes were cleared away and scoured, I put together a plate of scraps and took them out to our guest in the barn. He was still trussed to the post, but he was awake. I asked him how he was feeling, but he did not reply. A dozen questions tossed at him solicited no response. He was willfully stony and nothing I could say would prompt him to speak. With his hands bound, I was forced to spoon feed him, but he pursed his lips like a petulant child and turned away.

I laid the spoon back into the bowl. "That is quite enough, Mister Ephraim. You may choose to be silent if that is what you wish, but you must eat. Your wellbeing has been placed in my hands and I shall be very cross if you waste away under my watch."

The hardness in his face fell away and he relented to being fed. I set aside any pressing questions about his earlier claims and asked if anything pained him. He responded with nods or shakes of his head. Judging by his appearance and his wordless answers, he seemed much recovered. I wiped his mouth with a kerchief, gathered up the bowl and turned to leave. At the door, I heard him mutter something. I asked him to repeat it.

"Thank you," he said. "Not just for the food, but for your ministrations."

His expression was so low that it made me pity him anew. "I'm glad you're feeling better. I hope we can get on better in the future."

"Miss," he said in a plaintive tone, "will you loosen these bonds? I cannot stay here."

"That is not my decision, sir."

"And if I told you my life was in danger? Would you still refuse to help me?"

I turned away from those haunted eyes. "I will speak to my uncle. That's all I can do."

He closed his eyes and leaned back against the post, saying no more.

Returning to the kitchen, I heard a great bustle of voices from the front hall. Rushing in I was displeased to see Tom Hazard there in our home. Tom was a cruel boy, only a year older than Jacob, who often tormented me with catcalls. His father was Halton Hazard, fellow selectmen to Pardon. Mister Hazard stood in the doorway beside his son with his cap in his hand, the family much agitated around him.

"What's going on?" I asked.

"The boys have returned from Bountiful," Katherine replied, donning her bonnet. "And I fear the news is not good."

A cold tingle ran down my backbone. "Henry and James? Are they all right?"

"They're fine," said my uncle. "The selectmen have them at Beecham's inn and I'm wanted."

Prudence hurried to get her shawl. "I'm coming with you."

"The devil you are," he barked. "You're to stay and manage the house whilst your mother and I are gone."

Pru protested, and an argument broke out between the parents and their eldest child. I swept in to broker peace, but also to sway the disagreement to my own needs. Taking Prudence by the shoulders, I turned to my aunt and uncle.

"Prudence and I will stay silent and out of the way. Samuel can oversee the homestead while we're gone. Can't you, Sam?"

Samuel almost saluted, so eager to be in charge was he. I pushed Prudence out the door before another argument could ignite.

We hurried into town and rushed the doors of Beecham's Landing to find the tavern nigh packed. Henry and James sat before the fireplace and my heart thudded hard at the sight of them. Both looked haggard and spent as the men crowded around them, lobbing question after question.

"Are you sure, lads?" asked one.

"It's gone, all of it?" asked another. "Not a soul?"

James let his gaze fall to the floor before him. Henry looked up at the assembled crowd and spoke slowly. "It's true. Bountiful is gone. There is nothing but cinder and ash. Even the church."

A gasp went around the saloon. A voice let out a sob, and another cried out to God for mercy. The crowd parted as Ebeneezer Wickes pressed forward to reach Pardon, bending low to avoid rapping his tall noggin against the ceiling timbers.

"Pardon, you're here," he said, pulling my uncle away. "The others are in the green room, discussing the news. Come."

My uncle was swept away to confer with other selectmen secluded in the inner room. James was comforted by his mother and younger sister, Sarah. Martha Beecham took Henry's hand and led him away from the men and their questions.

Prudence could stand no more and she rushed over to be by her beau's side. The energy in the room dissipated a little as the patrons paired off in groups to discuss the matter over their mugs. I sat with Katherine until I saw Martha called away to attend to the men rattling their tin cups against the board for more drink. Excusing myself, I scurried over to speak to her son.

"Henry," I said, looking him over for any injury. "Are you hurt?"

His eyes rolled up, vacant and bald as if he didn't recognize me. "Hester?"

"Yes, I'm here." I took hold of his hand to help him focus. A bold act, but I didn't care. "Tell me you are all right."

"I'm fine." He shook his head as if to snap himself awake. "Nothing happened to us."

"I'm glad for that, but you witnessed something terrible. I can see it in your eyes."

His eyes reddened. I feared he was about to cry. "God, Hester, it was awful. I've never seen anything so terrible."

"There, there." I rubbed his hands, although they were not cold. I don't know if it helped, but it gave me something to do. I felt powerfully useless in the face of it. "You don't have to say anymore. Would a brandy help?"

His hand squeezed mine. "It's all gone. Every house, every building. It was still smoking when we came upon it. The horses refused to enter the place. We had to leave them on the road."

"There, there." My stupid mouth could not come up with anything more comforting.

"The only things left standing were the chimneys. In some of the ashes, you could even see the blackened bones of the souls lost in the fire. And then the churchyard. God."

The last detail confused me. "What of the churchyard?"

Henry relaxed his grip but did not release my hand. His hand was strong and lithe, and I never wanted him to let go. "The place was in chaos," he said. "Graves had been dug up everywhere. Coffins were struck open, the dead left exposed to the elements. It was madness. Why would they do such a thing?"

I had no way of knowing, let alone suggesting an answer. His words were baffling. Had they really seen these things or were the two of them suffering some shared delusion? I didn't ponder it long for I heard someone cry out Henry's name. The tap room was quite overcrowded at this time and it was unclear who had spoken until a lithe young woman pushed through all those elbows and embraced Master Beecham.

Elizabeth Wickes all but threw herself at Henry, startling him at first. Her cheeks were damp, but a relieved joy was beaming from her pretty face as she thanked the Almighty for his safe return. Her mother, Joanna Wickes, soon appeared, fighting through the brutes around us. Joanna Wickes was one of our village's great beauties, but she was a diminutive figure, shorter than even myself. When paired next to her towering husband, Ebeneezer, the pair struck a curious portrait of marital coupling. Elizabeth had been blessed somewhere between the two, taller than her mother but shorter than Henry. She had inherited her mother's pert nose and plump lips that always looked as if freshly bitten.

Under regular circumstances, the boldness of her embrace, now with her arms flung about him and kisses planted on his cheek, would have been scandalous and set tongues a clicking in disapproval, but the tragic news about Bountiful gripped everyone's attention and no one, I supposed, could blame young Elizabeth for being grateful for the safe return of the two men. We were all grateful for it.

The two of them fell into conversation and Joanna Wickes pressed a hand against Henry's brow, wondering if he shouldn't rest after his ordeal. More people crowded in and so I withdrew from the table. As I did so, I heard someone mutter the word "gargoyle" in my ear. This was in reference to my facial deformity, of course, and it was not the first time I had heard it. I snapped around to catch whoever had maligned me but saw no one looking at me, all taken with Henry as they were. I thought I saw young Tom Hazard through the throng, grinning at me. That was not a surprise. Tom Hazard never missed a chance to hiss a cruel word to me.

I made my way back to Mother Stokely, who was now comforting Prudence. Mother's face was pinched in disapproval at the noise and smell of the crowd.

"Time to go, girls." She tugged Pru to her feet. "The room is ripe with drink. Let's escape now before it gets any worse."

We pushed toward the door when another harangue went up and the men in the room began to part. The selectmen had adjourned their meeting and were now marching for the exit. Pardon stopped long enough to take his wife's hand and motioned for us to follow.

Half the room spilled onto the street, and Prudence and I kept at the heels of my aunt and uncle. I strained to hear what they were saying as the cacophony of noise seemed to carry with us.

"Where are we going?" Mother Stokely asked.

"Home," came my uncle's reply.

"I'll be glad to be away from this crowd," she said.

"Not just yet, Katherine. The selectmen are coming with us."

Katherine looked ill at the thought. "Whatever for?"

"They want to interrogate the man in our barn," he said. "After the testimony of the young men, they want to get to the bottom of the tragedy in Bountiful."

I quickened my pace. "Will they hurt him?" I asked. "Mister Fiske?"

"They will if he doesn't provide a straight answer," Pardon said. "This mob concerns me. Everyone is so riled up, I fear they might drag the man out to swing him from a tree."

As we approached our house, the selectmen waited for Pardon to catch up and lead the way. Arthur Beecham and Ebeneezer Wickes instructed the crowd from the tavern to wait outside our gate. Apparently they too were concerned about the mob at our heels. Pardon led the councilmen past the house where the faces of my cousins were all pressed to the glass at the hubbub in the yard. Marching to the barn, Pardon swung the door wide and led the selectmen inside. A few curses issued from inside, then the clatter of a pitchfork being hurled against the wall. For a moment I feared the council were executing the sick man then and there, but my uncle reappeared in the doorway a moment later.

The selectmen followed him out, their faces grim. In my uncle's hand was a length of hemp rope. Presumably the one used to bind up Mister Ephraim Fiske.

"What is it?" Mother Stokely demanded. "What have you done with him?"

"Nothing," Pardon said with a sad shake of his head. "The man's escaped."

11

SEARCH PARTIES WERE organized, men rushing into the woods with lanterns and clubs. A few were armed with flintlocks and others had retrieved the family sword from their mantelpiece. Halton Hazard brought out his hounds and throughout the town and the surrounding woods came the braying of the dogs and the howling of men long into the night.

The risk of a lynch mob was even greater now that blood was up and the hunt was on. Pardon loaded and charged his pistol, praying that wanton violence would not take over the mood of the search parties. Samuel and Jacob both pleaded to go with their father, but Pardon forbade it until Mother Stokely suggested that three of them could watch over one another better than a lone searcher among the rabble. Off they went after vowing to Katherine to keep each other safe.

Mother Stokely stayed out on the veranda, pacing back and forth as she listened to the distant hollers and whoops from the darkness. Twice came the report of gunfire. Prudence fretted at her mother's side and Faith sought to protect us all with prayers to the Almighty. I made tea.

Everyone stayed up, waiting for word. Hiram and Polly

refused to go to bed, so we settled them on the rug before the fireplace and wrapped them under a quilt. They fell asleep and the rest of us took to whispering around their lightly snoring souls.

At one point, we were all startled by a cacophony of dogs as they bolted around the house toward the barn. Hazard's hounds tore about the place, frightening the animals. One of them must have bolted into the paddock for we heard a dog cry out suddenly as if hurt. I can only assume that the hound made the mistake of harassing old Caesar and gotten kicked for his troubles. Polly woke from her nest before the fire, upset by the barking. Hiram slept through it all.

It was almost midnight when we heard the boots of our men clomping up the veranda steps. They were tramped with mud, their faces long with exhaustion. Following them inside were George Corwin and his son, James. Prudence's face lit up.

"Did you apprehend him?" asked Mother Stokely.

Pardon drew a chair close to the hearth to warm himself. "No. Not a damn sign of him anywhere." He looked down at the slumbering babes on the floor. "Why are the children laying about like house cats?"

"How could he have disappeared like that?" I asked.

Pardon grumbled something I didn't hear. Mr. Corwin spoke up. "The stranger is either as fast as the devil or he's holed up some place where even the hounds can't nose him. We'll renew the search in the morning. I'm sure we'll smoke him out in the light of day."

Pardon rose and thanked George for seeing them home. Prudence managed to sneak a few whispers to James before the Corwins bowed and left us. Faith and I gathered up the little ones and Mother Stokely ordered everyone to bed. She had had enough adventure for one night, thank you very much.

My slumber was neither deep nor restful that night. I kept waking, troubled by some vague unease, but when I sat up, the room was quiet, the house peaceful. This occurred two or three times before I saw a gray wash of light in the window. Dawn was not far off, and I despaired at how thoroughly wretched I felt.

There was a noise. A thud from somewhere in the house, followed by a pathetic cry. My first thought was that a door had been left open and one of the goats was rooting around the kitchen. I padded downstairs, the boards cold against my feet, but I found no stray animal. The front door, however, was quarterways open, letting the wind into the house. When I stepped out onto the chilly veranda, I flinched with fright at what lay there.

Prudence was flat on the boards, collapsed there in her thin nightgown. She did not respond to my voice or even my shaking of her. Her skin was cold. I shrieked for Mother Stokely to come as I tried to revive her.

My aunt and uncle appeared a moment later, groggy and confused.

"What the devil is going?"

Katherine fell at her daughter's side and pressed her palm against Pru's cold cheek. "What's happened?"

"I don't know. I found her like this."

"There's blood," Katherine gasped.

When Katherine rolled her daughter onto her back, we all saw the red blood staining her arm.

"Get her inside before she catches her death," growled Pardon.

I helped him carry her to the hearth in the parlor. By now the rest of the family was up, buzzing with questions. Mother Stokely ordered me to bind Prudence's wrist while she and Faith labored to rub the chill from Pru's hands and feet. Pardon started the fire and ordered Sam to get the quilt from their sister's bed to bundle her up.

Despite the shock, the family quickly closed ranks around their fallen member with marshal efficiency. It wasn't long before my poor cousin was bundled under a blanket before a warm fire. Katherine's attempts to revive Pru took a few moments longer. Prudence's eyes opened a slit but with lucidity came a sort of fright. She coiled up, covering her face, as if to protect herself.

"Easy now, girl," cooed her mother. "What's happened to you?"

Puzzlement and fear swirled in Prudence's eyes as she saw the family gathered around her. "Why are you all hovering?"

"Hester found you outside, dear. How did you get there? Did someone lay a hand on you?"

"No," Pru gasped. "I don't know. I'm so cold." She began to cry.

Little Polly curled into her side like a house cat wanting warmth. "Don't cry, Pru. Drink your tea. It will make you feel all better."

My aunt and uncle took a step back and scratched their heads over the situation, unsure of what to make of it. Pardon pulled me into their huddle but kept his voice low.

"Did you see Prudence get out of bed last night?"

"I did not. Nor did I hear anything until just a few minutes ago when I found her."

Pardon touched his wife's arm. "How badly is she hurt?"

"A small cut on her wrist. It must have happened when she collapsed. But what on earth was she doing outside in the middle of the night? In her nightgown no less."

I asked, "Could she have been sleepwalking?"

Mother Stokely shook her head. "It would be a first for her if she did. Night wandering was Faith's trouble when she was younger, but never Pru."

The couple studied their eldest daughter by the fire, surrounded by her siblings. Some color had returned to Pru's cheeks. Mother Stokely turned to peer out the window where the sky was a smoky gray.

"We'll let her revive a little longer before the fire," she announced. "Then we'll get her up to her own bed and keep watch. She's a strong girl. I'm sure she'll be fully restored by midday."

Pardon agreed. "The boys and I need to get dressed. They'll be renewing the search for that fugitive soon."

Katherine snatched her husband's wrist. "You don't think he attacked Prudence, do you?"

"I'm sure the man's long gone by now." Pardon planted a kiss on his wife's worried brow. "Will you be all right?"

"The girls and I will manage," she said. She hooked her arm round my elbow and pulled me closer to her. A small gesture but an oddly touching one to me, the family pulling together in crisis. "All this will be over and forgotten by supper time."

~

Mother Stokely's optimism was often the vessel that kept the family afloat when the troubles came, but in this case, it proved to be misplaced. Prudence's condition did not improve. Her complexion became whiter as the day wore on, and her rest troubled with fits. Her face would contort in pain and her hands clutched the quilt in a quaking grip. Occasionally she would wake and take water but had no stomach for food. I tried to spoon soup past her lips, but she expelled it violently. Her siblings crowded around, all needing to be helpful to their older sister, but when Pru returned the soup into my lap, Mother Stokely ushered them all from the room and told them to stay downstairs.

I scrabbled through the larder for something to remedy her situation. A cold compress for her burning brow and a poultice of myrtle, sweet gum, and blackroot that I plastered over her chest. Prudence's breathing was labored and racked with a croup cough. The vapors of the poultice were meant to clear her passageways, but I saw no improvement.

By late afternoon, Katherine sent Faith off to fetch the physician. The title was generous. Wickstead had not had a doctor for more than a year. We relied on an aged man who had toiled as a bonesetter during the war. He set the cracked bones of the townsfolk, and the barber performed the bloodletting when it was needed.

At one point, Prudence opened her eyes and seemed very much herself. Mother Stokely was downstairs seeing to the babies and Faith had not returned with the old man yet. I took my cousin's hand.

"Pru," I whispered. "How do you feel?"

"Terrible." Her eyes whirled about in confusion. "I can't remember feeling this wretched. What's wrong with me?"

"You caught a chill from being outside all night. Do you remember?"

"A little." She rubbed her eyes to clear them. "Was I really out all night?"

"I'm not sure. Do you remember going out to the veranda?"

My cousin wiped a hand down her face. "I was being foolish."

"How so?" I made a show of glancing around the room for I could tell she was reluctant to reveal anything further. "No one's here. Tell me."

She puffed out her cheeks in shame. "I was supposed to meet James."

"Corwin?"

"Is there another James?"

Stupid of me. "James was to meet you?"

"I was worried sick over him for three days. I had to see him. When the men returned from the search party, we spoke briefly and made plans for him to return at midnight, so we could reunite properly, without any prying eyes."

A lover's rendezvous. It was foolish but who could blame her? A troubling thought nagged at me and, before I could trap my tongue, I blurted it out. "Pru, did James hurt you?"

She recoiled at the idea. "Of course not. He would never harm me. He didn't even show."

"He didn't make the rendezvous?"

"No. I waited and waited, but he didn't appear. I started to get cold, so I fetched my cloak from the rack and settled into father's wicker chair. I must have fallen asleep."

"You don't remember what happened after that? Did you faint? How did you hurt your arm?"

She looked at the dressing on her wrist. "I struggled to stay awake. The next thing I remember is waking before the fire and mother rubbing my hands."

A troubled look must have clouded my eyes. Pru's tone became grave. "Did something happen while I slept?"

"Of course, not. You just gave us all a fright, is all. Rest now. The physician will be here soon."

She clutched my hand. "Hester, please don't tell mother or father about the rendezvous. Father would murder James if he knew."

I was uncomfortable with this. "Are you certain he didn't show up last night?"

"Positive."

I promised to keep her secret and then scolded her to rest. The bonesetter arrived an hour later, doddering up the veranda steps with his cane. Surgeon Bidwell, as he preferred to be called, was older than Methuselah and still sported a powdered wig. It was now yellow with age and it sat awkwardly on his broad skull. Prudence was gratefully asleep when he wheezed onto a stool at the patient's bedside. He thumbed open one eyelid, craned his ear to hear her strained breathing and, at one point, bent low to sniff at her.

Mother Stokely pressed him for a diagnosis but he would not speak aloud in the patient's presence. We proceeded downstairs to the parlor where I had set down a tea tray for him.

Between nibbles of seed cake, he said he was unsure about my cousin's malady but confessed he was concerned about her rasping breath and ghastly pallor. There was no immediate cause for concern, he assured us, and prescribed a night's sleep for all to see what the morning would bring. His declaration seemed to satisfy Mother Stokely. It was inconclusive but if it was good enough for Katherine, then it would be sufficient unto me. Who was I to doubt the great bone-cracker of Mr. Madison's war?

~

The men returned home just before sundown, spent and filthy, with nothing to show for their efforts. The elusive fugitive from Bountiful remained at large, although Pardon said it was his belief that the poor man had fled into the bog and drowned, in which case, he would never be found. Their wasted day was compounded by the news that Prudence had not recovered. They took this news very hard, Jacob more than most, as he and Pru were close. Their search party had returned with a fourth member, young Lefty Will, who had been out with them. Pardon asked me to fix him something to eat before he went home.

I took Will into the kitchen and fixed a plate of cold chops, yesterday's potatoes and Tuesday's biscuits. William was clearly ravenous and very grateful to have a full plate. I couldn't help but wonder if the larder in his mother's house was bare as bone and how often he was forced to skip a meal. He was a wiry young man, like coiled rope, but he was far too thin.

"This is very good," he declared. "Did you make it?"

I replied that I did and watched him eat. "So the search turned up nothing at all?"

"Not a thing," he said, tearing off another hunk of bread. "I think your uncle may be right. If he's sunk into the bog, even the dogs won't find him."

It was possible. The marsh was just a field over from our property, near the dreadful Cogburn Hall. The fugitive would not be the first person to vanish in the bog.

"I'm awfully sorry to hear about Prudence," he said. "Do you know what she's taken with?"

"No. The bonesetter was here, but he was reluctant to name it."

"Old man Bidwell? I wouldn't put much stock in his assessment. The man's half blind."

"I don't know about any of that," I replied.

"Was he sober?"

I shrugged. "Sober enough, I suppose."

Will put down his fork. He was nimble enough, what with one hand and all, but I noticed that he ate slowly. I couldn't tell if he was savoring the meal or simply being polite by not wolfing it all down in front of me. He looked at me. "What do *you* think Pru is laid up with?"

"It's not for me to say."

"You've a keener eye for malady than old man Bidwell. Go on."

Jacob passed through the kitchen and out the back door. I waited until he was gone and lowered my voice. "That wracking cough concerns me."

"Croup?" he asked. When I shook my head, his expression fell as he guessed my meaning. "Consumption."

The very word put the fear of God in me. "Like I said, it's not for me to say. But say nothing of this to Pardon or my aunt. It would only frighten them."

"What will you do for her?"

"That's just the thing. I don't know what there is to do. I wish we had some paregoric to help her rest, but our cabinet's empty of it."

"You should have nicked some off old Bidwell when he was here. He probably keeps a flask of it for his own use."

I laughed. "That's being mean."

"But it's not wrong," he said. "You could try the Beechams. I wouldn't be surprised if Martha keeps some hidden in her pantry for the guests."

He wiped his plate with the last sop of bread and thanked me. His eyes then narrowed. At first I thought he was staring at my scar as if seeing it for the first time.

"I'm sure she'll recover, Hester," he said. "Pru's a strong girl. We'll keep her in our prayers."

I suppose I must have let my worries betray my eyes. Something I try not to do.

Will reached across the table and patted my hand. A bit too personal, I thought. We weren't family after all. But his smile was earnest. "You look tired. You should get some rest."

"I'm fine."

"Yes, I know you're fine. You're always fine, but I also know that you're the one who'll be sitting up half the night with Pru and be down here at dawn to start the fires in the morning. You need to look after yourself, Hester."

He went through to the parlor to say goodnight to the others. I remained in my seat. For some silly reason, his words had bitten down on something inside me and I suddenly felt close to tears. I suppose I was more tired than I realized.

12

THE NEW DAY did not see any improvement for poor Prudence, nor the day after that. Her condition went from troublesome to alarming with frightening speed. She seemed to be wasting away before our eyes and there was nothing I could do to stop it. The coughing fits doubled Pru into twists and when the first spot of blood appeared on the kerchief, my worst fears were confirmed. My dear cousin was dying of consumption, the galloping kind that felled its victims quickly. I believe Mother Stokely knew it too although she dared not utter its name. Pardon, although an extremely intelligent man, possessed a blindness when it came to his own children. He insisted that Prudence's condition was temporary and that all she needed was rest. I saw no point in bursting his ignorance. The grim truth of it would come soon enough unless the Almighty found cause to intervene.

We tried everything. Setting up a cot on the veranda, we moved Prudence outdoors for some air. I had heard that clean air and sunshine were a balm to consumptives, and it did seem to relax her. With Pru outside, I burnt sage and juniper and wafted the smoke through our bedroom to dispel any miasma. I administered squills, iron salts and camphor to Pru but nothing helped.

Rum and cayenne on her throat did nothing to ease the croup. There were patches of St. Anthony's fire along her neck and chest, which did not respond to any of the balms Katherine and I applied. Again I scoured the pantry and the larder for an ounce of paregoric or even laudanum, which would at least make Pru rest, but there was none to be had.

As the illness wasted her body, it began to nibble at her sanity as well. Prudence was delusional at times, claiming to see dark shadows that menaced her or rats running the floors that none of us could see. She awoke in the night with a terrible scream, claiming that there was a serpent in her bed, biting at her over and over. Faith pulled her out and I flung the sheets open but found no vipers there.

By the fourth day, the physician Bidwell was summoned again and this time, he prescribed bloodletting. Prudence's humors were misaligned and the only relief he could provide was to drain some blood away to bring her vitality back into balance with her phlegm and bile. Pardon told him to proceed and asked that I assist him. The physician tapped a vein in her neck, and I held a bowl to collect the red fluid. We bandaged this, and he tapped a smaller geyser in her forearm to repeat the procedure. Working in close quarters with Mr. Bidwell was unpleasant for the man reeked of spirits. He remarked at my steady hand at such gruesome work. I told him to mind the spillage of the bowl.

Later that evening, James Corwin stopped in wishing to see Prudence. Pardon told him it wasn't a good time, but Mother Stokely, perhaps sensing urgency, overruled him and asked me to escort the suitor upstairs. It was obvious that James was not aware of how grave the situation was as he almost collapsed when he saw her. She looked ghastly.

He rushed to her side and took her hand, kissing it and whispering the sorts of things lovers say, which made me squeamish. I wanted to give him some privacy, but that was not possible. I lingered near the door and waited. When he had settled, he motioned for me to come. I took the stool on the opposite side of the bed and tried not to stare at his wet face.

"How has this happened?" he asked of me. "And so quickly? She looks close to death."

"I wish I knew. We've tried everything. I am sorry, James."

Prudence lay asleep, her breathing labored and heavy. He

stroked her thin hand.

"Please be well, sweetheart," he whispered to her. "How can I go on without you?"

I flushed at the intimacy and wanted to leave. "We should let her rest."

"Of course." He released her hand.

At the door, I stopped him and kept my voice to a whisper. "James, Pru told me that the two of you planned to meet on the veranda the night you returned from Bountiful. Is this true?"

His already flushed face turned a darker shade of red. "It is."

My hand squeezed his arm. "Did you hurt her? How did you leave her when you left?"

He looked alarmed and confused. "I didn't see her that night. I had wanted to, but I was exhausted after the search party. I fell asleep at home. Poor Pru must have thought I abandoned her."

"I see."

We spoke no more of it and I saw him out. I felt relieved, knowing that James hadn't hurt Pru. The mystery of her collapse remained. I doubt we would ever know its cause.

~

When dinner was over and the pots scrubbed, the family sat quietly in the parlor. My aunt returned to the quilt she was making, this one with a distinctly garish pattern. Samuel read a broadsheet from Providence that was three weeks stale. Faith read the lives of the Saints, of course. Jacob whittled at a length of wood. He was not one for reading but was a fair hand at carving. His current handiwork was a likeness of a bear in chestnut. The aroma of the wood settled over the room. The younger ones had been sent to bed and Prudence was asleep in her bedroom. Drying my scalded hands on my apron, I knew I was expected to go sit with my sick cousin, but I was reluctant to do so. A flush of resentment passed through me just then, at being the nursemaid while the others were allowed their leisure.

When my uncle announced that he was walking to the inn for his evening constitutional, I asked to accompany him. I explained that I wished to speak to Martha Beecham about anything she had in her larder that might help Prudence. This was a half-truth, of course. I wanted out of the house and away from the sickbed for a while. I had seen nothing but the four plain bedroom walls for days and was beginning to feel like a prisoner. Selfish of me, I know, but there it is.

Katherine refused, saying it was too late for a young girl to be gadding about town like a trollop. Faith agreed, but of course she would. Pardon, bless his heart, swept aside his wife's concerns and said the walk would do us both good. He believed that vigorous exercise in the evening air kept his rheumatism at bay.

The night air was crisp and the web of stars overhead brilliant and bright, illuminating the road before us. I adored nights like these and the distraction from the woes at home lifted my spirits. Within minutes, we approached the glowing windows of Beecham's Landing and pushed through the doors into the taproom.

Peg-Leg Wilkins sat at a table with the bonesetter, Mr. Bidwell, both of them clumsy with drink. Martha Beecham was behind the long bar, setting clean glassware onto a shelf. Her husband, Arthur, sat at the long table near the hearth with Ebeneezer Wickes and Halton Hazard. These three looked austerely sober and grim. Pardon joined their table while I went to see Martha. I did not see Henry anywhere, which disappointed me, I don't mind saying. I was worried about him after the harrowing events he told me of in Bountiful.

Mrs. Beecham kissed my cheek in greeting, the good cheek, and asked after Prudence's health. I told her she was still ill but neglected to mention how dire it really was. What would have been the point? I related to her that I was after some paregoric or laudanum to help Pru sleep and asked if she had any to purchase. She didn't know but led me round to the pantry to search. Nothing turned up, but she pressed upon me a packet of dried mugwort from her own garden, suggesting I try this on a night with a quarter moon, when it would be most effective.

Henry appeared suddenly in the pantry with us, reaching for a bottle of glycerin.

"Henry," said his mother, "would you check the storeroom for any laudanum? Hester needs some."

Henry led me out back to a shed in the rear courtyard. "Is it for Pru?" he asked, unlatching the bolt.

"Yes. Her sleep is not restful."

"Sorry to hear that."

Moving past the barrels, we searched the shelves. He seemed in a rush, so I grasped for a scrap of conversation. "I hope you've recovered from the expedition to Bountiful. I can't imagine how awful that must have been."

He seemed almost surprised by my concern. "To tell you the truth, I've had nightmares about it."

I touched his arm. "I'm sorry. Perhaps I shouldn't pilfer your supply of paregoric. It might help you sleep."

"It doesn't matter either way," he said with a shrug. "It seems we don't have any."

We closed up the storeroom and he excused himself. I returned to the saloon to find my uncle speaking in a heated, yet hushed tone, with his fellow selectmen. Their faces were dour and their voices stony.

"Are you sure it was him?" queried my uncle.

Ebeneezer Wickes held a glass of claret in a dainty grip. "Who else would be out skulking in the middle of the night?"

"The fugitive is still on the loose," added Halton. "And we must capture him. Hence the night watch."

I wanted to ask what they were discussing, but I knew all four would clam up if I did so. So I remained invisible. This was not difficult for me. As the one holding the serving tray at home or tending to the children, I often found myself invisible to everyone. But it did have its advantages. I stood apart from the table, waiting on my uncle as was my duty. The men continued to talk, oblivious to my craning ear.

"Who spotted him?" asked Pardon.

Ebeneezer nodded to Peleg Wilkins across the room. "Old Peg-Leg there, walking home late last night. Said he saw a dark figure scuttling about the street, looking into windows and such."

"Clearly foraging for food or looking for a house to burgle," added Halton.

Ebeneezer raised his glass. "The fugitive is still among us. He may have eluded our dragnets, but he still has to eat. Clearly, he's venturing into town after nightfall to scavenge and commit God knows what kind of mischief."

My uncle frowned. "And this is why you propose a night watch?"

"One man, walking round the town from midnight to sunup," replied Halton. "A rotating shift, with every able-bodied young man taking a turn to spot this rogue and apprehend him."

My uncle shifted in his chair, uncomfortable with the idea. "Every man?"

"A democratic approach, in keeping with the spirit of any Republic. That means your son, Samuel." Hazard turned his attention to the innkeeper. "And Henry. James Corwin and Prewitt's two boys. Lefty Will."

Pardon clasped his hands together, looking solemn. "Yes, that sounds reasonable. But why on earth is the man still here?"

"Presumably, he has nowhere else to go," suggested Arthur. "Which brings us to the question of Bountiful. Henry and James reported that the dead lie among the ashes there, unburied."

"And the strange disturbance to the graveyard," added Ebeneezer. "The exhumed graves and open caskets. We cannot leave the place in such a state. Even if there's nothing left to it."

"Of course," my uncle said. "Those poor souls need Christian burials."

"Or reinterment," said Ebeneezer. "If the report is to be believed."

"What do you suggest?"

Halton Hazard reached for his glass. "We'll have to dispatch a team to go up there and perform the unpleasant task of collecting and burying the dead."

Pardon shook his head. "More strain on our resources. How many can we spare now that sowing season is on us? In addition to this new night watch you propose."

"The parson will have to go as well," said Arthur. "To perform the burial rites."

Ebeneezer Wickes agreed. "It'll be a grim business, make no mistake."

I remained silent in all this, waiting for Pardon to rise and signal that it was time to leave. If any of the men were aware of my presence, they didn't seem to care. Why would they, really? A plain country girl waiting on her master.

There was a disturbance near the door and, as I turned, I saw Martha there speaking to the strange woman in black that I had seen a few days earlier. She remained a striking figure, even at a distance, draped in mourning clothes as she was. Martha came scuttling toward us with a grave expression on her face.

"Arthur, gentlemen," she said addressing the men at the

table. "Our guest wishes to speak to you."

Ebeneezer looked across the room. "Ah yes, your mysterious lady guest. Arthur, have you learned anything about her?"

"No," replied the innkeeper. "She hasn't said much at all."

"She said she is the Widow Fiske," cut in Martha. "And she wishes to address you all."

"Fiske," sputtered Mr. Hazard. "Pardon, isn't that the name our fugitive gave?"

Before my uncle could reply, the lady in question approached the table. Her face remained shaded behind the mourning veil. She wore no gloves, which I thought curious for what was obviously a woman of wealth. She was also a bit damp having come from outside. A light rain must have started.

The men stood and bowed and Arthur Beecham, being the host, introduced his fellow selectmen.

"Good evening, Madame," he said with a slight bow. "May I introduce Mr. Pardon Stokely, Mr. Ebeneezer Wickes, and Mr. Halton Hazard. We are at your service."

The woman nodded at them each before addressing Arthur. "I am sorry if I appeared rude when I booked rooms, Mister Beecham. I had wished to be anonymous."

Pardon offered the woman his chair. "Do sit, madame. We are pleased to meet you."

The woman took a seat. I slid another chair to my uncle.

Arthur motioned to his wife to bring another glass for their guest. "No offense taken. We believe in respecting our guest's privacy here at the Landing."

Ebeneezer was so intrigued he was teetering over the table. "Martha announced you as the Widow Fiske. Do I have that right?"

"You do, sir," she said. "I am Lady Szabina Constantin Fiske."

There was a lilt of an accent to her voice, but I could not place it. I had heard Dutch and French and even some Italian in my time, but hers was none of these. German, perhaps, or something further east. I have no ear for foreign tongues. I studied the face behind the laced web of the veil, trying to distinguish her features, but all I could make out was the strong nose and dark lips.

The men around the table sat up straight at the widow's

surname. Pardon leaned forward. "May I ask, Widow Fiske, if you have a relation by the name of Ephraim Fiske?"

"I do. Ephraim is the reason I am here."

The men stirred and exchanged glances. The Widow raised the veil and tucked it back over her hat. I can say with all honesty that I had never seen a woman so stunning. Her eyes were dark and intense. They could have been green or hazel, I could not tell. Her complexion was milky as befitted a lady, her nose Roman and noble. The men seated around her were, for the moment, speechless.

The Widow went on. "Ephraim Fiske is my late husband's brother. And his murderer. Ephraim is mad, and he is very dangerous. I am here to track him down and make him answer for his crimes."

The men remained mute. The wind rattling the window was the only sound as everyone, myself included, recovered from the woman's bold statement.

Ebeneezer craned his long neck. "This man, Ephraim, murdered your husband? His own brother?"

"He did," she replied. "I know he fled here. And someone gave the heathen shelter."

"We did," I blurted out, forgetting my place. I immediately blushed.

The Widow trained her eyes on me with a hard expression, and I felt suddenly exposed as if standing in my night shift. Her tone was imperious, and it frightened me.

"And you are?"

Pardon spoke up. "This is my niece, Hester. Madame Fiske, I'm afraid I am the one who sheltered your brother-in-law. We had no idea who he was, but he was clearly in distress. If I had only known…"

"Forgive my tone," she said. "It was the charitable thing to do. Did he say anything while in your charge?"

"He was unconscious for most of it. He gave his name, but other than that, it was fevered gibberish. He fled in the night."

She frowned at this information. Arthur turned to her. "Madame, if you are related to this man, then you are from Bountiful?"

"I am."

"Pray, tell us what happened? We sent a deputation to your

village, but they found it burned to the ground."

The hardness in the woman's eyes fell away, replaced with something more sombre. "I am still unsure of the details myself. Tragedy had befallen us, striking down one household after another with illness. Consumption, to be precise. Whole families were laid low, taken to their graves. No family was spared. A sort of panic took hold and people became convinced that the Devil had come to roost in Bountiful. Ephraim, who was always of a strange frame of mind, believed it to be true. He and a group of fellow conspirators tried to burn the Devil out. Starting with my house, with his brother inside. The fires took hold and ripped through town. I fled. But I was one of the few who made it out."

"My God," Pardon said. The other men sat with their mouths gaped open.

"What a monster," said Hazard. "And to think the man is here in Wickstead."

The Widow narrowed her eyes on him. "So you believe he is still here?"

"We do. We organized search parties when he escaped, but to no avail. However, we believe he is still in the vicinity. In fact, we were just discussing a night watchman to patrol the streets."

"Only one?"

The council men seemed unsure. Mr. Beecham addressed her again. "And you mean to exact revenge on your brother-in-law?"

"I do."

"That hardly seems the task for a lady, if I may say so."

"I am no longer a lady, Mr. Beecham," she said. "I am a widow with nothing left. Respectability is meaningless to me."

Ebeneezer Wickes turned his nose up at her boldness. "Beg pardon, madame, but we are well equipped to apprehend this fiend. We have plenty of arms for the task."

"As do I." The Widow turned to Martha, who looked a little pale at the conversation. "Mrs. Beecham, may I have a hammer?"

"A what?"

Arthur barked across the room for Henry to fetch the tool requested. We all stood confused until Henry returned with a hammer and offered it to the Widow.

"I want this man caught and brought to me. And I am willing to reward anyone who catches him." From a hidden pocket, she produced a large coin and held it aloft for everyone to see. It was gold and roughly the same size as a double eagle, but it was clearly not the currency of our Republic. She crossed to the grand fireplace and proceeded to hammer a nail through the coin, fixing it to the mantelpiece. "One hundred crowns to whomever brings me his corpse. Two hundred if he is brought to me alive."

Again, all were stunned into silence. The gold coin gleamed in the firelight where it was pinned to the mantel.

"Thank you, Mrs. Beecham," the Widow said, returning the tool to Martha's hand, and then she crossed the floor to the stairs. "Goodnight, gentlemen."

13

"A WOMAN!" EXCLAIMED Mother Stokely. "Traveling alone?"

"Not just a woman," replied my uncle. "A proper Lady."

"And a widow," I added.

Katherine sputtered, the needle in her hand forgotten. Pardon and I had returned home still reeling from our encounter with the woman in black and related our adventure to the rest of the family. My aunt gaped in disbelief.

"She can't be a lady, traveling on her own like that," declared Mother Stokely. "And a widow no less. Has she no shame?"

My uncle settled onto a stool before the fire with a glass of brandy in his hand. The brandy was usually for guests as Pardon rarely tippled. Tonight's events had rattled him. "She has nothing at all now. I'd imagine propriety is a low concern for her."

Samuel perked up. Both he and Jacob were consumed by the telling of the gold sovereign nailed to the crossbeam of the fireplace. "Did she really offer a bounty for this man? Ephraim What's-his-name?"

"Fiske," I corrected him.

"A hundred crowns?" Samuel went on. "Two hundred to

catch him alive?"

"What's a crown?" asked Jacob.

"A foreigner's currency," said Sam. "Is it English, father?"

My uncle gazed into the glowing embers. "A crown? It could be from any nation, really. I did not recognize the coin."

"But it was gold?"

Pardon nodded. "It was. What other metal could one drive a spike through?"

A strange glossiness came over the eyes of the boys. Jacob seemed very far away. "Imagine that," he said. "Two hundred gold coins."

Pardon raised a finger at his sons and issued a warning. "Never you mind that bounty. You'll not take any part in it."

The boys groused but Mother Stokely scolded them to heed their father.

"That bounty will prove nothing but trouble for this town, mark my words," announced Pardon. "Every fool will be out there stomping the woods with a musket for that wretch. Fired up by the thought of that reward, they'll blast at every shadow in the woods. And someone is going to catch a musket ball in the back."

Sam and Jacob demurred and shut their gobs, knowing better than to argue the point. Katherine sat down at her spinning wheel. A dull thud from upstairs interrupted my thoughts.

"Where is Faith?" I asked. "Has she gone to bed?"

"Watching over her sister," replied Mother Stokely. "Will you go and relieve her? She's looking a tad pale herself. The rest of you off to bed."

I found Faith curled up in a chair next to the bed, eyes closed and a book in her lap. I touched her shoulder.

"Faith? Go to bed. I'm here now."

Faith sat up, blinking slowly. She flattened her palm against her sister's brow. Pru looked smaller somehow, like she had shrunken.

"No change, I see."

Faith shook her head and rose lazily to undress. A sudden cough took her, and she sat again to catch her breath. She seemed pale, and I palmed her forehead for fever.

"Are you getting ill?"

She shooed me away. "I'm just tired. It's Pru that needs

seeing to, not me."

The thought of another member of our household becoming ill was troubling, but I said nothing. I would wait until morning. If Faith's color had not returned, I would tell Katherine.

I dragged my cot next to the bed and checked Pru before turning in. Her lungs were gurgling, so I rubbed more of the mustard poultice on her chest to ease it.

Faith climbed into the bed next to her sister, watching me with her churchmouse eyes. "I don't think she's long for this world," she said.

"You mustn't say such things."

"What's the point in deluding ourselves? You can see where she is headed."

I wanted to smack her. I have never gotten on with Faith, and there were times when she could be so obtuse or blind to other's feelings that it shocked me. In my darker moments, I sometimes questioned whether she was Pardon's daughter. All the children bore some mark of the Stokely to them, whether it was the big ears or high brow or the knobby knees. All save Faith. The second born daughter resembled Katherine in a small way but bore no likeness at all to my uncle.

Sometimes I shocked myself at how dark my thoughts turned.

"Read your prayer book, Faith."

She watched me with those dark eyes of hers, glistening wet in the candlelight.

"Why do you hate me so, Hester?"

"Don't be silly. I just wish you would think before you speak sometimes."

I blew out the candle and we spoke no more.

~

I awoke early the next morning, dressed in the dark and crept downstairs to light the fires. I didn't mind being the first one up. I would make myself a cup of tea, or sometimes coffee if we had any, and would sit in peace to watch the sun come up over the southern meadow. The air was eerily still as a mist rose up in vapors as the sun's first rays touched the dewy earth. There was something divinely magical about this hour and I had it all to myself. This serene moment was where God existed for me, not the church or the braying of the parson or the puckered faces of pious churchwomen. The silence, pristine and whole, was where our world overlapped with the next.

Sipping my tea on the back veranda, I saw two brown hares munching stalks in the garden, but I did not bother to chase them off. That would have spoiled the quiet, and I wanted to savor it for as long as I could.

"Eat it all, you greedy beggars," I whispered to them. Their ears twitched in my direction.

There was something out of place in this tableau: a small bundle lying on the top step. Had Samuel left some tool out to spoil in the elements? I picked it up and unwrapped the burlap to find a narrow bottle of blue glass. The label read "Tincture of opium." It was the paregoric I had been after! But who had brought it and why leave it on the back stoop like some secret gift? Clearly, it was someone who knew I would be the one to find it.

Henry.

Who else would it have been? He must have found some in his mother's pantry and, knowing I was desperate for it, brought it round like a thief in the night and left it for me to find. I could feel my cheeks warming. Even the scar tissue felt flushed as I stood there clutching it to my chest, feeling as giddy as a ninny.

The tincture would ease Pru's suffering by inducing a deeper sleep and easing her ragged breathing. I had seen its effects before and my hope was that, when mollified into its slumber, my cousin would begin to heal properly. I hurried back inside and up the stairs with my prize in hand.

I heard Mother Stokely stirring behind her bedroom door as I tiptoed past her room. In the girl's bedroom I found little Polly sitting on her older sister's bed.

"What are you doing up so early?"

Something wasn't right. Polly was rubbing Pru's hand. She looked up at me.

"Pru's cold again," she said. "I can't warm her."

The bottle slipped from my hand. It did not break, only thudded clumsily against the rug. Prudence's eyes were open, staring at the ceiling rafters, but the dark pupils were milky.

"Come away, Polly." I snatched the girl out of the bed and set her down. "Run and fetch mother."

"But Hester—"

"Now!"

The girl scampered away. I touched Prudence's cheek and recoiled as if stung. She was as cold as iron in December and the blue bottle at my feet would not help her now.

"Faith, wake up! Pru is gone. Faith!"

Faith did not stir. My blood ran as cold as Prudence's flesh. I touched Faith's cheek and almost fainted with relief when I felt her warm skin. She was alive, but she was burning up and senseless. Helpless and frightened, I wanted to run back outside to the quiet morning and the stupid rabbits chewing up Katherine's vegetable garden. I wanted to crawl under the bed and hide.

Everything after that was pandemonium. My aunt and uncle were in the room and a profound wailing rose to the rafters as they fell upon their dead daughter. The chaos doubled when they saw Faith's low state and feverish brow. Polly was crying and now so too was Hiram. Jacob and Samuel appeared and sputtered in groggy disbelief until comprehension set in and brought them low. It was like a madhouse with all the shrieking and weeping and beseeching unto God for deliverance. I sat down on the floor, too numb to do anything.

I saw an errant foot kick the blue tincture bottle under the bed and out of sight. My cherished little prize now a useless article of clutter.

14

WE HUDDLED IN the parlor in our grief. No one went up-stairs for hours. Faith was brought down and settled into a chair where she slowly recovered. Neighbors came and sat. Some brought food. By mid-afternoon, Mother Stokely rose and brushed her hands as if she'd been dusting flour.

"Enough," she declared. "There is work to be done."

The younger ones were packed off to the neighbor, Mrs. Beasley, who had children around Hiram and Polly's age. Pardon went outside with the boys to root through the lumber shed for materials. Soon the sound of sawing and hammering sang from the yard as they carpentered a coffin out of pine boards.

Mother Stokely and I cleared a space on the floor of the scullery and threw down a sheet of unbleached muslin. Then we went upstairs and brought Prudence down. I was surprised at how light she felt in my hands and wondered if our souls have weight to them. Is that why Pru felt no heavier than Polly?

We laid her out on the muslin sheet and Katherine warmed a bucket of water over the fire. Faith, who had regained some strength, was sent upstairs to fetch Pru's best dress and her silk bonnet. Then we began preparing my sister-cousin for her final rest.

There were no undertakers here. People in Wickstead did the preparing themselves and we were no different. There were women in town, shrouders as they were called, who would lay out the deceased and prepare them for burial if the family was not up for the task, but Mother Stokely wouldn't hear of it.

"I'll not have some stranger's hands on my sweet girl," she stated. "Only those who loved her."

The sentiment was touching, and I was moved to be considered among those loving hands. Removing the shift was difficult as Pru's limbs had stiffened, but we managed to get it off. Mother Stokely covered her mouth when she saw her daughter's bare form.

"My God," she uttered. "How wasted she'd become. I didn't realize."

My own eyes gaped, for here was the reason my cousin weighed so little. Her ribs were poking through the skin like the iron hoops under a wagon canvas. Her belly was sunken, and her hip bones jutted up like the tips of icebergs. The consumption had eaten her alive with none of us the wiser.

Faith carried in the bucket of water and collapsed onto a stool. She watched as we washed the body and combed the hair. Employed thus, my eye was drawn to a white scar on Prudence's thigh. It wasn't new.

"When did this happen?"

"A long time ago," Mother Stokely replied. "When Pru was nine or ten. Samuel had taken the hot poker from the hearth and, without meaning to, burned his older sister in the leg. How she wailed."

I had no idea. Why would I? Yet, I found it upsetting, this long strip of ruined flesh. Pru and I had both been branded by burn scars. I never knew.

"I don't care for the look of all this blotch on her," Mother Stokely said, pointing out the red rashes on her daughter's body. "Did the illness do that I wonder or was there some other cause."

"I'm not sure. I don't think St. Anthony's fire is brought on with consumption. I could be wrong."

"Let's not mention that word for now," Katherine remarked, her eyes flicking over to Faith dozing in the corner. "And what of this? Was this blemish from the bloodletting?"

The blemish was a puckered rupture over the left breast. "No, ma'am. Blood was let from the neck and the wrist here."

"Look, there's another here and here," she said, pointing to another break in the skin on the collar bone and the belly. "What caused this?"

I was baffled. "I don't know. Could she have done it herself, in one of her fits?" My cousin had thrashed about in her bed when the fever struck hard and it was possible she injured herself. But looking at these strange puncture wounds, I recalled Pru's complaint about a snake in her bed, biting her. I dismissed it as a nightmare, but could there have been some truth to it? Perhaps some asp had lain a nest in the feather and straw stuffing of the mattress? It seemed so unlikely that I chose not to mention it.

With the body cleansed, I took down the dress hanging on a hook.

"Getting her dressed will be difficult." I touched Pru's cold hand, but the fingers would not bend. "With her limbs like this."

"We'll have to slit the dress up the back just to get it on. We can run a stitch here and there to keep it in place."

The going was troublesome, but in the end, we managed to get Prudence attired in her church clothes. My cousin's eyes were open when she died, and Katherine had shut them before we began washing but the left eyelid raised up again on its own and would not stay closed.

Mother Stokely let out a sigh. "Sweet Pru. Stubborn to the end."

"I may able to fix it," I said. "You can start with her hair."

As Katherine combed her daughter's hair, I lit a candle until it was hot and dabbed a finger into the taper and applied the soft wax under the eyelid as a bond to keep it closed. With this accomplished, I looked over to see Mother Stokely take her good sewing scissors to my cousin's hair and snip off seven locks. These she set onto a plate and handed to Faith.

"Plait these for me, dear," she said. "Seven braids in all."

Faith was clearly failing, but she did as she was told. I looked at my aunt. "What are those for?"

"Mementos. One for all of us, to remember her by."

I was unfamiliar with this custom, but there were many things that were still new to me in this place. Customs and taboos, odd observances, and rules of etiquette. It seemed I was constantly confronting some ritual that baffled me.

Katherine finished with the hair, combing and pinning it in place. We looked down at our handiwork. I wish I could report that cousin Prudence looked as she did in life, but she did not. The hair was as she wore it, the dress complimentary, but there is no mistaking death. Even a peaceful one in bed. In life, Prudence's face was beautiful and glowing, robust with flushes and the cheeks ripe with apples. In death, she seemed like some distorted reflection in a warped mirror. Her skin sagged and her eyes had sunken deeper into their sockets. Her full lips had flattened as if pressed with an iron. She did not look like Pru. She did not look like anyone.

"There," Mother Stokely said, wiping the pomade from her hands on her apron. "Now she is ready."

Prudence's boots lay under the table. "Her brogues need shining," I said.

Katherine looked at them. "We won't need those."

"Why not?"

"Boots are too costly to bury. Prudence will walk barefoot into Paradise."

I glanced out the window to the yard where the men were. The coffin was complete, propped up on the wobbly workhorse frame. Samuel and Jacob and my uncle were sitting on a log contemplating their work. They neither spoke nor wept but sat in silent contemplation of the receptacle that would ferry their deceased relation to the afterlife.

"Faith," my aunt said, "are you done with the braiding?"

"She's asleep," I whispered.

On the china plate lay seven delicate plaits of Prudence's dark hair. Faith remained on her stool but slunk against the wall with her eyes closed.

"The poor thing's worn out," my aunt said.

"We should carry her to bed."

Each taking an arm, we took Faith up the stairs and into her bed. She was still in her nightgown so there was no need to fuss with her. We drew up the quilt and neither of us mentioned her pale complexion or labored breathing.

"All she needs is a good rest," said Katherine.

"Yes." I had no wish to contradict her in the moment. I prayed with all my heart that she was right.

~

The coffin was brought in and lain next to its recipient. It was a plain affair of pine boards and penny nails. Prudence was gently lifted inside and Mother Stokely struggled to arrange her daughter's hands together. The wax applied to the left eye was shaken loose in the process and the eyelid rolled back once more. An unsettling tableau as I felt her milky eye staring at me, but I was tired and brainless from the grief. The coffin lid was fitted on and tacked into place with a few more nails.

A place had been cleared in the parlor for her. The wooden workhorses were brought in for a bier and placed before the window and the coffin set atop. We disbursed to our rooms to dress in our church clothes. Now would come the waiting and the visiting as callers would come to pay their respects.

Returning to the parlor, Mother Stokely stopped cold, a hand going to her mouth. "Oh no. The mirrors. I forgot the mirrors."

My uncle, who had been staring at the floor in some reverie of grief, looked up. "Hurry, woman. Before anyone arrives."

"Hester," she said to me, "run and fetch the bolt of black cloth. We'll cut pieces from there."

I knew not what the problem was with the mirrors, but I did as I was told. Katherine cut lengths of the material and the two of us went about draping them over the mirrors in our home. There were only three.

Like other customs, this was strange to me. "Why are we covering the mirrors, mother?"

"To deny vanity in a time of mourning," she said, arranging the material so it draped with a shapely fall. "And to not confuse the dead."

"Confuse them how?"

"The soul must find its way out, but if it passes by the mirror, the soul will be trapped in the looking glass. We must do what we can to usher Prudence's spirit onward to the Almighty."

"Of course," I replied, though, in truth, I did not comprehend it. I said no more.

Visitors arrived to pay their respects and soon the parlor was filled with people standing about and platters of food were lain on the sideboard. Everyone was kind and sympathetic, the women helping to see to the food and refresh glasses of cider and beer, while the grieving family was allowed to sit and mourn. I have never been a great socializer and grew uncomfortable with the constant press of people and their mournful looks of sympathy. I imagine Pru would have appreciated it. She loved a gathering. Faith's strength ran out on her. She was sliding against the wall in her exhaustion, so I took her upstairs to bed.

When I returned to the parlor, Henry was there. He bowed as I approached.

"I am sorry for your loss, Hester," he said. "Prudence was a kind soul and we will all miss her."

I had been "bucking up" all this time, what with the preparations and looking after the little ones, who had been returned from the neighbor. I was sad, of course, but the gravity of Pru's passing had not had a chance to settle on me. Until now. Henry, of all people, brought it home. There was something to the look of genuine concern in his eyes and the gentle way he touched my arm. The tears erupted so fast I lost my bearings and would have fallen had he not caught me.

I dampened his coat with my tears and pressed my brow into his chest. He held me up and I'm not ashamed to confess that, in the moment, I never wanted it to end. To curl up against him and weep onto his shoulder. But I couldn't, could I?

"Thank you." I withdrew and dabbed the tears away. "You are a sweet man, Henry Beecham."

I stepped away, needing some air. I almost ran back, wanting to thank him for the gift of the paregoric, but I couldn't face another moment in that stuffy overcrowded room and continued on to the kitchen and through the back door.

The night air was cool, and it revived me, the breeze blowing away the fuzzy-headedness of grief.

"Hello Hester," said a voice.

I turned to see Will Treves on the back veranda. He was leaning against the post, looking in through the window at the house of mourners.

"Why are you lingering on the back porch? Come inside."

"I can't." He removed his cap and looked down at his threadbare jacket and the empty cuff of the right sleeve. "I'm not dressed properly. I was hoping one of the family would step outside so I could pay my respects. I'm glad it was you."

"Nonsense," I said and took hold of his arm. "Come in and

say hello to Pardon. He'd be happy to see you."

He wouldn't budge. "I mustn't. Please."

I followed his gaze to the window where the mourners shuffled through the house in their church-going clothes and realized that Will had no Sunday best to change into. I let the matter go.

"Are you hungry," I asked. "Let me fetch you a plate. There's too much food as it is."

"I can't stay. I've been called up for duty."

"Duty?"

"The night watch," he said. "The selectmen picked names out of a hat to schedule the rotations. I get to go first."

"Oh. I'm afraid you'll be in for a long night, then." I remembered the words of the Widow Fiske. "Do be careful. Have you heard about the widow at the inn? And what she said about the fugitive who was in our barn? He sounds dangerous."

"I heard." He folded and unfolded the cap in his hand. "Such a terrible story."

"Will you be safe? Pardon has the flintlock pistol he confiscated from the man. Perhaps you could borrow that for tonight?"

"No need. Ebeneezer is loaning me his weapon and Mr. Hazard has a whistle for me in case I spot the fugitive."

"Well, maybe you'll get lucky and catch him," I said. "Then you can claim the Widow's reward."

He looked down as if uncomfortable at the idea. "I'd be lying if I said it hadn't crossed my mind. Did you see that gold coin she nailed up in the tap room?"

"I didn't get a close look at it. What do you make of her, the widow?"

Will offered a slight smirk. He had kind eyes. "She's not from around here, I'll tell you that for nothing. I've never known a woman to act so bold."

"I suppose grief does strange things to people," I agreed. "She seems determined to bring her husband's murderer to justice."

"Is that justice? Putting a bounty on his head?"

I heard my name being called inside the house. Samuel's voice, bellowing away.

"I should go," I told Will. "Good luck with your night watch."

"Again, my deepest sympathies, Hester." Will put his cap

back on and squared it. "When is the burial?"

"Tomorrow. In the morning, I believe. My uncle said something about going to church afterward."

"I'll be there. And tell your uncle I'd be honored to bear the pall if needed."

He touched his cap and bid me goodnight before going out through the back gate to the road. Will Treves was a capable young man, even bereft of one wing as he was, but I felt a certain unease at his task of being the night watchman. I'm sure I was worrying for nothing, but I offered a quick prayer for his safety before retreating into the crowded house with its mourners and misery.

15

THE MORNING BROKE bright and clear, as fine a day as spring could provide but a contrast to the sad business ahead. Unable to sleep, I got out of bed and went down to the parlor where I sat with a cup of tea contemplating the coffin. I tried to fashion some sort of farewell to my sister-cousin but my heart was too broken and my brains too feeble to relay anything but tears. I didn't want to let Prudence go. Not just in the spiritual sense, but the physical as well. I didn't want her to leave the house where she was safe and make that awful journey to the church-yard. The thought of leaving her there was awful.

The family rose and dressed and went without breakfast. By nine of the clock, Arthur and Henry Beecham arrived, along with tall Mr. Wickes and the physician Bidwell. Samuel fetched our horse Phantom out of the paddock and into the traces of the wagon. My uncle would have preferred Caesar, but his favorite horse would be too troublesome for the task. Arthur offered to drive the bier wagon so the family could walk together into town. Jacob suggested we take the shortcut by the marsh road but Mother Stokely was in no mood to see the awful Cogburn house, so we took the high road.

A good number of people stood on their porches as we walked past and stepped out to fall in line behind us as we made our way to the churchyard. It was respectful, of course, but there was something oddly touching about it as the residents of Wickstead removed their hats as we passed and then joined the funeral procession behind us.

Reverend Crane stood waiting before a freshly dug grave. The sexton stood near the mound of unearthed soil with the spade behind his back. The wagon was already arrived, and the pallbearers brought out the coffin and bore it forward. James Corwin, Prudence's beau, was at the head, looking like a broken man, his face drawn, and his eyes red. Henry was across from James, with his father behind. Edwin Hendershot and Will made up the rest of the pallbearers. Will had done his best to make himself presentable after spending the night as first watchman. He must have been exhausted, but he didn't show it.

The pall men were almost to the grave when James Corwin stumbled and fell to his knees. The coffin pitched forward and was almost dropped, but the men quickly righted it. James remained on his knees and was weeping openly, and it was clear that he had not slipped but rather was broken by his grief and unable to contain himself. The sight of it was like a knock to the chest, it broke open our own grief and soon we were all sobbing along with him. George Corwin hurried forward and helped his son away and the coffin was laid alongside the grave.

The Reverend Crane performed the rites and gave a eulogy but not a word of it could I recall. My ears were blighted with sadness and deaf to anything but my own grief. The narrow coffin was lowered into the grave with ropes and then the sexton came forward with two spades for anyone who wished to help. Every man present stepped up to take a spadeful of earth and fill the grave. Henry and his father, one-handed Will, tall Ebeneezer and even James composed himself long enough to scatter the sandy soil over his beloved's coffin. I found myself moved by this small, but intimate act of kindness.

Pardon tugged at his family to leave, but Mother Stokely wouldn't budge until the grave was backfilled and the dirt pounded hard with the flat of the spades. Katherine's eyes had taken on a stony, distant sheen. Prudence's grave was next to her other four children, their small headstones slanting in the grass.

"All of my babes in a row," she uttered in a low voice. "Take care of your sister, little ones."

I feared I would drop to my knees in grief the way James had. I couldn't bear anymore and stood in disbelief at my aunt's composure and clearness of eye. How she could bear another loss was beyond me.

We left the churchyard the way we had entered, the rest of the mourners moving only after the family led the way. Katherine held tight the hands of Hiram and Polly as if she feared to let them out of her grasp. At the gate, Hiram turned and looked back at the grave site.

"Come along," Mother Stokely said. "You mustn't look back."

Hiram looked confused, but it was Polly who asked the question. "Why not?"

"Your sister may think we're beckoning to her and she might follow us home."

Hiram protested. "But I want Pru to come home."

"Hush now," scolded his mother. "Prudence must find her way to Heaven now and we shan't confuse her."

I'll admit I was as baffled as the children, but I had not the stomach to question it. I had given up trying to make sense of these strange customs and odd notions. I am sure that, in time, these beliefs would become my own, such is the way of these matters.

~

Grief can be so very exhausting; spiritually, mentally, and even physically. The days after the burial were ones of tears and sorrow but the tedious drudgery of life carried on, our prescribed toils performed with salt dried on our cheeks. We went about our routines like sleepwalkers trudging through a bog, slow and mindlessly. Adding to the misery was Faith's ailing condition. Her lethargy and whooping croup indicated the same awful trajectory of her older sister with the rest of us watchful and fearful of its worsening. There were times when Faith's eyes wheeled about so in their sockets that it frightened me. At bedtime, I asked her to read to me from her book about the lives of the saint's. She seemed to enjoy this as she became clear-eyed for a little while. I felt wretched about every harsh word I had ever spoken to her.

On the third day after Prudence's burial, my uncle asked me

to help him groom old Caesar. It was out of the ordinary as that task fell to Samuel, but I did as I was told, even though that obstinate horse never liked me and the feeling was mutual. He brushed the chestnut hair and I combed the tangles from the black mane, chatting quietly about nothing until he came to the point.

"What do you make of Faith's condition?"

"It's worrisome," I replied. "But Faith's always been a bit fragile." This was the truth. What was a sniffle in others became a bout of bedrest for Faith.

"But its characteristics are similar to what ailed her older sister, yes?"

I agreed with his observation but added nothing more. My uncle was not usually a man inclined to directness. He liked his words and preferred to use ten when two would suffice.

"Do we call in the physician again? Was he helpful? I cannot decipher these things the way you can, Hester. Should we ask Bidwell to return to perform his nasty bloodletting?"

"I'm not a physician, sir. I doubt my opinion matters."

He was displeased with my politeness, which was odd for him. The grief had whittled away his manners. "Do you think the bloodletting helped Pru? Be forthright, child."

I cleared my throat. "I do not. I think it weakened her when she needed her strength."

"Very well. We won't fuss with the bonecracker and his tubes."

He said nothing more, and we resumed our grooming. I tugged too harshly at a knot and Caesar swung his head round and tried to bite me with a clap of his monstrous teeth.

My uncle laughed at my shriek and then asked if I minded running into town. He had some correspondence he wanted in the post. I said I'd be happy for the walk. This was true. Then he added another errand.

"Do you mind stopping in to see Arthur? I want to know how the night watch is getting along. If there's anything to report and so on. I trust your discretion with any news."

I must have sounded far too eager to carry out his request, but if I did, he made no remark on it.

~

I was grateful to be away from the house and all of its misery.

There was no break from the grief. One person's tears would bring low another and then, like dominoes, the bout would run its course through the entire family. I found my mood lifting as I walked into town, eager to hear outside news and see faces that were not heavy with mourning.

I stopped at the postmaster and then went round to Beecham's Landing, where I found Arthur at a table going over a ledger with Mr. Hazard. The taproom was busy with a few patrons to whom Martha was serving pots of soup.

"Ah, Hester," Arthur replied when I approached their table. "How is everyone at the Stokely farm?"

"We carry on best we can."

"Of course," he said. "I should stop in soon and see how your uncle is. How is young Faith? She seemed quite under the weather the last time I saw her."

"She is still ill, but we hope she will recover soon."

There was an exchange of glances between the two men, a dark look that left me with an uncomfortable feeling. Had I said something wrong?

Mr. Hazard seemed to sense the awkwardness. "She's a strong girl. I'm sure she'll be right as rain soon."

"My uncle wanted to know how the night watch was coming along. And if there was anything to report?"

Again, there was a side-glance between them and then innkeeper smiled up at me. "There was a sighting last night in town, of someone skulking about. And a window was broken over at the Corwin house. But other than that, there's been nothing."

"A window was broken?" I repeated. "Did the fugitive try to burgle the house?"

Mr. Beecham glanced over at the patrons nearby and lowered his voice to me. He clearly did not want to broadcast this news. "We don't know. It may have been an accident. Tell Pardon I'll stop in later today and give him a full report then."

"Thank you, sir." That was an end to the discussion, so I said good day to them. Scanning over the saloon, I asked, "Is Henry about?"

"He's out back unloading a wagon. Why?"

"I just wanted to thank him for his kindness."

I went on through to the back, saying hello to Martha, who seemed quite harried. The rear of the inn was a rough courtyard where a rattletrap wagon stood in the dust. Henry was rolling a keg down a plank to the open bay doors. His sleeves were turned up and his arms flexed as he labored.

"Hello, Henry."

He looked up with surprise and, thankfully, he smiled. "Well, hello. What brings you into town?"

"Just some errands. My uncle wanted to know about the night watch. Your father said there'd been a sighting last night?"

The oak keg rolled to a stop and Henry sat back against it to rest. "I wish it was just a sighting."

I was puzzled by the remark until the realization came. "Oh dear. You were on watch last night?"

"I was."

"So you saw the fugitive?"

Henry popped a kerchief from his pocket and ran it over his face. "I saw *someone* last night, but it was dark. I hollered at them to stop but they just vanished into the shadows."

My hand, of its own accord, touched his arm in concern. "That could have been dangerous."

"I had a pistol on me."

He glanced down at my hand. I withdrew it. "That must have been frightening."

"That wasn't the half of it. The fool tried to break into Corwin's house and then later he killed a dog."

"A dog?"

Henry nodded toward the eastern edge of town, which was not the most prosperous quarter of Wickstead. "It was dead in the street with its skull crushed. The man must have bludgeoned it with a rock or something."

The horror of it made me shudder. "To think that madman was in our barn."

"I heard Faith is under the weather," he said. "Is she any better now?"

"She's still pretty weak, thank you for asking. I think Pru's death has sapped her strength."

"Such a terrible loss. We remember her in our prayers."

The sentiment was touching, but before I could thank him for his concerns, two figures ambled into the courtyard with their bustled skirts and fancy gowns. Miss Elizabeth Wickes and her friend, Mary Hazard, waved to Henry.

"Ah, Miss Wickes is here," he said. "She'd asked for some help with her chaise. Excuse me, Hester."

His face lit up, and he ran a hand through his hair to straighten it. Gazing across the yard to where the two interlopers waited, I felt an abrupt distaste for young miss Wickes, which was uncharitable of me, I know. But the heart is an unruly thing that thwarts logic and manners with equal aplomb. I forced a polite smile to my pursed lips as he strode off across the dusty path.

He was halfway across the courtyard when I remembered something. "Oh, Henry! Before I forget, thank you for the gift. It was very thoughtful of you."

He stopped in his tracks. "What gift was that?"

"The bottle of paregoric I needed. It was a pleasant surprise."

A puzzled look came over him. He shrugged and continued on his way. "Wasn't me, Hester."

I must have looked comical, standing there with a ridiculous expression. Elizabeth and Mary were huddled close and giggling and I could only conclude that it was at my expense. I rushed back inside before my face turned red.

16

"**AN ANGEL CAME** to me in the night and sat at my bedside. Its eyes were red, like holy fire."

I dipped the cloth in the basin of cold water and wrung it out. "Hush now," I cooed. "Save your strength."

Faith was consigned to bed, too weak to even sit up. Her color was almost as white as the bedsheets and her feeble voice was broken repeatedly with a coughing jag that left her winded. I was back to my poultices and remedies in an attempt to help her, but in truth, the best I could manage was to make her comfortable.

"Its touch was cold," Faith wheezed. "Isn't that strange? I expected an angel's hand to be hot. Scalding even."

I folded the damp cloth and draped it over her brow. The fever had scrambled her brains, leaving her with strange delusions. "It was just a dream, Faith. Rest and they will go away."

Her eyes were wet and glassy, staring up at the rafters. "It didn't feel like a dream, Hester. I believe the Almighty is telling me to prepare myself. Why would I want them to go away?"

I think Faith always believed herself to be like the ecstatics of old, or the saints she so often read about; taken with some vision of Heaven in a fit of ecstasy. Her condition was not only sapping her vigor, but nibbling at her mind.

"The angel," Faith went on, "had a strange purpose. She told me that it would consume a small part of my heart each night until it was all gone. Then and only then, would I be prepared to meet the Maker."

"She?" I asked. "I thought angels were sexless?"

"It looked female. I don't know. Her face—its face, what have you—was too glorious to gaze on."

My cousin frightened me when she got like this, whipped up in her ecstatic visions. The blue glass bottle of paregoric stood on the night table with a spoon next to it. I had retrieved it from under the bed where it had been kicked and I was grateful for it now. Even if its origins remained a mystery. Faith needed to cease her prattling and rest. The tincture would ensure that.

"Take your medicine," I said, spooning a thimbleful into her mouth. "No more of this talk."

Faith's eyes drooped and then closed and she was gone. Even in sleep, her breathing was rumbled.

The rest of the family wasn't doing much better in the aftermath of our recent loss. Pardon kept himself busy with work or taking his beloved horse for a run. I suppose riding took him away from it all. Mother Stokely was a different matter, going about her duties in a sort of haze. She refused to quit her mourning clothes for days afterward. The younger ones had become quiet and even boisterous Jacob was sullen. Samuel was not himself. He seemed tired and without energy, but when I inquired about his health, he became irritable. I feared the sickness was creeping into his veins, no matter how much he tried to hide it. Katherine was either in too much of a fog to notice or she wanted to go along with the ruse. I suppose I couldn't blame her.

I was also in something of a haze but that had more to do with being harried in ten different directions than with grief. With Mother Stokely lost in mourning, the duties of the household fell to me and these, combined with nursing Faith, were testing my strength. Yesterday I had fallen asleep at the spinning wheel, waking to find my fingers garroted in thread.

My cooking was getting sloppy as a result, but if anyone noticed, they didn't say a word. Perhaps their tongues were as deadened as their hearts. Grief strips the color out of everything in that way.

I was preparing turnips in the kitchen, making a right hash of it all while Polly and Hiram sat at the table with me. I had asked them to help me, to keep them occupied, but their ministrations of the vegetables were almost criminal. Pardon came through the back door and asked where Samuel was.

"He's gone into town," I said. "To see the cooper about mending a barrel. Why?"

"Caesar has a loose shoe," he said. "I need one of the boys to steady him while I tap in a few nails. Can you holler at Jacob to come help?"

"He's gone with Sam, I'm afraid."

My uncle frowned, hat in hand there in the doorway. "Well," he said, "you'll have to do. Put that aside and come out to the paddock."

"I need to finish this, and your horse despises me."

"He'll behave himself if I'm there. Children, finish up your cousin's chore there. Come along, Hester."

He vanished out of the back and I almost swore in front of the poppets. I wiped my hands, instructed Polly and Hiram to quit mucking about and do it proper, and followed my uncle out to the fence.

Caesar stood in the clover as haughty and menacing as ever. Fourteen hands tall, his bay coat rippled in the fading rays of twilight. Pardon had groomed him well, and he stood waiting for me with a hammer in his hand. "Just take hold of the bridle and keep him steady while I tack the shoe back into place."

Wincing, I did as I was told, but the moment I grasped the leather strap, the evil horse pulled away from me with a great snort of his nostrils.

"He won't take his lead from me, uncle. Perhaps if you hold him and I nail?"

"Very well," he said, pressing the hammer and three stubby nails into my hand. He took the bridle and spoke softly into the horse's ear, calming him. I leaned my shoulder into the withers and tapped at the hoof until Caesar relented and let me raise up the foreleg. My aim with the hammer was clumsy, and I walloped my thumb but managed to secure the nails.

A voice rose out of nowhere. "Hallo Pardon!"

Ebeneezer Wickes came cantering up on the back of a dun

horse. His long legs and absurd height gave the suggestion of a grown man trying to ride a foal.

My uncle smiled. "Ebeneezer! What are you doing about?"

"Contessa needed some exercise," Ebeneezer replied, patting his horse's neck. "I thought I'd say a hail fellow as I passed by."

"That's thoughtful of you." Pardon wagged his chin in the direction of the house. "Will you stay for dinner?"

"I can't. But I did want to have a word with you."

Mr. Wicke's eyes flitted to me for a moment. My uncle took his meaning and turned to me. "Hester, walk Caesar round, see if his limp persists."

The notion did not sit well, but I took the reins and led the horse away. The distance provided by the reins seemed to suit the animal since he let me lead him without fuss. I saw no limp in the leg with the mended shoe. We traversed a wide loop and circled back to the two men. Caesar contented himself with the lush barley at his feet and I stood waiting while the men conversed. Invisible as usual.

"And you're sure it is consumption?" asked Mr. Wickes.

Pardon nodded his head. "Bidwell seemed sure of it. I can't think of what else it would be."

Ebeneezer Wickes was grim-faced at the reply. He was always grim-faced, but now more so. "That is a frightening prospect. Our little town has been lucky so far, eluding the plagues that have decimated other places. We had assumed that the natural bulwarks of hills and creeks had sheltered us from it."

"You think our luck has run out?"

"I think we need to be vigilant unless we want to be caught out when it comes." Ebeneezer cleared his throat, reluctant to proceed with his query. "I hear Prudence's sister is ill. Is it the same ailment?"

"It appears so. Although we don't know for sure." Here my uncle pivoted around to address me. "Hester, what do you think? How similar is Faith's condition to Pru's?"

"Very similar, sir."

The conversation stalled out. The horse munched loudly, clapping its teeth at the strands of barley.

Ebeneezer patted his horse's nose. "I suppose we have that wretch to thank for it."

"The stranger?"

"Who else? The man has repaid your kindness by leaving illness at your doorstep. And now he's running wild through the streets."

Pardon turned his gaze west where the sun had finally dipped behind the line of trees. "I'm surprised no one's gunned him down yet, what with that foolish bounty on his head."

"He's a wily fox, that one." Mr. Wickes slipped his foot into the stirrup and launched his mighty frame into the saddle. "I best get back before dark." He touched his hat to us and was about to guide the horse on, but then he lingered.

"I hope you won't take offense to this, Pardon, but there has been some discussion among the other selectmen that Faith remain secluded here on the farm."

"She's in no condition to go anywhere."

"The thinking is that, until we know more, that we try to limit contact for now. To prevent the malady from pulling anymore into its web."

I could see my uncle bristle at the notion. "I see. Does that include me?"

"Of course not. Just the ones who are ill." Ebeneezer touched up the reigns and the horse cantered away. "We need your guidance on the council, Pardon. Now more than ever. Good night."

We watched the rider gain the road where he brought the horse into a trot until both horse and man disappeared behind the row of sycamore trees that bordered our property. My uncle shook off any ill feeling like a dog emerging from a lake and asked me to walk Caesar again. The animal was displeased to have its repast interrupted and harried me as I tugged him along. Pardon seemed satisfied that the limp was gone and his cherished horse was as fit as ever.

The clap of the back door sounded across the yard. Hiram came bounding through the weeds toward us.

"Father! There's a visitor to see you."

"Who is it?"

"A widowfish."

Pardon wrinkled his brow. "A what?"

"Hiram," I said, "do you mean the Widow Fiske?"

"Yes. That's it."

My uncle did not look pleased. "What on earth does she want with us?" He steadied his horse and began unfastening the bridle. Waving me onward, he said, "Hester, go greet our guest. I'll be there momentarily. I suppose we'll need tea."

17

RUSHING INSIDE, I stopped to hang the kettle in the fireplace, wiped my dirty hands on my apron and bustled into the parlor. Our guest was near the hearth, studying something on the mantelpiece. The widow was a tall woman, perhaps matching my uncle's height, and of slender build. Dressed in black as she was, she appeared as an imposing column of night within the comforts of the room.

"Ma'am," I said. "My uncle will be in momentarily."

She turned. "Thank you. You are one of Mr. Stokely's daughters?"

"His niece." I gave a small curtsy. "Hester."

A smile peeked through the web of the veil. "I remember you." She lifted something from the mantle, which I could now see was one of the thin braids of Prudence's hair. "These are mementos, yes?"

"My cousin Prudence. She passed."

"I heard. My condolences." She laid the hair back onto the mantel, alongside the others. "It is a sweet custom, these remembrances. No one likes to be forgotten."

A squeak sounded in the room. Little Polly sat on the

ottoman as quiet as a churchmouse, staring at our visitor.

"Polly, I didn't see you there." I patted the top of her head. "Go and play, dear."

"But I want to stay."

I shooed her along. "I believe the hens need feeding. Take your brother and see to them, please."

Watching the child run off, the Widow seemed to relax a little. Not everyone likes children, I supposed. With Polly gone, the woman raised her eyes to me and her eyes narrowed at the scar marring my features. I was accustomed to this but something in the open boldness of her stare unnerved me.

"The tea will just be a moment," I said, turning my chin a few degrees to the side to block her view. "Won't you have a seat?"

"Thank you," she replied, but did not sit.

My uncle swept into the room, clipping the awkward moment. He gave a small bow. "Mrs. Fiske," he said. "This is a pleasant surprise. Welcome to our home."

The widow did not curtsy. Rather she extended a gloved hand to shake like a man. I scuttled off to the kitchen and hurried to make the tea. I returned a moment later and laid the tray on the sideboard. Our guest, now seated before the fire, had raised the veil and was folding it back onto her hat. With the web-like material gone, the woman's features were lit by the firelight. She was like something out of a painting, a Helen of Troy or Joan at the stake. Even my uncle was taken aback at her glamor, losing his place in the conversation. They were still trading pleasantries, the widow offering her condolences and so on. I hadn't missed much.

"Thank you for receiving me at such an hour, Mr. Stokely," the Widow said, "And without notice."

"My door is open to all, neighbor and newcomer," my uncle replied. "I must say, you've caused quite a stir in town with your arrival. We are unaccustomed to such… excitements."

I poured the tea and placed the cups onto the table positioned between the two chairs. One rattled against the china saucer as my eyes were on our guest. Her gaze locked onto mine and did not break.

"A stir was not my intention," she said. "I dislike attention."

Pardon lifted the dainty cup and saucer from the table.

"Placing a bounty on a man's head is not a discrete act, if you'll excuse my saying so. Especially in a peaceful village like ours."

"I suppose not. But it is done."

"But it could be undone," he said. "Could I persuade you to rescind the reward? My concern is for the recklessness of men with gold in their eyes and muskets in their hands. Someone is going to be shot."

"One man's carelessness is not my concern, Mr. Stokely. A dangerous man is running riot and he must be stopped."

"But surely this is a matter for the authorities?"

The woman looked at the fire. "What authorities? The council in Bountiful has gone up in flames. No, I will see justice done and by my own hand to see it performed right."

There was a lapse in the conversation. I remained by the sideboard, studying this strange creature. It was impossible not to stare. Her comeliness and her curious mannerisms drew one's attention the way a fire does, holding it and lulling it into a kind of trance. The Widow raised the teacup to her lips, took a small sip and returned the cup to the table, unsatisfied. Perhaps she was accustomed to a finer blend of tea than the course leaves we had.

"I hope the Beecham's are treating you well at the inn," Pardon said. "Their blood pudding is the finest in all the parish."

The woman's expression grew sterner, if that were possible. Her countenance was difficult to decipher; cool and sober, a little aloof, but with flashes of amusement in her dark eyes. I supposed it was her foreign nature that confounded me.

"My accommodations are the reason for my call, actually. I cannot remain at the inn, and it's my own fault."

"How so?"

The Widow folded her hands in her lap. "The knocking at my door won't stop. Men asking about the bounty or details about my brother-in-law's person that might aid them in his capture. It is too much for me. I cannot exist without quiet and so I am forced to find other lodging."

"That might prove difficult, ma'am. Beecham's Landing is the only inn for miles around."

"Yes. I discussed the problem with Mr. Beecham, and he mentioned that you have a property for lease not far from here. Cogburn Hall?"

My uncle's expression was almost comical. Tea spilled from

his cup into the saucer.

"Cogburn Hall?" he repeated. "I'm afraid that house is not fit for habitation."

"I disagree," she replied. "I took a walk out to see the property and I like its distance from town and its seclusion. I would like to lease it from you immediately."

I closed my mouth. Who on earth would wish to live in that decrepit old house near the swamp? Let alone actually pay good money for it? Was the widow partially blind? Perhaps she could not see the broken glass and rotting shingles, or the moss creeping its way over the north facade?

"I'm sorry Mrs. Fiske, but I cannot allow anyone to move into it in its present state. Much less a lady. I'd be worried the rafters would dislodge and come crashing down on top of you. You should speak my friend, Abraham Wharton. He has a lovely little cottage near the river that is without a tenant. It is small but quite a cozy little nook."

Our guest raised her cup again in her slender hand and held it without sipping. "That is kind of you, but no. My heart is set on Cogburn Hall and I won't take no for an answer. How do you require your tenancy; by the month or the season?"

Pardon stuttered for a moment, spilling more tea into the saucer. "But the house is so old and in disrepair."

"I much prefer old houses," she said. "The smell of newly milled lumber and paint makes me ill. I like history and worn-out floorboards. Cobwebs don't distress me."

My uncle sat up and carefully poured the spilled tea from the saucer back into the teacup. "Speaking of history, you should be aware that the house was the sight of a tragedy. Which is why it's lain untenanted for so long. A troubled man murdered his wife before hanging himself from the ceiling beams."

"I don't pay any mind to ghost stories. Do you, Mr. Stokely?" Without waiting for an answer, the woman dipped into her dainty black purse and the sound of coins rattling could be heard. "Let me lease the house for the season and we will revisit the price again in the autumn, if I am to stay longer. I believe the sums will be generous to you."

She counted out two large coins onto the small table between them. They were gold and of uncertain vintage, like the one nailed to the post at the inn. A fortune, whatever the currency was.

I wondered how much longer my uncle was going to refuse the woman, but he seemed entranced by the bounty before him. The Widow turned to me and smiled. "Could you warm my tea, dear?"

I brought the pot over and poured only a little as the cup was still full. Her eyes scrutinized me in a way that left me feeling vulnerable. I did not care for it.

"Thank you," she said. "Hester, isn't it?"

"Yes, ma'am."

She continued to study me. Gawking was not something unfamiliar to me. She reached out to touch my arm. "You look familiar to me, Hester. Is it possible we've met before?"

"I don't believe so, Mrs. Fiske. I would have remembered someone such as yourself."

"I must be mistaken, then. My memory is long but details become muddled." She smiled again but did not touch her warmed cup. She turned her attention to my uncle again. "The sum is agreeable, yes? Is there a key?"

Pardon shook his head, bringing himself back to the present. "Are you sure, madam? I would not want you to think you've been taken advantage of somehow."

"On the contrary, I am very pleased and wish to move in immediately. The key, Mr. Stokely?"

My uncle waved at me and I went to his desk and found the ring of keys and brought it to him. I was sure the key to Cogburn Hall was unnecessary. The lock was most likely seized with rust. Pardon unfastened the iron skeleton from its ring and placed it in the widow's palm.

She rose from the chair. "Thank you for this, Mr. Stokely. And thank you for the tea, Hester. Now I must get on. I will not spend another night at the inn."

Pardon rose also. "Do you have to go so soon, Madam Widow? I was hoping we could speak of the events in Bountiful as there is much that is still a mystery to me."

"I'm afraid I must get on," she said, moving to the door. "But I will be back for a proper visit. Or perhaps I could invite you over to my new lodging. Good night."

She swept out the door and into the evening air. My uncle stood there with a baffled expression on his face. I believe the notion of stepping foot inside that old house was as disagreeable to him as it was to his wife.

18

KATHERINE DID NOT receive the news well. She was livid at the very idea of a tenant at the detestable house on the marsh.

"How could you?" she seethed at her husband. "Have you lost all reason?"

"I thought you'd be pleased," he said. "The place is tenanted. At thrice what the property is worth! How can you argue against it?"

Mother Stokely slammed the ball of dough she was kneading onto the table. It was baking day. "That woman or lady or whatever she is, is scandalous! Setting out to hunt down her own kin like some mercenary. Offering blood money for his head. And you offer her shelter among us. What will people say? The tongues are already wagging with one daughter gone and another on death's door."

"Katherine, no one is telling tales about such things," my uncle protested, but it was to no avail. My aunt declared that the widow was a sad individual who would bring shame down on all our heads. She marched from the room.

She wasn't far from the mark with regard to the wagging tongues of town. The looks of pity the townsfolk had bestowed on us had altered over the weeks to that of suspicion and fear. Illness had marked our door like the plague crosses of old, with death following thereafter and our neighbors were fearful of it spreading. The women gave a curt nod where before they smiled. The menfolk touched the brim of their hats and kept walking rather than stopping to converse.

And they weren't wrong. Faith's condition deteriorated in the days that followed and all expected the worst. The bonesetter Bidwell had been sent for but when he prescribed a round of bloodletting, Katherine chased him from the house, vowing she would never allow anymore of his barbarous methods. She called him a barber and a drunk. Her husband scolded her, but I secretly agreed with my aunt's assessment of his skills.

Sadly, Samuel was failing too. He tried to hide it and be brave, brushing aside any concerns for his pale complexion or weakened state, but we all witnessed him gasp for breath or reel with dizziness after exerting himself. A touch of fever, we all lied to ourselves. Too much sun and not enough shut-eye, we assured one another. No one wanted to face the truth, which was that we were powerless to stop the consumption that had settled in like dry rot in our family. All we could do now was to pray, but the prayer-leader among us was on death's door as it was. What was to become of us if Faith passed?

Bad news piled on in the days that followed as we learned that James Corwin had fallen extremely ill with symptoms common to consumption. The severity of his condition was missed at first as most assumed it was profound grief at losing Prudence. He had been shuffling through the days sporting a black arm band when the illness hit hard, confining him to his bed. The suspicious looks and whispering gossip grew worse after that, as it was assumed that Pru must have passed her plague onto young James with a kiss, condemning him.

On Tuesday, I went into town for supplies and received a cold welcome. Mrs. Van Tassel, the shopkeeper, who was usually quite a chattering bird, said hardly a word to me. The coins I paid with were left on the counter with a small cloth placed over them as if the currency were anathema to her. The following day, Mother Stokely went to the Corwins with a basket of holly cuttings for young James but she was told that they were not receiving visitors. Flummoxed, Katherine left the holly on the step and hurried home. On Thursday came word that the oldest Perkins boy had been killed out near the Derrick farm. He had been mistaken for the fugitive Fiske by two men eager to collect the bounty and shot in the neck.

When Saturday came, Pardon asked Samuel if he would take a walk to Cogburn Hall. He wanted to know how his new tenant was getting on, but Mother Stokely would have none of it. Sam was too ill, and she would not allow their firstborn son to cross the threshold of that woman's abode. Jacob was eager to perform the task, but he was dismissed, and the task passed onto me. I was feeling low myself, spending my nights watching over Faith, but I was happy to comply. My curiosity with the Widow Fiske had only swelled since she graced our parlor.

I prepared some gifts for our new tenant, a few basics such as salt, butter, and oil for the lamps, and set off on the footpath along the marsh's edge. Cogburn Hall rose from the bulrushes in all its forlorn glory, the shutters drooping and the creepers meshed over the veranda like webbing. The place looked as abandoned as before as I went up the broken steps, and I wondered if the Widow had delayed her relocation from the inn. The front door was ajar.

I knocked on the lichen-encrusted wood and announced myself. When no one answered, I stepped inside and called out again. The house, which had once been quite grand, was huddled in gloomy shadow and swathed in years of cobwebs. Great strands of it wafted from the dulled chandelier and more of it netted up the balustrades of the staircase. The air was thick with the smell of mold and damp wood, the floors strewn with the dry bones of small animals. An opossum scuttled along the gallery of the second floor. It leered down at me briefly before waddling away, unconcerned with my presence.

"Can I help you?"

The voice startled me and I dropped the bundle I was holding. The Widow emerged from the gloom to my left, silently.

"Beg your pardon," I said, kneeling to gather up the bundle. "I called out my arrival, but no one answered."

The woman closed in on me. "So you barged in?"

"I am sorry."

Between the fright and my clumsiness, I did not get a proper look at the tenant until I got to my feet. I almost didn't recognize the Widow. Gone was the veil and hat, along with her fine dress. Her long hair fell loose, and she was clad in a kimono of black silk. The sash was loosely cinched at her waist and the folds hung loose, revealing a disquieting amount of pale flesh.

"You were resting," I said, trying not to stare at her. "I'm sorry to have disturbed you."

The suspicion in the widow's eyes fell away as she saw I was no threat. I must have startled her as much as she did me. "Hester Stokely," she said. "What brings you to my door?"

"My uncle wanted to know how you were getting along. Is there anything you need?"

"Oh," she replied. She seemed unsure of how to respond. "That's very kind of him. All is fine. I adore the house."

I could not stop my eyes from scanning our surroundings with its mold and cobwebs and frayed curtains. The place was a tomb. "I apologize for the state of the house. Perhaps Mother Stokely and I could help you clean it up or at least sweep out the cobwebs."

"There's no need," she said. Stepping past me, she led the way further into the gloom. "Come this way. I have one room prepared."

This turned out to be the library, a massive room with walls paneled in dark wood and shelves upon shelves of musty books. The library had been partially tidied up and swept clean. Dying embers glowed in the fireplace and the Widow stirred the coals to rekindle it.

"Are you managing, Mrs. Fiske, in this big house all by yourself? Wouldn't you prefer it was made habitable?"

She cast her gaze over the room. "I suppose it does look a fright, doesn't it? But it doesn't matter. Little does anymore." She nodded her chin at the bundle in my hands. "What have you got there?"

"A few essentials to help you settle in." Near the mullioned window stood a wide table that had been cleaned of dust and held only a large map. I set the bundle down and withdrew the items I had brought. "There are candles and a quart of whale oil for the lamps. Some sage to cleanse the air. Also some tea and some sugar."

The widow came alongside me and looked over the meager offerings. "That is kind of you. And what is this?"

One unaccounted for item among the others, a brown glass jar that she picked up.

"A gift of salt," I replied. "It's customary here. Good luck and all that."

She dropped it forthwith, and the jar thudded against the table but did not break. Something like disgust flashed briefly across her face before she recovered with a weak smile.

"My clumsiness," she said. "Thank you for all of this. You may take the salt back. I have no use for it."

One may as well say they have no use for air or water. Foreigners have such strange notions. I placed the jar back into the sack and set it aside. My eye went to the map flat on the table.

"What is this?" I asked. "Is it a map of Wickstead?"

"Yes," the widow said. "An ordinance map of the area. Mr. Wickes loaned it to me."

I studied its curious configuration of acreages and roads, the river and the marsh. Small squares had been drawn to represent the houses and the church, the town green. "How interesting," I said. I pointed to a figure near the swamp. "Oh, look. There's Cogburn Hall, where we stand."

"Indeed," she said, fitting one of the candles into a pewter holder.

"What is it for?"

She tucked her dark hair behind her ear and looked down at the map. "I wanted to get the lay of the land, to see where the murderer could be hiding."

"You really are determined to find him."

Her eyes were focused and intense. "Vengeance is not a trifle, it is a vow. And like all true vows, be it of marital bonds or fealty, it is sacred. Once committed, one cannot stray from it."

The notion puzzled me. "You make it sound almost holy."

"It is holy. What could be more sacred than a promise to avenge the wronged? Even God in his Heaven is honor bound to recognize that."

The log in the fireplace popped, throwing a handful of sparks up the flue. The Widow came out of her reverie and straightened the loose folds of her robe. When she looked at me again, some of the fire in her gaze had dimmed. "Your family was the one who found my brother-in-law, yes? You gave him shelter?"

"He collapsed in our yard. I was the one who nursed him."

"Come sit." She motioned to the two high-back chairs before the fire. "What was his condition then?"

I took the seat offered. "Not well. He was weak and feverish. I wasn't sure he would survive that first night. I dressed his wounds as best I could, using a poultice to draw out the bad blood. He began to recover over the next few days. His constitution must be considerable, considering his state."

"I see. His wounds weren't fatal, then? Describe them to me."

"There was a nasty gash to his neck and a deep cut on his head. Another on his chest, near the collar bone. Those were the worst. His hands and face were raw with scratches as if he'd clawed through a thicket."

She studied the fire as I spoke. The glow from the flames was complimentary to her. "Did he speak? And if he did, what did he speak of?"

"He was unconscious for most of his time with us. When he did speak, it was a fevered ramble that was difficult to make sense of. Fanciful nonsense, really."

Her gaze latched on me. "Fanciful how? Tell me exactly what he said."

The woman had a forceful nature that made me want to please her. It was strange. "He said something about the end of the world. How it was already here. He told us his name and where he was from. And then he said that Bountiful was gone, taken up in flames. He broke down and wept after that, refusing to say more."

The widow relaxed, easing back into her chair. "The guilt of his crimes was eating at him. Even in his madness, it claws at him. But not enough to compel him to face the consequences."

She grew contemplative again. Her moods seem to swing wildly from pole to pole. Reflective one moment, hot with passion the next. The extremes of grief, to which I had become recently acquainted with.

I sat quietly for a moment before venturing a question. "Was he always mad, your brother-in-law?"

The woman started to reply, but then paused as if to reflect on her answer. "Not always. He was a zealot, and very pious. But when I first met him, he was simply a bit dull in his sermonizing.

Piety can be so tiresome. I believe he truly meant to lead everyone to a greater understanding of their maker. But as time went on, the zeal became overbearing. When the tragedy settled on our village, something changed in him, turning him manic. And dangerous."

"How so?"

Her eyes dimmed, casting back into the past. "He saw the Devil everywhere, his hand behind every death as the consumption cut down our ranks. I always suspected him of being a Puritan. A nascent witchfinder, seeing the Devil behind every shed."

"Did you know this about him when you married his brother?"

"No. Nathaniel, my husband, and I met in Europe when he was traveling abroad. I didn't meet Ephraim until after we had wed and my husband brought me here to the New World. I remember thinking how different the two were, Nathaniel and his brother. Like night and day, really."

That was no surprise to me, given the clash of personalities within my own family. How different Samuel was to Jacob, how unlike somber Faith was to the effervescent Prudence.

Pru. Dear sweet Pru.

"Are you all right, child?" she asked, sensing my caprice.

"I'm fine," I replied. "So you are from the Continent. Which part, may I ask?"

"Rasnov. A forgotten corner of the Hapsburg Empire, away in the mountains."

"I've never heard of it," I remarked.

"No one has. We were a dead dynasty, trapped in a crumbling castle."

Details. I hungered for them. My uncle would have called it being nosy. What of it? "You are a noblewoman?"

Her lips stretched into a wry smile. "I was, once. It sounds grand but in truth, it was an empty title from a forgotten era. I was Lady Szabina Constantin. Descendant of the Emperor Constantine himself."

I blanched. "The Holy Roman Emperor?"

She laughed. "Or so my ancestors claimed. I don't know. The past becomes cluttered with glories and treasures as time grinds on." She traced a finger along the lines of her palm as she spoke, the way gypsies are said to do when telling one's fortune.

"My family had fallen in stature, cut down by the intrigues of the court. Our lands were overrun and taken, and we starved until there was only me and a few servants left in a crumbling keep. That's where Nathaniel found me. He proved to be my savior. Like a knight of old, he stormed the tower to rescue a fallen princess."

"That sounds terribly romantic," I said.

Her eyes narrowed as she smiled. "It was. Nathaniel was like no man I knew. He was handsome and brave and adventurous, but he had something of the poet about him. A kindness that saw a common bond with every creature, a warmth that extended to everyone he met. He stole my heart. When he asked for my hand, to take me to his home in the Americas, I was lost. I would have followed him anywhere."

The glassiness in her eyes deepened as she spoke, caught up in the remembrance of her departed husband. Clearly there was great loss and great tragedy, but only because of the love she had shared with this man. It tweaked a rash of envy in my own heart, callous monster that I am. I longed for a passion that pure, a love that cherished. I was under no delusions that it was within my grasp, deformed and unworthy as I was. I was no princess locked in a tower awaiting rescue by a charming knight. I was the gargoyle leering over the parapet, frightening off any invader.

My expression must have betrayed my thoughts for I nearly fell off my chair when my hostess posed a question.

"Someone has stolen your heart," she said. "Haven't they?"

My back went rigid. I played the fool. "Me? No, no."

Another wry smirk. "You are unconvincing as a liar, little sister. What is his name?"

"It doesn't matter," I said. "Because it will never be."

"Oh? And why is that?"

How did the conversation swing this way? I despised being the focus of attention. By way of an answer, I simply squared my features to her so that the light of the fire illuminated the mangled rip of flesh on my cheek. Words are clumsy things at the best of times. I let the horror of it sing out.

She was gracious. "We all have scars, Hester."

"But we aren't all blind. Most of all, the male of the species."

A thin smile and dip of her chin, but no rejoinder. Some truths are naked on the face of it. I thought that the end of the matter, but the widow reached out a slender hand and took hold of my chin. She turned my face east, to cast more firelight on the devastated side.

"How did you come by this?"

"A fire," I answered. "I was twelve. Asleep in bed. My parents threw me from the window to save me. But not before a blazing timber fell over me."

"I see. And your mother and father?"

"Perished." I pulled back a little, to withdraw my chin from her cold fingers. A thought occurred to me then. "We lived in Bountiful at the time. I was born there. Is there any chance you knew my parents?"

The Lady Szabina, as I thought of her now, cocked a fine eyebrow on her high forehead. "I can't say. What were their names?"

"The Reverend Steadfast Stokely and his wife, Jane Ervin."

Her eyes narrowed in recollection. "I don't recall. You said you were twelve when you lost them. What year was that?"

"Eighteen-seventeen," I said. "The year of starvation, as it's known."

"Nathaniel and I came to Bountiful the year before. The summer without sunlight."

I remembered those days. Gray and heavy with sleet from May until October. There had been one day, and only one, where the clouds parted and there was sunshine that whole summer. It was dreadful. No crops that year, nothing grew, which yielded the following year of starvation. The Lord had tested us all.

"We are all tested, each in our own peculiar way," she said, which startled me. It was as if the woman had intuited my thoughts.

The widow rose from her chair, indicating that the visit was now concluded. "Thank you for the gifts, Hester. Please tell your uncle that I am quite happy with the house."

She saw me out, said goodbye, and I went on my way. I found nothing changed when I returned home. Faith was in a desperately low state and Samuel was causing a ruckus with his croup.

The Widow's love story stayed with me as I slipped into bed and pulled the quilt over me. The silly fable of a damsel and a knight, the notions of love and fealty. Although I had vowed to cease any thoughts of Henry last time, I found he crept into my mind like a burglar; stealthy and fox-like. I dreamed of him, the kinds of dreams that are not safe to say aloud, but the dream ended badly. I had relented to his kisses when a sudden pain sprang upon me out of nowhere. Sharp and bright, like a bee stinging my lip. The salty taste of blood afterward. I spasmed and woke. My lip was still stinging and when I pressed a fingertip to it, it came away red.

I must have bitten it in my sleep.

19

FAITH WAS DYING. There was little we could do but cool her brow and hold her when the coughing jags brought up blood. When she thrashed in a fit, we administered the paregoric to calm her. Like Pru, she was wasting away into a frail husk that barely resembled the quiet and pious girl we knew.

After calming another fit, my uncle shooed the younger children outside and assembled the rest of the family in the parlor.

"The end won't be long now," he said to the downcast faces before him.

Jacob began to cry. Samuel sat mute and pale, himself laid low and too weak to react beyond a lowering of the head. I do not remember if I wept. I must have, I suppose.

Mother Stokely knelt before her children and clutched their hands in turn. "We must be strong for her. She needs that of us now. One of us will sit with her at all times. I will not have her die alone."

As a people, we abhorred the idea of anyone dying alone. When someone's time was nigh, a family member would be with them at all times to prevent this. If this was not possible, there were neighbors who would help or even some women in the village who were known 'watchers' who would sit vigil with the dying. Some were even remunerated for this task, although I have never witnessed this.

This was our duty now and all, save little Polly and Hiram, were required to do their part. There was a moment of dissension when Pardon suggested that Sam be left to rest, but the oldest son wouldn't hear of it. He insisted on doing his part. The day was allotted into three-hour vigils with a rotating shift for my uncle, Mother Stokely, myself, Samuel and then Jacob. Thus began our death watch.

It was on the third night of vigil that I awoke with an ominous feeling. I had suffered another nightmare and woken with a start. The house was quiet. The pocket watch taken from the fugitive lay on my night table. I turned its face to the moonlight through the curtain and saw that it was past three in the morning. Mother Stokely should have woken me for my bedside duty a half-hour ago. I rose and tiptoed into the bedroom where Faith had been sequestered since the illness. The lamp was low, but I saw Mother Stokely slumped in the chair beside the bed. I gently shook her shoulder to rouse her, but she did not respond. When I shook with more vigor, she slumped forward and tumbled to the floor.

"Katherine!" I exclaimed as I rolled her onto her back. "Wake up."

My aunt let out a low moan and her eyes pinwheeled about in their sockets. She was senseless and did not reply to my cries. Had she taken a spoonful of the opium tincture? It seemed ludicrous, but how else to explain her delirium? I propped my aunt into a sitting position against the bed and called out for Pardon.

I then turned to rouse my sister-cousin. "Faith, wake up. Something's happened to mother."

But Faith couldn't hear me. Her mouth hung slack as if her soul had fled in mid-scream.

Pardon was suddenly in the room and now Jacob, now Samuel. Then the wailing began as the family huddled around the narrow bed of another lost daughter.

~

How grim our home became, how the days dragged like molasses in November. Where there was once lively chatter and the thump of feet running the floorboards, there was now silence. Mother

Stokely could not be consoled. She took to her bed with a blasted expression and did not rise. The rest of us shuffled about like monks under a vow of silence. With the exception of the children, we were all still wearing our mourning clothes from Pru's death.

What followed was grim repetition. Faith was carried downstairs to the scullery room where I washed and prepared the body. Alone this time as Katherine lay infirm with her grief. Samuel and Jacob brought out their saws and awls to carpenter another coffin. Pardon did not help them this time. He saddled his horse and he rode off for the day.

I asked Polly to bring me Faith's church dress and the tortoiseshell broach that she liked best. When she returned with the clothes, she asked to help prepare the body, but I didn't think it appropriate. The little thing stamped her foot and became adamant.

"She is my sister. My last sister. I want to help Faith find her way to Heaven."

How could I refuse? I relented, and she prepared a bowl of hot water while I removed the shift. Together we began washing the body.

"She's so bony," Polly said. "She doesn't even look like Faith."

The girl wasn't wrong. The consumption had left behind a wasted husk of my sister-cousin. The rib slats poked through the flesh over the sunken hollow of the belly, the limbs like gnarled branches. Like Prudence, there were rashes and contusions to the flesh that I assumed were the results of her many fits.

"We will make her look as good as we can," I said, rinsing the cloth in the basin. "Like how we knew her best. Do you want to comb her hair?"

The little girl took up the brush and moved to the end of the table. The scissors were on the windowsill. I set them down near Polly. "When you've done the hair, you can snip locks to braid. For mementos, the way Mother did with Pru's hair. Would you like that?"

"Yes."

Polly combed through her sister's sandy locks with great care, gently tugging out the tangles although Faith could no longer feel pain. "Do you think she is already in Heaven?" she asked. "Along with Prudence and all of mother's little ones?"

Spiritual matters were not my ken. Faith had been our guide in all things ecclesiastical. "I don't know. If her spirit is not there yet, it will be soon."

"It must be hard to leave."

I looked at her. "What do you mean?"

"If I died and became spirit," she said, "I would find it hard to say goodbye. Even though Heaven is a wonderful place, I wouldn't want to leave my family. I'd miss them too much."

The musings of a child can be devastating. Not because they are wrongheaded or simple, but because they can speak with a bluntness that cores one's insides out. Why is that? Is it because they have not yet been corrupted by the civility around them?

"Saying goodbye is always hard," I replied. "Even when the hereafter beckons."

Polly's eyes flashed up at me. "Is that where ghosts come from? Spirits that don't want to leave their family?"

"No talk of ghosts, please Polly. Now is not the time."

We pressed on until, out of nowhere, I flinched as if I'd stepped on broken glass. "Put the comb down, Polly," I said. I took the spare sheet and furled it over the body. "I forgot something."

"What?"

I rifled through the upper cupboard for the swathes of black crepe. "We must cover all the mirrors, just as your mother did last time. Hurry. And we must open the windows."

"Why?"

"Because that is our way." I shooed her on and we got busy. Polly's talk of spirits and ghosts made me remember the mirrors. I had a ghastly vision of Faith's spirit trapped inside the house. With the mirrors bare and the windows shut, it would have no means of egress from our bleak home.

"We must help her spirit find its way to Pru and the other little ones. Hurry now." Faith had earned that much. She did not deserve to be trapped here with us in our misery.

~

The burial took place two days later. Seventeen days after our last visit to the graveyard. No one outside the family came with us, no visitors came to our door with condolences and pies. In life, Faith had always lingered in the shadow of her older and more vivacious sister and so her death proved no different. I don't think Faith would have cared, she had little time for the empty vanity of society. What mattered to her was her family and her devotions. Standing next to the narrow pine coffin and the open grave that awaited it, we gave her that as best we could. Her father was as low as I had ever seen him, and Katherine's hands trembled as they clutched her kerchief. Jacob and the children seemed dazed as if they didn't comprehend what was happening. Samuel started to list from his feeble state and would have fallen had Jacob and I not propped him.

At the end of the last prayer, Katherine seemed to falter and my uncle steadied her. Her voice was as ragged as a rusted gate-hinge.

"We have buried our Faith," she rasped. "What will become of us now?"

I do not know if Mother Stokely meant to put a poetic spin to her lament. That was not her way. It troubled me, nonetheless.

Aside from the parson, there was one person outside the family that I did not notice until Reverend Crane dropped the first handful of soil onto the coffin lid. Will Treves stood to the side with his cap clutched in his one good hand. I didn't know if he had been there all along or had arrived late. When the ceremony was concluded, he spoke a few words to my uncle and aunt before taking up a spade to help the sexton backfill the earth.

He gave me a nod in acknowledgment as we passed him. No one looked back at the grave this time, not even the children.

20

GRIEF CAN BE a tedious grindstone, eroding the afflicted to vacant-eyed shadows shuffling from room to room with no purpose, no hope, and little sense. It stretches the days, shortens the temper, and clips patience to the quick. Mother Stokely withdrew into her bedroom, closed the door, and did not emerge for three days. She did not eat and refused to speak to anyone, her husband included. Pardon slept on the divan in the parlor.

The children were confused and when they asked too many questions, they were shushed. Jacob stayed outdoors, spending his days in the barn and the paddock. He came in for his meal and left when it was over. Samuel became weaker but redoubled his efforts to hide it, to be strong. On Wednesday he collapsed in the yard, dead asleep in the clover under a hot sun. Friday he dropped to the floor in the kitchen, upending bowls and dishes as he went down. He was ordered to take his bed and had to be wrangled physically there by his father and brother.

I lost track of time. Had it been a day since Faith's burial or a fortnight? I could not tell. The days came and faded in a dull-eyed routine of chores and child-minding. I tried to recall what month it was. Was it still May or had the calendar turned to June?

Did it matter?

News from outside trickled in and it was not good. Pru's sweetheart, James Corwin, had been laid low with consumption for days. He died in the night, hurried into an early grave the same way as his betrothed. A funeral was set for three days hence. Then came word that Edwin Hendershot had been taken to bed with a debilitating cough and sallowness of the flesh. We all knew it to be the deadly consumption, but no one spoke it aloud. Like a conjuring spell, no one wished to name the thing for fear of attracting its awful attention. Denial was the handiest tool, ignorance a blessed shield.

Pettiness was often its outlet, which I discovered anew when I made my weekly trek to the merchant's in town. Mrs. Van Tassel was outright belligerent to me, her customers hostile. Leaving the merchant's, I ran straight into the dreaded Tom Hazard. Tom has always hated me, and he never missed a chance to taunt me with cries of 'gargoyle' and 'wretch.' I do not know why he despises me, I can only assume it is my appearance that displeases him. This time, however, his chiding torments were of a different nature.

"Keep away," he shouted, backing away with a melodramatic flourish. "Don't curse me with the pox the way you've done to others. Look away, you foul Medusa!"

The brutish boy clearly blamed us Stokelys for the consumption that was felling other families. Ours was the first household to be struck low and now the townsfolk were keeping their distance from us. Clearly Mrs. Van Tassel believed it, which explained her frigidity. The Van Tassels were kin to the Corwins and with the illness of James, they had closed ranks against us. How medieval of them.

Hazard Tom continued on with his taunting as I marched away. Men on stoops watched, the women from behind their parlor curtains. It was humiliating. If no one were about, I would have taken a stick and thrashed some sense into his brutish little skull, but the watchful eyes of the townsfolk stayed my hand. He followed me down the high road, calling out his tweaks and insults. He even hurled a few stones at my back but missed. In my heart, I cursed him, wishing the consumption would silence his poison tongue.

That was wicked of me. Later that night, I repented of it in my bedtime prayers. When I snuffed the candle, the darkness was disrupted by the sound of coughing through the house. It issued from the grand bedroom where Katherine slept alone.

~

On Saturday came word that another family, the Caulfields on Wexeter farm, were laid low with consumption. That made four families afflicted with the white plague. On the Sabbath, Pardon instructed us not to bother dressing for church. Katherine was in no state to attend and, given the temperament in town, he thought it best if we were truant. We would pray together in the yard, under the apple tree where Faith used to read to the children. Our absence must have been noted, for in the late afternoon of that day came a harsh banging at the front door. I answered it to find a deputation of selectmen on our veranda. All five of them.

They needed to speak to my uncle. I told Jacob to run and fetch his father while I ushered the men into the parlor and offered to bring tea. Mr. Hendershot and Mr. Hazard asked for beer, Mr. Corwin inquired if there was something stronger to be had. Ebeneezer Wickes towered in the room, scraping the ceiling beams with the crown of his head. There were two other gentlemen among their number, Mr. Spaulding, the cobbler, and Mr. Tillinghast, a farmer. Both had served terms as selectmen in the past. Their faces were stern and their postures stiff. Something unpleasant was afoot.

Pardon entered and greeted his fellow councilmen. The assembled men offered their sympathies to him and asked after the health of Samuel and Katherine. That surprised me as I thought no one outside the family knew of Mother Stokely's condition. I scurried from the study to the kitchen bringing tea and mugs of ale, catching only snippets of the discussion. Mr. Hendershot stated that something needed to be done immediately about the illness that was stretching its tentacles into our village. Halton Hazard, father to the sick Edwin and the odious Tom, questioned my uncle about the steps he had taken to treat the consumptives in his house. That was harsh and Arthur Beecham told him to temper his remarks.

Ebeneezer asked me if there were any seed cakes to go with his tea and Mr. Hazard added that a wedge of cheese might be nice. The selectmen had come with grave business in mind but they had also brought their appetites and so back and forth I went, gathering up provisions from the larder when all I wanted was to be a fly on the wall during this heated discussion. As it was, my understanding of the meeting was spotty and clouded with things I did not understand.

Ebeneezer, dipping a biscuit into his black tea, spoke of a cure for consumption that was radical but known to work. Pardon refuted this, saying he had heard of the prescriptive measure but did not believe in it. Mr. Tillinghast vouched for its efficacy, saying he saw it work for a distant cousin in Exeter. Mr. Spaulding also offered testimony of his own relations in Vermont some years earlier. My uncle would have none of it, calling it tommyrot and gruesome to boot. Unfortunately I had missed the reveal of this controversial remedy and its nature remained a mystery.

The discussion grew more heated, with the selectmen seemingly ganging up on my uncle. His only ally was Arthur, who implored his fellows to stifle their passions and keep heads cool. We are all in this together, he told them, and we must row in the same direction or drown one by one.

The terms of the disagreement were confusing. Someone mentioned the 'purifying fire' and another used the term 'cleansing.' Ebeneezer spoke of fresh blood and uncorrupted flesh while Halton Hazard argued the presence of malignant spirits. Through it all, Pardon was unmoved by their entreaties. Arthur asked him to reconsider and Mr. Hendershot accused my uncle of holding the entire town of Wickstead hostage if he continued to refuse.

Then something changed within the room. Voices lowered as a new presence was felt in my uncle's study. Mother Stokely stood in the doorway, clutching the jamb to keep herself upright. She was pale and trembling but there was a fire in her eyes.

"Get out of my house," she growled at them. "How dare you suggest such a monstrous thing?"

Pardon rushed to her side. "Katherine, please. The council—"

"I know what the council is suggesting," she said, waving her husband back. "But I forbid it! No one will touch the graves of my children and that is the last word on it." She took a step back and motioned to the front door. "Get out. All of you."

Scolded, the selectmen lay down their cups and marched to the door with their heads bowed. Only Arthur offered an apology for upsetting the household at such an awful time.

When the last one had stepped off the veranda, I turned to my uncle. "What on earth was all that about? What remedy did they suggest?"

His face was ashen. He thrust his chin in the direction of my aunt, who was wheezing against the door frame. "See to mother," was all he said before he closed the study door on me. I stood gape-mouthed for a moment. From within the room I could hear my uncle curse the names of his fellow council men.

~

A strange air settled over the house after the visit from the selectmen. It wasn't just the grief that was smothering us all like a pillow to the face, but an odd tension that left Pardon brooding and Mother Stokely seething. I still hadn't a clue what the council had proposed as my aunt and uncle refused to speak of it. Word came the next day that the selectmen had finally come to a decision about the problem of Bountiful. A deputation of strong backs was to be sent out immediately to begin the grim task of collecting the dead and giving them a proper burial. A handful of men were chosen, with Reverend Crane leading them on their journey. He would perform the funerary rites for the poor souls.

At supper that night, Jacob announced that he was one of the deputations traveling to the ashen ruins of Bountiful.

My uncle choked on his broth. "The devil you are. The selectmen know better than to recruit you. Especially at a time like this."

"Yes, I know," said Jacob. "That's why I volunteered."

Now it was Katherine's turn to spit out her food. "It's too dangerous. You will retract your offer."

"I'll do no such thing," Jacob countered. "I want to go. I can't stand another day in this grim house and all its grief. I'll pack tonight and be gone before sunup."

A quarrel spilled across the supper table, ruining everyone's meal. Not that it mattered, really. None of us had much of an appetite anymore. Pardon forbade it, but Jacob said he didn't care. He'd just as soon leave now and nothing was going to stop him. I watched the argument bounce back and forth across the table like an errant ball of India rubber. Jacob was adamant, and who could blame him? In fact, I was envious. I wanted to get shed from all this grief as well. As odious as the mission to

Bountiful would be, it would be a change of scenery from all of these sad faces. Pardon grew sullen and capitulated with his silence. Mother Stokely said she would prepare him some dry sausage and bread to take with him. The matter was settled.

True to his word, Jacob was gone before the sun rose and our house became a little bleaker for his absence. Katherine roamed about in a haze, sometimes distracted, often weeping. Samuel continued to weaken, despite his protestations that he was fine. He put on a brave face, but we all shuddered at his sallow complexion, fearing the repetition of another slow decline in the sickbed.

Ebeneezer Wickes darkened our doorway the following day with a small wheel of cheese for Pardon. From what I could gather, it was something of a peace offering after the quarrel with the selectmen. Pardon was appreciative of the gift. I heard tall Mr. Wickes entreat my uncle to reconsider the plan, adding that the mood in town was becoming a bit frantic and the proposed plan of action would do much to bring peace of mind. Even if it didn't work. Mother Stokely came late to the conversation, but she was not so resolute as last time and when Ebeneezer took his leave, the two began to debate the idea. No agreement was reached as my aunt left the room in a bit of a huff just as I entered. My uncle sat brooding in his chair. It was all he seemed to do lately.

He nodded at the cheese wheel on the table. "Will you take Mr. Wicke's gift to the larder, please."

I complied, gathering up the bundle, but I lingered a moment. "Uncle, may I ask what it is the selectmen want?"

His hand gestured with a dismissive wave. "It is nothing."

I should have let it go but my curiosity burned. "Is it a remedy for consumption?"

"It's a ghastly business. Don't trouble yourself about it."

"But if it could help Samuel, or prevent any further illness, should you not try it?"

His mouth set into a grimace. "It is a barbarous notion, no more effective than that fool barber and his bloodletting. It would do nothing but pour salt on our grief." Annoyed at my pestering, he withdrew into his study and did not emerge until dinner.

21

YOUNG JACOB HAD been gone two days when Mother Stokely declared that she wanted him home. She had had a terrible dream.

"I was in the orchard," she told us, her face bloodless that morning. "The trees we planted when we first married. The sky darkened and then the apple trees began to wither before my eyes. The fruit blighted instantly, boiling with worms as they tumbled around my feet. The trees split and crashed to the earth. Half the orchard was felled within minutes from some powerful corruption. Then I saw the culprit; a great serpent writhing from tree to tree, poisoning them all with its venom. When the awful viper was done with its destruction, it slithered across the heather and came for me."

Neither my uncle nor myself spoke for a moment, stunned with such a strange narrative. Dreams are bothersome things, thrashing us about in our beds with their merciless whimsy.

"Twas just a dream, dear," Pardon said, patting his wife's hand. "Brought on by an undigested bit of beef."

She snatched her hand away. "Don't patronize me. It was a warning."

Katherine was in a temper and I knew better than to provoke her when her blood was up. I let my uncle dig his own grave.

"Of what? Crop failure?"

"Don't be so dense, Pardon. Honestly." She stepped here and stepped there, agitated. Mother Stokely took her omens seriously and with good measure. She was the one who dowsed for water when new wells needed to be dug. "The orchard is our family. I will lose half of them before this nightmare is over."

Pardon rallied, seeing how upset she was but I feared it was too late. "Katherine, please. It was just a dream. Dreams mean nothing."

A spoon was flung across the room. It missed my uncle and clattered against the wall. Something diabolic flashed hot in Mother Stokely's eyes just then. If I hadn't been standing there, I sincerely believe she would have attacked her husband.

"Death has taken two already," she cried. "Now Sam is ill, sure to be taken the same way. How many more, Pardon, while we dither about, unable to stop it?"

My uncle stayed on his side of the kitchen table and said nothing. He must have realized that any response would only make things worse. Katherine was sensible and cool-headed most of the time, but her passions ran deep and, when riled, she became volcanic. When that occurred, there was little any of us could do except to hang onto something and ride it out.

Her eyes flashed again but this time it was with terror rather than rage. "And Jacob has gone. Gone to that awful place of ash and death. I need him back. Pardon, go saddle your horse and fetch him. Bring him back to me."

"Jacob will be fine. The other men will watch out for him. I promise."

"Promises?" Mother Stokely spat back at him. "The way you promised that Pru's illness would pass? That Faith would recover?"

Even I felt the sting of that one. Pardon had said such things to her as a way to keep her from worrying. Now those empty words returned to cut him.

"Go and bring my son back to me! Or I will take your beloved Caesar and go after him myself."

"I cannot go, Katherine. Not now. It's three days round trip. I cannot go now. You know this."

Mother Stokely snatched up another utensil to hurl at him. A knife this time.

I stood. "I'll go," I said.

"Don't be stupid, Hester," Pardon spat. "Sit down."

"It's not stupid," I argued. "I don't like Jacob being there either. It makes perfect sense for me to make the trip. Both of you are needed here. I will put Phantom in the traces and take the wagon so Jacob and I can both return."

The two of them countered my argument on numerous points, but I would not relent. And it was not selflessness on my part. I wanted to get away from this house and here was a rare chance to do so. To escape and be alone for a while. What a rare thing.

Cracks appeared in their defenses and I wedged them open with my reasoning until they split like an oyster shell. "If you want your son home, then I will be the one to fetch him."

"But it might be dangerous," Katherine mused. "What with that madman running loose."

"To say nothing of the inappropriateness for a young girl to be running about on her own."

"I'll take the pistol," I replied.

My uncle slunk down in his chair as if fatigued. "Someone must escort you. Samuel is out of the question. I will fetch Will Treves. He will accompany you there."

The idea was not without merit, I thought. Will was pleasant enough, but my greedy mind raced ahead, and I spoke before thinking it through. "Very well. But Will is busy helping the Browns with their new barn and he may not be able to get away. Perhaps Henry Beecham is available. He's a fine horseman, and he knows the way."

Mother Stokely rose from her chair. "We will not burden the Beecham's with this. Will is a lad we trust. He's the one for the task."

I kept my trap shut after that. I'd pushed my luck far enough for one night.

~

Will was agreeable to the request, and we set out early the next day. We outfitted Caesar in the buggy traces rather than Phantom since he was the stronger and could get us there faster. The obstinate creature obeyed Will and did not try to bite him as he did me. We took turns at the reins, trundling along the rutted track that took us through the woodlands and skirted the foothills to the east.

Will and I talked for the first leg of the journey, mostly pleasant banter about our respective families. He asked how my aunt and uncle were holding up since Faith's passing and inquired about Samuel's health. I knew little of his life, so I asked after his mother and learned that she was laid up with dropsy, which is unfortunate. When I asked after his siblings, he reported they were fine but offered little detail. By midday the conversation dwindled to nothing as we shook and rattled with every jarring brace of the wagon wheels in the rough track.

We rode until twilight and then stopped to make a simple camp next to a creek. Will made a fire and I warmed the cold rabbit I had packed. We had tea after the meal and listened to the hoots of owls and the croak of frogs in the reeds.

Will sat cross-legged on the ground, gazing into the fire. "When was the last time you saw Bountiful?" he asked.

"Four years."

He seemed surprised. "And you've never been back?"

"I had no reason to, really. We had no other kin there."

"It won't be the return of the prodigal for you then," he said. "Are you worried about seeing it reduced to ashes?"

I tilted my head, considering the question. "It's hard to imagine, isn't it? A whole village gone. I don't remember much of the town, which is odd. I don't know how I'll feel when I see it."

He took a stick and prodded the fire. A coil of sparks rose into the night air. "Twelve is a tender age to lose both parents. What were they like, your mother and father?"

"They were good people. Pious and industrious. My father was a kind man who always treated others fairly. My mother was gentle and protective. She brooded at times."

"Over what?"

The question stopped me cold. "I couldn't tell you, really. She never confided in me what she brooded on. But she would often withdraw from everything and seek solitude, going on walks in the forest outside of town. In winter she would shut herself up in her sitting room for hours on end. My father referred to these occasions as her 'moments of contemplation,' although I know not what she contemplated. She was a curious soul."

He picked up his tin cup and flung the dregs of his tea into the fire. "And do you have those, too? These moments of contemplation?"

"I wish I did," I said with a laugh. "I'd be content with some quiet at times. The house can be such a riot of noise and running about that I can't hear myself think. The dinner table is a catastrophe of voices talking over one another." The log in the fire popped and spit out a tiny ember that landed on the hem of my skirt. I brushed it away. "Although, the house won't be half so noisy now, I suppose."

Will turned to me and the expression of sympathy in his eyes was too much to bear and I looked away. It was probably just a trick of the firelight. "You've all suffered a terrible loss," he said. "I can see the strain it's had on your aunt. Poor woman, two children lost like that."

"She's a strong woman."

"Are they good to you, your aunt and uncle?"

"Very," I said. "They are kind people who took me in when I had no one."

Another spark flew. It landed on the ground and glowed briefly before it snuffed out.

"Did you censor your thoughts just now?"

"Did I?"

Will smiled at me with that lopsided grin of his. "I sensed there was something more to add, but you clipped it."

"You think yourself clever, don't you?"

"Come on, out with it. What were you going to say?"

I sighed. The conversation had turned a little too intimate, but I decided to be forthright in this moment. "Pardon and Katherine are good to me, as I said. And my cousins treat me squarely, but there's always a certain distance. I am not my aunt's daughter. I am not sister to my cousins. I am a step removed from that intimacy, and I am grateful and try to be helpful, but there are times when I am little more than a servant to them all. A helpmeet who is allowed to sit at the same table, but only after the privilege is earned through toil."

I gasped for air as if I'd been held underwater. I'm not sure what possessed me but it all just came pouring out. Will sat stiffspined, taken aback at my confession.

"I am sorry," I said demurely. "That came out so ungrateful."

"No. Just honest." He got to his feet and fetched the bedrolls from the wagon. "We'd best turn in. You can sleep in the box of the wagon. It'll be drier. I'll sleep out here."

I rose and brushed my hands together. "I want to sleep next to the fire."

"Are you sure? You'll be damp with dew by morning."

"I'll survive."

We laid out the bedroll and the blankets on opposite sides of the small campfire. I unlaced my brogans and kicked them off. The ground was hard beneath me.

"I'm such a ninny, Will. Prattling on and on. I never asked you about your family."

"You know all there is to know," he said from across the flames. "I've a mother and three siblings. Nothing much to tell."

I knew those basic facts, but little else. "There must be more. What about your father?"

"He left when I was young. He never was much to speak of. We get by. That's all there is." He adjusted a satchel for a pillow and lay down. "Goodnight, Hester."

The conversation was replaced by the crickets and the crackling of the dying coals. My bones ached from the day's traveling and sleep was tugging my eyelids closed. I was just about gone when I heard Will's voice.

"I meant to ask if the opium tincture helped," he said. "I left it on your back porch."

I do not remember if I replied.

22

OUR NOSES DETECTED the town long before our eyes did, a deep smell of wood smoke that grew stronger as we trundled along the road. When we came onto a clearing, we saw the first charred stumps of trees where the fire had reached and then, cresting a low hill, we looked down on the cinders of Bountiful.

It was all gone. Where there had once been cottages and barns, there was now only blackened timber beams collapsed into jagged heaps or the sooty stones of chimneys rising from the ruins. Ash was everywhere, clotted on the road beneath us and blowing in the breeze like snowflakes. Here and there rose coils of smoke from embers still burning deep within the cindered remains.

I was speechless, mouth agape at the horror of it all. Will, trundling beside me on the bench, was also struck dumb. Even Caesar sensed the wrongness of it, coming to a stop in the track and he would go no further.

We climbed down and led the horse back up the trail where there was still greenery and secured him there so Caesar could graze without looking on the village of ash.

We proceeded on foot, treading in awed silence as we

passed the charred ruins around us. I tried to recall the village as it used to be, the blacksmith's shop on the corner, the church on the west end, the merchant's wide veranda. It was never a large community, more hamlet than village, but there was nothing for me to orient myself to what it had once been. No landmarks remained. I tried to remember where my parent's house stood but I could not. How long before the wind blew the ash away, and the forest crept back to reclaim it, erasing any sign that a settlement had once stood here?

I felt Will's hand on my arm as he stopped me. "Hester, are you all right?"

I said I was, but he did not look reassured. "Stay here. I'll find Jacob and we can be gone quick as you like."

"I'm fine, Will." I continued on, the hem of my frock now gray with ash. "Let's find my brother."

Brother is how I thought of him now. Poor Jacob, working in this horror of a burned village. I wanted to gather him up in my arms and run from this place.

Picking our way through the ruins, we came upon a horse and wagon standing in the road. Two men moved slowly among the cinders, poking through the ash with spades. They were so covered in soot from crown to toe that I did not even recognize Jacob at first. I called his name as I hurried to him. At first he did not react, his eyes blinking as if he didn't recognize me. The spade fell from his hand and he ran to me, crushing against me in a tight embrace. He buried his head against my chest, and I felt him sobbing.

The other man was Tobias Finch, the barber's son. He too had the same dazed look in his eyes as if he'd witnessed something awful. And indeed they had. I looked over to the wagon where charred bones lay collected in the box, an ashy rattle of ribs and skulls.

Will came up and greeted Tobias. They shook and Will's one good palm came away darkened with soot. The two waited silently as Jacob calmed down and finally let go. His tears had mired the soot into some strange black mask. I took my kerchief and cleaned his face until he stopped me.

"Why are you here?"

"We've come to take you home," I told him. "Mother needs you."

Jacob glanced at his crew mate and shook his head. "I can't. We have work to do."

"You must. Mother is sick with worry."

"She speaks the truth, Jacob," Will said. "Where is the Reverend? We'll explain it to him."

Jacob nodded to the west. "He's at the churchyard."

Tobias stepped forward and put his hand on Jacob's shoulder. "Go on home, lad. We'll see to this just fine."

"Are you sure?"

"Go," assured the barber's son. "They never should have brought you in the first place."

We left Tobias and the bone cart and followed Jacob through the rubble. I stumbled here and there for my eyes were stinging from the ash blown up on the breeze. Coming onto the western edge of Bountiful, the debris cleared as we came to the small churchyard. The church, a wooden structure of whitewashed clapboard and cedar shingle, was completely gone.

We saw another wagon of bones and two men carrying the spindly remains from the cart to an open grave. The bones were passed to a third man standing in the pit who would then arrange the tangled bits of skeleton along the bottom. The men moved in a slow, plodding gait, their hearts heavy with the morbid task they performed. I shuddered to think of the horrors Jacob had already witnessed toiling here. I was glad we were taking him away.

The Reverend Crane was overseeing the mass burial of the people of Bountiful. He squinted his eyes as we approached as if unsure of what his eyes beheld.

"My goodness," the Reverend cried. "Lefty Will and Hester Stokely. Have you come to join our merciful deputation?"

"No, sir," said Will. "We've come to collect young Jacob and bring him home."

The Reverend turned to my cousin, his eyes scanning the lad. "Are you ill, son? Why is my crew to be reduced?"

Catching the shameful cast on Jacob's face, I spoke up. "Pardon and Katherine want him home, sir. Our family has suffered, and we need to close ranks to see us through. I'm sure you understand."

"I understand I'm to lose one of my hardest workers," he said, perturbed.

"I'm sorry, Parson," Jacob said. "Maybe I should stay after all."

I thought the reverend was being miserly on the matter and I told him so. "He shouldn't have been allowed to come in the first place. Not after what we've been through."

He sputtered on about doing God's work in a Godless place, and I readily agreed but said he would have to do so with one less pair of hands. Will glanced at me, uncomfortable with my sass. I am sure he was right for it is never wise to contradict a man of the cloth, but I would not allow Jacob to toil a minute longer in this unpleasant business. For all of Jacob's bluster and bravado, he was still only a boy of thirteen for goodness' sake.

Will removed his cap. "Reverend," he said, waving his hand at the small graveyard around us, "what happened here?"

"I wish I knew, son."

The churchyard had been terribly disturbed, and it was horrid to see. A number of graves had been dug up, and not neatly either. The moldy coffins had been hauled to the surface and broken open, their ghastly inhabitants left staring up at the sky or disturbed in their rest, tumbled about as if someone had taken them up, danced the dead about and dropped them back into their coffins with no thought to their dignity. The headstones of some of these unearthed graves had fallen in and lay in the pit so it was impossible to read the names inscribed there.

"Some malicious act was conducted here," the Reverend announced, shaking his head at the state of these graves. "To what purpose I know not."

Jacob's face was downcast as he surveyed it all. "It's as if they all went mad, digging up their dead."

"I doubt we'll ever know why," Crane answered.

I had a brief thought to searching for my parent's headstone, for they were buried here, but I did not want to tarry any longer. Had their resting places been disturbed also? I couldn't bear the thought and took hold of my cousin's hand.

"We should press on," I said, curtsying to the pastor. "I shall tell my uncle that more labor hands are needed here immediately."

Reverend Crane nodded sagely. "I should be very grateful, Hester. Thank you."

We said our goodbyes and strode back through the razed

town to where we had left our outfit. Jacob asked about his brothers and sister, to which I assured him they were well.

Caesar, the big fool, had pulled free of his mooring and had wandered, cart and all, further down the glen to munch on the barley stalks there. Will fetched him round and soon we three were bouncing along in the wagon. I let Jacob ride on the bench with Will while I sat on an apple crate in the box. Will ticked at the horse's flank with his crop, prodding him into a quickstep march. He said he wanted some distance between us and the cindered village before the sun went down.

Jostling along on the crate, I watched the ruined town draw away behind us when movement caught my eye. A dog had emerged from the ashes and was trotting along behind us. My heart went out to this last denizen of Bountiful who had no doubt lost its master in the fire. I thought the mutt would stop and turn back after a while, but it did not. I touched Will's arm, telling him to stop. When the cart lurched to a halt, I climbed down.

Jacob looked confused. "Hester, what are you doing?"

"We have a traveling companion," I said. "Wait a moment."

The lone dog was some hundred paces behind us on the trail and when the cart stopped, so too had the dog. He sat watching me approach with his long tongue lagging from his chops. I snickered and called for him to come, but he slunk into the brush when I closed the distance and vanished from sight.

I continued to call and coo to the dog until the others complained.

"It's just a dog," Will said.

"He doesn't want to be tamed," added Jacob. "Come, Hester. The daylight is fading."

Disappointed, I returned to the spring wagon, and we continued. Sure enough, once we were ambling forward, the dog slunk out of the forest and followed again.

"Look," I said. "He's come back."

Will refused to stop again and we jostled along with our strange follower behind us. The poor mutt matched our pace for quite a while, but after an hour, he began to fall further behind. This vexed me to no end, and I do not know why. He wasn't my pet. Finally, the dog simply lay down in the road as if he could walk no further.

"Stop the horse," I said.

"No."

"Stop!"

I clambered down with the cart still rolling and marched back down the road. Will and Jacob called after me, scolding me not to waste my time. The dog lay there in the dry track watching me approach. He was a good sized hound but of uncertain breed. His brindle coat was filthy with ash and his forepaws looked badly used up. I slowed as I came near and cooed to the mutt softly. His eyes watched with the wariness of an animal that had reason to mistrust, but I continued to whisper sweet nothings until the tail came up and started wagging.

The poor beast was rail thin and terribly dehydrated, judging from the chalky foam along its jaw. I gathered it up in my arms, fouling my clothes with its sooty mess, and carried it back to the cart.

"You're mad, you know that?" said Will. "What do you aim to do with that cur?"

Jacob agreed. "It could be half-wild, Hester."

"Don't be silly," I said. "Help me get him into the back."

Will took the animal from me and settled it into a corner of the box cart. I cupped water into my hand from the leather bladder and the dog lapped it up. Will started the horse again, and we trundled on. I settled onto the bed of the cart and cradled the poor dog's head in my lap. He was asleep by the time the sad sight of Bountiful was lost in the distance.

23

THE DOG IMPROVED as we made our way home. He was fearful of the boys and would only take food from my hand. His hide was thick with burs and one foreleg bore a wound that had turned mealy. We made camp beside a creek and I tried to wash the poor beast, but he seemed fearful of everything. The creek water tasted of iron.

We ate a cold breakfast and started off at first light. Old Caesar proved to be a steady drover, and we made good progress. We gained the high road and by late afternoon we could see the church spire of Wickstead rising from the distant trees. It gave us heart to see it for nothing will take the starch out of you like a day's journey in a cart. We three, or four if you count the mangy dog, were a sorry sight when we trundled into town.

It was late, about supper time, when Will let the horse stop. "Hester, up ahead," he said. "Is that your family?"

Jacob and I both turned in that direction and sure enough, there was the Stokely clan walking through town. Pardon and Katherine were linked at the arms, with a sad-looking Samuel behind them. Hiram and Polly brought up the tail end.

"Have they come out to greet us?" asked Jacob.

"They were lucky in the timing of it," Will replied.

I squinted as I watched the family approach and saw that all were clad in their black mourning clothes. "Something isn't right," I said.

We clambered out of the wagon on wobbly knees and stiff backs to greet our family. Mother Stokely trotted ahead and Jacob limped toward her and the two embraced, despite Jacob's filthy state. The boy was enveloped into the bosom of his family. Katherine kissed my cheek in greeting.

"Has something happened?" I asked. "Another death?"

Their reaction was strange. Katherine looked away and my uncle lowered his head sadly. With the entire family present, I could only assume that a neighbor had passed. Pardon dismissed the assumption.

"No one has died," he said. "But there is work to be done. Come. They are waiting for us at the graveyard."

My uncle and aunt linked arms again and strode on. I stood there like a buffoon. "Who is waiting for us? What is at the graveyard?"

"Come," said Pardon. "Our salvation is nigh."

The couple proceeded onward, and their children followed. A tingle of unease wormed up my spine at this strangeness. Samuel was still ill and fairly shambled along in his state and poor Jacob needed a bath, a meal and a bed in strong order. I asked again what was afoot, but Katherine hushed me.

The dog stood in the cart watching the procession pass. I asked Will if he made any sense of it but, of course, he was as mystified as I. He took the horse by the bridle and fell in behind the party.

I followed them to the cemetery gates. The dog had leapt from the cart and was limping along on his bad leg at my side. My thought was this: I must find a name for this mutt. How silly, given the circumstances that I should be dithering about naming a lost dog.

The sense of unease was confirmed when the family finally halted, and I came alongside them. The horror of it. Two sextons were neck deep in the ground, spading out the dirt as they dug up two graves. The simple wooden markers above each read PRUDENCE PARDON STOKELY and FAITH KATHERINE STOKELY.

My knees buckled and I clutched at my uncle's sleeve. "What in God's name is going on? Why are those men desecrating my sister's graves?"

Pardon was irritable. "We are doing what must be done to save us all. Now be silent."

I couldn't stop my mouth from running, demanding to know what was happening. Mother Stokely was sobbing and Sam's eyes were filled with tears. I was spent and exhausted from the journey and wondered if I was dreaming it all. Perhaps my brains had been shaken loose in that rattling cart and I was simply insane. I turned to look at Will. He kept back aways from the family, out of respect I suppose. When he saw my eyes, he only shrugged in mutual confusion.

There were others with us at the grave site, but whether they had just arrived or had been there all along, I could not say. The five selectmen stood observing the exhumation, along with the two former members of the council, Spaulding and Tillinghast. Parson Bell, a hawk-nosed curate to Reverend Crane, hovered near the headstones with an officious air, directing the toil of the gravediggers.

The spading came to an end and one sexton climbed out of one grave to join his fellow in the pit of Faith's open grave. Guy ropes were thrown down and threaded up again. The men hauled and strained, and the dirt encrusted coffin emerged into the light of the day and was pulled onto the grass.

A hammer and a chisel were put to use, tapping at the seams of the coffin lid. When it fell to the ground, the sextons stepped back and covered their noses from the coffin gases. Parson Bell and the selectmen approached, handkerchiefs pressed to faces, and peered down at its contents. The men conferred amongst themselves for a moment, nodding their heads as their eyes watered. Mr. Spaulding took a knee and, reaching into the moldy pine box, he prodded and poked around, but I could not see at what. Another round of nodding heads and whispered communication and then Arthur Beecham waved my uncle and aunt forward.

Samuel did not move but Jacob began to follow and the children with him. I took his arm. "Jacob, no. Keep Polly and Hiram back."

The boy seemed confused and unsure what to do, but he

relented, taking the younger ones by the hand.

I did not adhere to my own advice, hypocrite that I am, and I paid for it. Two paces forward were all I took, but it was enough to see the withered flesh and skull-life face of our lost Faith. It was a ghastly, unrecognizable sight, and it seared itself into my memory, never far from recall to this day.

Spaulding and Tillinghast, along with Ebeneezer Wickes, were motioning to the desiccated corpse to elaborate certain articles of truth to my uncle. My ear caught only the rag ends of phrases. "A true death," said one. "Proper corruption, as it should be," said another. Ebeneezer agreed, saying, "No fresh blood. There is no sign of evil with her."

All withdrew from the coffin and Ebeneezer, towering over all as he did, directed the gravediggers to retrieve the second receptacle. Down the sextons went into the other open grave with their spades and ropes to bring the coffin to the surface. Again, the hammers clanged to break the seal and unseat the nails. The lid was pushed aside, but this time the gravediggers scurried away from what was inside the casket. One of them made the sign of the cross.

The council men gathered around the wooden box and there was much discussion between them. Some shook their heads and others turned away, their faces pale and frightened.

Ebeneezer waved at my uncle. "Come, Pardon. See. The culprit is here."

Mother Stokely refused to go. Pardon took her wrist, but she snatched it back and turned away, so my uncle went alone. I could not stop myself from following him despite the awful thing I had seen.

Prudence Stokely lay before us in a profoundly unchanged state. Her flesh was not withered or sunken like that of her sister. Her cheeks bloomed and were, to my astonishment, almost rosy. In fact, she looked much better than she had when she perished. Then she had been thin and much wasted from her illness, but the form before us was like the Prudence of old. Beautiful and full of life. She looked asleep, not dead. There was, however, a few things amiss about her appearance. Foremost was the blood on her chin, with more of it foaming from her mouth. There was more blood on her hands, some of it fresh and some of it old and dried black. Her fingernails were encrusted with it.

Mr. Spaulding stood with his wide brimmed hat in hand and said, "Here is the source of your troubles, Mr. Stokely. The presence of an evil spirit is locked within this poor girl."

Pardon swayed a little on his feet, his eyes bald with horror. This is what he said: "No."

"The signs are here, sir," said Mr. Tillinghast. His voice was gentle, as he could see the distress in my uncle, but he leavened it with authority. "Though she has lain dead for a month, there is no corruption to her. The blood there on the mouth is fresh. She has feasted on the life force of her siblings. That is the root of their illness. It must be stopped now."

A heavy wallop was heard, a force brushed hard against my knee. Uncle Pardon lay flat on the ground, overwhelmed by the horrors before him. Katherine wailed and rushed to his side. I loosened his collar and Ebeneezer fanned his face with his hat to give him some air. The men raised him up and pulled him back from the open pits and their putrid vapors. Within moments he came around but remained seated on the ground like a sack of grain, leaning slightly. I had never seen my uncle look so old or frail as he did in that moment.

The smell of smoke wafted over me and for a moment I thought the smell had followed me from Bountiful, but this was not the case. A fire had been built near the graves and Mr. Hazard and Mr. Beecham were adding logs and more kindling, building it up into a high blaze. It seemed odd to build a bonfire in the churchyard as if we were attending some country cookout, but my wits were scrambled, and I could not think straight. How could Pru be as uncorrupted as those old saints in their glass tombs in Rome? And what gibberish had Mr. Tillinghast meant by feasting on blood or the presence of an evil spirit?

The selectmen had gathered round the coffin, and some disagreement was in play among them with one pointing to the other and he pointing at yet the next man. A large cleaver, like the kind a butcher favors, was being passed from man to man, but none seemed to want to possess it. It was not unlike a child's game of blighted potato, the way no man wanted to take the blade. They bickered on until the knife lay in the hand of Mr. Spaulding who now accepted it with his head hung low.

He clenched the blade in his teeth while he shook out of his coat and rolled his sleeves well above the elbows. Then he turned and knelt by the coffin with the butcher's blade in his right hand. Mr. Tillinghast was on the opposite side of the coffin and he too had a knife, much smaller and daintier. He ran this blade up the laced front of Prudence's burial dress and, to my shock, tore open the material to expose the naked belly. The horror compounded as Spaulding asked the Lord for forgiveness and sliced the massive blade across the stomach. Blood spurted up and bubbled forth, but the man did not stop. He cut and sawed and eviscerated the dead girl. Her innards were pulled out and swept to one side and he plunged his hand inside the cavity all the way up to his elbow. His face contorted with disgust and sweat beaded his brow as he worked at some unknown toil. He withdrew his hand and looked at the thing it clutched, a small slippery mass, dark in color. The liver was my guess.

Tillinghast had now turned and wretched up his supper onto the grass. He crawled away from the ghastly business on his hands and knees. Mr. Spaulding blinked stupidly at the organ in his hand and then threw it down in revulsion. He fell back on his rump and hung his head. He was slathered with gore.

"I can't," he gasped. "I cannot locate the heart."

Ebeneezer hissed at him with anger. "You must! You assured us this was the way of it. Now extract the organ."

"I cannot!" Spaulding spat back. He rose to his feet and thrust the cleaver to the tall selectman. "I am no butcher nor surgeon. I suggest you find the prize."

Ebeneezer backed off with his hands up and away from the bloodied knife. Spaulding held the blade and offered the haft to every man before him, but none would take it.

"One of you must do it," said Mr. Tillinghast, barely recovered from his vomiting. "If we do not have the heart, the evil will continue and there will be more deaths." Here he turned to everyone within earshot. "Please. Anyone. This girl's soul cannot find release unless it is done."

There was silence and then there was a voice. To this day, I know not who spoke up, but this is what it said: "Hester can do it."

My senses were dulled, my thoughts numbed. A hand nudged me from behind, another took my elbow. Voices around me pleaded and beseeched.

"Do it, Hester. Find the heart."

"We must have it. A moment's unpleasantness and it will save your family."

The heavy cleaver was in my hand and I was led to the coffin. They wanted her heart. That was simple enough. Who am I to refuse them all? I looked down at the butchered stomach. Spaulding had been clumsy in his work so I made another cut as close to the ribcage as I could. The cut was clean and the cavity open. I made the mistake of looking at Prudence's face. Spaulding's rough handling had somehow caused the eyelids to roll back and now Pru lay staring with glassy eyes at the sky above her. I looked away and thrust my arm into the breach and felt my way in. Here was a kidney, there a lung. Further in, my fingers locked around it. It tore away quite easily, and I plucked it out and held it up for all to see. Prudence's heart dripped with dark blood in my hands like a purpled jewel. Ebeneezer Wickes moved in to claim it and, for a moment before he did, I thought I felt the heart beating against my palm. Not the steady beating of a heart at rest but the quick pounding of a rabbit in terror.

The heart was taken to the fire, which was now a roiling inferno that shot sparks into the air. A drizzle of black pitch was poured on Prudence's heart to make the rubied meat burn all the quicker before it was laid onto the flames. Arthur Beecham stoked the flames and banked the hot coals against the muscle to make it burn.

I remained on my knees with my senses blasted and my arms dripping with gore. Someone raised me up and led me toward the fire where the rest of my family was assembled. From the flames issued a greasy black smoke, and I knew the heart was ablaze.

"Come closer," said Ebeneezer, huddling us together. "All of you together. Samuel and Katherine in front. Let the smoke bathe you and wash over you, cleansing you all of this profane evil."

More madness. The seven of us stood weeping in the smoke from the cremating heart of our dear Prudence. Did any of us understand what the purpose of it was? Or was I alone in my ignorance, glassy-eyed in the dazed acceptance of some ritual outside of my ken? My only coherent thought was an urge to run home to the pump and washstand to scrub away all the blood from my hands.

24

THE REST OF the evening was spent in a kind of stupor as we shuffled home. No one spoke of the terrible things that had been done. No one wanted supper. Pardon retreated into his study and the rest of us took to our beds in hopes of forgetting the whole profane event. The flesh of my hands burned from scrubbing them at the pump over and over. I could not get shed of the smell of the blood nor the sensation of it on my hands, even when I resorted to using a bit of lye to scrub with. It left my hands pink and raw.

When morning came, it was as if the horror had never happened. No one spoke of it. When I brought it up, I was hushed to be quiet. Moreover, Samuel seemed miraculously revived when he appeared at the breakfast table. Gone was the white pallor and croup-like cough, so too was the sluggish lethargy that had robbed his limbs of energy. His appetite had returned, eager to make up for lost time as he asked for a second and then a third helping.

Mother Stokely was also transformed. Her cheeks glowed as she hurried about the kitchen and fussed over her children. Jacob, too, had recovered from his toils in the ashy remains of

Bountiful. The sun rose bright and cheery on our homestead and I was left so baffled that I wondered if I had dreamt the whole outlandish experience at the graveyard.

Afterward I went out to the barn to check on the brindle dog we had brought home. Perhaps I had dreamed him up too, but no, there he lay in the bed of straw I had made for him, his tail thumping loudly when he saw me.

"How are we today, my little friend?"

The tail thumped harder, and he emitted whiny yips as he nosed my hands. The wound on his leg was not improved, but it looked no worse and I wondered if I should wrap it in something or let the clean air do its work. The dog ate from my hand the few table scraps I had brought him and then settled into my lap. I picked away the burs in his hide, happy to have this small distraction. What is it about dogs that can lift one's spirits? Is it their cheerful nature or their guileless eyes that appeal to us? Cats are wicked and I have no use for them.

"Do you have a name?" I asked him. "What became of your master, hmm?"

The ears flattened, and he nosed my palm again although all the food was gone.

"I suppose we must have a name for you. What should it be? Ashes, maybe? Vagabond?"

Neither appellation suited him as they recalled the sad state I had found him in. Another thought occurred to me.

"How about Lucky? That carries a ring of truth to it, yes? What do you say, Lucky?"

He rose up, wagging his tail all the harder, and I decided that he liked the name. I know he was simply responding to the rise of enthusiasm in my voice, but I preferred the conceit. Here is my thinking: A story has flavor; truth can be bland porridge.

But it was truth that was nagging my brains the way a mouse gnaws at the oat sack, nibbling at the edges until the grain pours out. What madness had gripped all of us in the churchyard? Had I really plunged my hand into my sister's breast and plucked out her heart? Had I truly felt it beat in my palm or was that a story my addled brains had improvised on the spot?

"Stay here, Lucky," I said as I rose to my feet. "I'll bring you some fat from the larder."

Lucky would not stay. He kept at my heels, reluctant to have me out of his sight, so I let him out of the barn. He loped across the yard, happy to have room to run but when he spotted the chickens near the coop, he went straight at them. He seemed to have some strange dislike of yard fowl as he barked at them and chased them around. I scolded him and brought him into the house with me. I was sure Mother Stokely would banish the mutt from her home, but she was not to be found. Polly said she was in the front garden and then she squealed loudly at the sight of the dog, wrapping her arms around Lucky's neck.

The door to the study was closed. I told Polly to watch the dog and crossed into the hallway. I knocked and pushed inside without waiting for a reply. My uncle stood at the window, gazing out at the meadow. He seemed annoyed at the intrusion.

"Not now, Hester," he said. "I don't wish to be disturbed."

"Uncle, I do not understand what happened yesterday. I don't even know where to start."

"Does it matter? The remedy worked. That is all that is important now." He turned back to the window.

How could I let it go? I would not. "What was that all about? Disturbing the graves of poor Pru and Faith? Violating their corpses and burning Pru's heart? It was madness, to say nothing of sacrilege."

My uncle's face hardened. "The parson was there. He, along with the others, sanctioned it."

"But to what end?" I demanded. "All that talk of evil spirits and fresh blood? As if Prudence was some sort of blight reaching out from beyond the grave? Make me understand. Please."

Pardon withdrew from the glass and slunk into his chair. The room was dark and it was chilly, for the hearth was cold. I gathered the kindling and a few slight logs to get a fire going. I needed its cheery warmth now. With the first flames eating up the dry spindles of wood, I knelt before the hearth and waited for my uncle to speak.

He brooded a moment longer before turning his eyes to me. "How much illness have you seen in your short lifetime, Hester?"

"More than I care to remember," I said. "Cholera and small-pox. Camp fever and now consumption. Leprosy, even."

"And how much of it do you understand? The source of each, the remedy. The cure?"

I folded my hands in my lap. I knew of tonics and remedies,

but I had never come across an actual cure or a definite cause for any of them. I said nothing.

Pardon looked at the fire. "Some plagues cannot be treated because they have a sinister root. Where some pox is carried in a miasma of bad air or rises from the ground to afflict us, others are simply diabolical. And they must be treated as such if they are to be stopped."

I laid a small log of cherrywood across the kindling, careful not to snuff out the tender blaze. "Are you saying the Devil had a hand in my cousin's deaths?"

"Not the Devil himself, but some agent of his. One that slithers into our lives under a mask of disease and tricks us into not believing in it. It is guile played by a master hand."

Anger fluttered my ribs. "I do not have a head for riddles, uncle. I need simpler terms."

"Bring me that cognac, would you?"

I rose and fetched the brown glass bottle from its perch on the bookshelf and brought it to him. Returning to my place at the fire, I waited as my uncle poured a draught into a glass and downed half of it.

"What took Pru and Faith was not natural consumption. It appears as thus, but the root of it is an evil spirit. It wastes away its victims, but it does not stop at death. It persists, even in the grave, and reaches out to afflict the next of kin. It feeds on the lifeblood to keep it alive in its tomb." He reached for the bottle again. "That is what happened to your eldest cousin. The malign spirit nested in Prudence's breast and then it fed on poor Faith until she too was dead. Then it turned its appetite to Samuel. I suspect Katherine also. And it would have claimed them if the selectmen had not bullied me into action."

A ball of ice formed in the pit of my stomach. His words seemed without sense or meaning. "Are you saying that Pru did not die? That she was somehow alive in her grave?"

"Not Pru, the spirit within her. Nay, it thrived after her death as it fed on her sister's blood. Did you not see her condition when the coffin was pried open? She was healthy and blooming. It is a cruel spirit, this thing."

Would I ever forget that horrid vision of Prudence in her grave, with her rosy cheeks and glowing flesh? The blood on her mouth, the gore chalking her fingernails? No matter how long I live, I will never escape that image.

"And that butchery is the way to destroy it?" I asked. "To carve out and burn the heart?"

"The heart is where it resides. The flames purify it, ending its threat to all of us."

I gazed down at the scuffed floorboards, no wiser than before. The narrative was difficult to swallow.

Pardon was quiet for a moment, perhaps granting me time to take it all in. His eyes were brimmed with sympathy as he watched me struggle.

"I did not want to believe it either," he said. "When Ebeneezer and the others came to me with their plan, I refused to accept it. The selectmen feared the evil would spread once it consumed our family. Their concerns were for the community at large. As it stands, we are too late. The wickedness has claimed James Corwin. I can only pray that no others will be afflicted."

My sympathies reflected back onto him. How horrid it must have been for him, with the council demanding this terrible rite to be performed on his children. I recalled the earlier disagreements, and how Katherine all but threw the men out when she learned of their schemes.

"It is difficult to comprehend," I said. I considered myself somewhat astute in the ways of remedies and curatives, no matter how queer they seemed. Oyster shells in the bed of a dropsy sufferer or scalding lemon water to flush the ears of the deaf. I said, "How have I never heard of this"—I groped for the appropriate word—"solution?"

"It is an old belief. One never spoken of unless necessary." He drained the second glass of cognac and studied the bottle, contemplating another draught. "I hope word of what we have done does not travel. Outsiders would not understand. They would mock us for it. So, we shall speak of it no more."

With that, the matter was settled. I rose and took the cognac bottle and returned it to its shelf. Another taste of it would only lead to more brooding on my uncle's part. I lingered there, a thousand questions buzzing round my head like blowflies on July meat, but I settled on one.

"How did this evil find Prudence? Where did it come from?"

He sighed. "The stones on the road to Hell are laid with the best intentions. I believe we brought it on ourselves."

"What do you mean? We are lacking in some spiritual way?"

"No." he rose and took the bottle down again. "Our good-will laid us low. That vagabond we sheltered, he brought this wickedness to our door. May God curse his rotten soul."

~

I was not myself for the remainder of the day, sniping and stand-offish to my cousins. Despite the cheeriness of Samuel's recovery and the renewed roses in Mother Stokely's cheeks, I could not shake off the terrible events of yesterday. The abhorrent images were always there in my mind's eye. The shriveled husk of Faith in her narrow coffin or the sight of Prudence's eyes rolling open as my hand violated her. What I wanted was some time alone and away from the bustle and chores of the house.

Katherine was of another mind on the matter, disapproving of my long walks at dusk or hours spent alone by the creek. Solitude, she declared, is not a habit suited to a young girl. This is what I have to say on the matter: A head that does not need solitude is a head that is probably empty.

There was a lull in the afternoon chores, so I informed Mother Stokely that I was going for a walk. She objected and asked where I was going, but she grew quiet when I said I was going to visit with my departed cousins. I picked daisies and blue-bells on the way, stringing together garlands to lay over the stones of their disturbed graves. Lucky the dog ambled by my side, glancing up at me at regular intervals as if he did not want me out of his sight. His limp was improving.

Arriving at the churchyard, I found that I wasn't the only visitor to the graves of Pru and Faith. Will was there, holding a spade in one hand as he stamped the earth at the foot of Faith's wooden headstone.

"William," I said, strangely glad to see the one-handed lad after our adventure to Bountiful. "This is a surprise."

He removed his cap and regarded me with a look of concern. "Hello Hester. I hope you've recovered from yesterday?"

"I have, thank you. And so has Samuel for that matter. He got out of bed this morning looking as fit as a fiddlehead."

"That is good news," he said. His lopsided smile was sincere. He nodded at the dog leaning against my knee. "Is that who I think it is?"

"It is. I've named him Lucky. Say hello, Lucky."

Will nickered for the dog to come to him. "How is he getting along?"

"He has a strange dislike of the chickens," I said. "Otherwise, he's quite docile."

He gestured to the dog again, but Lucky remained aloof and wary. "Not the friendliest fellow, is he?"

"He's a shy one. God knows what he's seen." I ran my fingers over the flat pate of his head and Lucky's tail thumped anew. My gaze went to the spade in Will's hand and the newly compacted soil around the headstone. "What are you doing there?"

"Just straightening the markers," he said. "They were knocked askew in yesterday's disturbance."

I tucked my chin in. "And you came to set them right?"

"The sextons did a poor job of it. They were eager to quit the place."

Not for the first time was I surprised by the man's decency. "That was very sweet of you."

"I'd hate for your aunt to see the stones listing the way they did." He stamped the earth under his boot a few more times. "Or you, for that matter."

I did not know what to say. I scratched Lucky's ear before I embarrassed myself with some mawkish display. Simple acts of kindness can bring tears to my eyes. I am a ridiculous person.

"You've brought garlands, I see." He meant the wildflowers in my hand.

"Yes. I felt the need to do something after yesterday. Silly of me, I suppose."

"Who doesn't love bluebells?" He hooked the cap back on his head and squared it. "I'll give you some privacy, then. Goodbye Hester."

We watched him make his way through the graves, Lucky and I. The dog seemed to relax with his absence, but my reaction was the opposite. I wished he had stayed. Why, I could not tell you. My silliness was overflowing this day.

I laid the garlands over both their graves and knelt in the clover before them to say a small prayer. To my left was a ring of stones and the sooty remains of the fire that had blazed yesterday. The furnace that had consumed Prudence's heart left a deep scorch mark on the earth and the smell of it lingered still. I thought of calling Will back to help me scatter the ashes and cover the blemish on the ground. I did not want any remembrance of yesterday's horribleness.

I was sure Will was long gone, but I rose and turned to the gates anyway. A lone figure stood among the tombstones, watching me from a distance. Not Will, and not even Henry, but a disheveled figure that I did not recognize at first. My blood ran cold when I placed the man's face. Ephraim Fiske, the madman.

25

THE FUGITIVE CAME shambling toward me and my limbs iced solid with fear. I looked about for help, but the graveyard was empty save for him and me. Lucky stirred against my leg, ears up, and hackles rising. He seemed to grow in size, and I was grateful for his protectiveness, but he was still weak and would not last long in a tussle. I thought of running but I have never been fast, and the skirt and bustle are impossible to run in. My boots were sturdy. Perhaps I could kick him.

His coat was in tatters and his face was grimy, but the man Fiske was much recovered from the last time I had seen him. He was armed as before, with a pistol and a knife tucked into his belt. God only knew where he had acquired these, possibly some roadside banditry. He slowed his pace and stopped some distance from me. The look in his eyes was not savage or mad as I had anticipated. Wary yes, but also saddened. Lucky bristled at my side, but my own fear throttled back a notch.

"Stay back," I warned him. "I'll scream for help if you come any closer."

He removed his threadbare hat and made a small bow. "These were your sisters, yes?"

"What do you want? Half the town is out hunting for you."

"Your name is Heather, is it not? You're the one who saved my life."

"I should have let you die," I spat. "It's not enough that you destroyed your own village, but you had to bring death to our home? After we took you in?"

He gripped the hat tightly. "I am not the issuer of their demise, Heather. I swear. I tried to warn you all."

"Hester!"

"Beg your pardon?"

"My name is Hester," I said. "Now let me pass. I want no violence."

Ephraim Fiske stepped aside, allowing me a wide berth on the path to the gates. "I will not keep you. I only wanted to ask what happened here yesterday."

I made no reply other than to advance on the path toward the road. My feet wanted to run but I would not give him the satisfaction. He spoke as I passed him.

"What did they find when the bodies were exhumed? Whose heart was plump with fresh blood?"

I stopped flat. "What do you know of it?"

"It's happening all over again," he said. "The consumption and the deaths. The madness in the graveyard."

I lashed out at him. "You brought this madness on us! After we took you in, this is how you repaid us. With death and illness!"

I must have cut him to the quick for he hung his head in shame.

"I suppose I did," he sighed in a low voice. "It was not my intention, Hester. You must believe me."

"It is not my nature to heed the words of murderers," I returned. I don't know why I didn't dash for safety or call for help. Ephraim Fiske was collapsed against the stone in a lowly state and posed no real threat. I should have shrieked my lungs out that the wanted man was here, the reward was ripe for the plucking, but I held my tongue.

"Where have you been all this time?"

He squinted up at me. "On the run. I was halfway to Providence when I turned back."

Lucky was still agitated, bristling at the stranger. I patted his head to calm him. "Why come back? There is a bounty on your head."

The fugitive's brow rose sharply at my remark. "A bounty? That's rather mercenary for country gentlemen."

"It was not they who set the wage," I corrected him. "It was your own sister-in-law."

An expression of despair came over his paling face. His chin dipped to his collarbone, and he shook his head sullenly. "Of course she did. Clever woman."

"Can you blame her? After murdering her husband, your own brother? You are no better than Cain."

Ephraim Fiske shot to his feet. Anger flushed away the despair from his features. "I was not the one who killed him." Then he laughed, like the madman he was. "How cruel she is, to blame it on me. His blood is on her hands entire!"

The madman paced the ground in an agitated state. Lucky began to snarl, and I cursed myself for not running when I had the chance. But no violence ensued. Not from him anyway, for a voice cried out over the graveyard.

"Stop where you are, man! Or I will cut you down with a musket ball!"

It was Henry Beecham! Stalking through the stones from the south glen, he shouldered a musket with the business end trained on his target.

Fiske sprang into action with remarkable grace. Like quicksilver, he had the pistol out and up and let off the shot at his pursuer. Henry dove for cover as the shot chipped the granite of a headstone. The fugitive bolted for the trees, but Henry was already on his feet and drawing his sightline down the long barrel of the gun.

A thunderclap of sound and a cloud of smoke, the air acrid with the smell of powder. Fiske went down.

Henry let out a roar and chased after him, holding the gun high overhead in victory. When I caught up to them, the man named Fiske was flattened against the clover with a patch of red pooling through the coat on his back.

Henry whooped and hollered with the gun overhead and his boot on his prey. "I got him!" he railed at me, his face beaming. "The bounty is mine!"

The swiftness of the action had left me senseless. Before I knew what was happening, Henry swooped me up in his arms and kissed me passionately on the lips. My knees went wobbly. I must have faltered in that moment. When I opened my eyes, he still held me about the waist with one hand and brandished his weapon in the other. There were other men now, running into the graveyard, alerted to the report of gunfire. I tore myself away from Henry's arm, terrified of being caught out, my lips stinging from his kiss.

~

A great hullabaloo commenced when word went out about the capture of the dangerous madman and the heroic courage of our own Henry Beecham. Hurrah and good fellow they cried as the whole citizenry seemed to rush into the churchyard. Ephraim Fiske was dragged away while Henry was borne aloft on the shoulders of the men, past the gate to the town green.

Fiske was not, as I had assumed, killed by the musket fire. The ball had somehow missed a vital organ and Mr. Fiske was still conscious, although spitting blood through gnashed teeth. He was taken to Bidwell the bonesetter under the guard of the watchmen. If the projectile hadn't taken his life, then Bidwell's ghastly treatments surely would. The prospect of his death was not reassuring, despite the reign of terror he had imposed on our pastoral existence. Why this was so, I could not articulate. I think the recent deaths of my sisters had knocked my senses askew, making me sentimental and ridiculous. It was not a pleasant sensation, this muddling of justice and passions.

Arthur Beecham and Ebeneezer Wickes questioned me as to the chain of events and then walked me home. I hurried through the back door to find Katherine in a state, bustling and grumbling as she prepared our supper. She scolded me soundly for leaving her to cook alone and she was not moved by the reasons behind my tardiness. She was distracted and clumsy, dropping pots and spilling beans as she fussed and spat harsh words at me. Lazy, useless, indulgent, and other epithets. I hold no shame in admitting they stung, but they blinded me to her state. Mother Stokely was ghastly pale and sweating profusely. Her hands trembled as if chilled and her coughing fits doubled her over more than once.

I began to set the table, and she barked at me to count the plates again, dullard that I was. I had set a table for seven, the family only, and asked if we were expecting company.

"We need nine settings, you goat," she spat. "Can you not count?"

Nine had been the usual number of mouths round the supper table. Until recently, of course. Katherine was insisting on setting places for Prudence and Faith. I softened my tone and reminded her of this. Liar, she called me. A plate flung at my head shattered against the wall. She swayed suddenly as if astride the rocking deck of a ship and then her gray eyes rolled over white. She thudded heavily against the floor.

Jacob and Samuel helped me carry her upstairs where I loosened her corset and patted a damp cloth over her hot brow. Another coughing jag had her coiled into a ball. Polka dots of blood stained the cotton of the pillow. I ordered the boys downstairs to feed the children and boil some water. I did not want them to see her in this state. The signs of consumption were unmistakable, and no one deserves to see their own mamma cut down thus.

Pardon had not returned from the clamor of the fugitive's arrest and I dreaded his return now. How was I to inform him that the consumption was back and was now laying his wife low? How would I tell him that our horrendous efforts in the exhumation of his children were all for naught?

Polly and Hiram were relentless in their questions about their mother's absence at the dinner table and soon pried the truth out of Samuel, Jacob, and myself. Upset at hearing she was ill, they dashed to her room where they clung to her like burs on a horse's tail. I didn't want them near Katherine while she was this feverish and I whispered so to Jacob and Sam. Clutching at their mother, the children wept and became furious with me for banning them from the room. More harsh words, more stinging welts to my heart. I would have thought my heart was a toughened piece of leather by now, but it was not. Their childish rantings cut like glass.

When the children were finally in bed, I went to the kitchen to brew a poultice that might ease Katherine's labored breathing. There was still the bottle of paregoric, which would help her sleep. My uncle returned home as I crushed blessed thistle in the mortar and pestle. He looked weary and unwell.

"I kept a plate warm for you," I said as I fetched his dinner. "Come sit."

With a heavy sigh, he dropped into a chair and said nothing.

I set the meal before him and dipped a cup into the cider pail. "You look tired, uncle," I remarked.

"It's been a difficult day." He drank the cider but only picked at his plate. "I should be hungrier."

"What's become of Mr. Fiske?"

Pardon barely managed a shrug. "He lives, but for how long, I cannot say. Bidwell patched up the wound, but he does not expect him to last long."

"Where is he now?"

"Taken to the stockhouse and put under guard. It'll serve as a gaol for now."

The stockhouse was a remnant of the original settlement of Wickstead, back when it was a simple garrison. A rough building of log palisades and a heavy door, it had served as an armory during the war. It was now a storehouse and, on occasion, a gaol when needed.

"What will happen to him now?"

"Would you refresh this for me, please?" He pushed his cup forward. "The council will decide his fate. Whatever that may be."

"Did you speak to him?"

"Not yet. The injury has left him senseless." Taking the cup from me, my uncle leaned to one side to peer into the parlor. "Where is Katherine?"

Now it was my turn to sigh. I told him as plainly as I could that she was seriously ill and taken to bed. I added that she bore all the signs of a galloping consumption. And then I said I was sorry.

To my surprise, he did not burst into wailing or dash for her bedside. Instead he simply pushed his untouched plate away from him. "Then it was all for nothing," he said darkly.

I said that I was doing all I could to make her comfortable. I looked at him again. "You don't seem shocked."

"You know Sarah Corwin?"

"James's sister?" I said. A year younger than James, Prudence's deceased beau. Sarah and I knew one another, but we were not friends. George and Alma Corwin had six children in all. Now reduced to five, and possibly reduced by one more now. "Is she all right?"

"She is deathly ill," he said. "Consumption. Bidwell assured us of it."

"That poor family. So soon after losing James."

"There are whispers that one of the Van Tassel boys has also been taken to bed with a similar fever." He drained his cup and set it on the table. "All that wretched business in the graveyard was for nothing. I'm such a fool."

Pardon was not a man accustomed to strong emotions. Or at least, revealing them to the world. His sorrow riled up with his anger, and back and forth the two moods played over him.

"That is not true. You did what you thought best. For us all."

He patted my hand and then leaned forward, becoming suddenly earnest and severe. "Hester, listen to me. I think we are in for a rough go of it. You need to steel yourself against what may come. Sticks and stones and whatnot."

"What do you mean?"

"The cleansing ritual did not work. The consumption has escaped our little family and is laying others low. This is exactly what the selectmen feared. They will blame us now. Not all of them, but enough. There will be cruel words said. Perhaps even a rotten cabbage flung at our heads. Toughen up."

He pushed his chair back and said he was going to check on his wife. I remained at the table with a sickening dread growing inside my belly.

26

A SCREAM BOILED up inside me like a pot left too long over the fire and I feared its release would be messy. With Katherine taken to her sickbed, I took up the slack of duties and had scarcely a moment to clear my head between the meals and the chores and the caring of the ill. The memory of Henry's kiss still stung my lips and my frantic mind churned relentlessly over its meaning. Did he love me or was he simply caught up in the thrill of the moment? Had he always longed to kiss me? Did I dare think there could be something true between us? I felt lost. His kiss had swept the rug from under my feet and my entire existence seemed upended.

Henry Beecham kissed me.

He saved my life.

Henry kissed me.

I crafted a plan. I shrugged some of my usual chores onto Polly and Hiram, who were getting underfoot anyway, and conjured up a poultice that I could bring to the prisoner in the stockhouse. A brew of saltpork and bread to draw out the poison blood and foxglove to promote the healing of the flesh. How could Pardon refuse such a Christian gesture as aiding the downcast? The stockhouse gaol was not far from the inn. I would go there first to find Henry before going on to deliver the remedy to the gaol.

It wasn't until late in the day when I made my dash. Dinner was a simple hominy warming over the fire which could easily be doled out by Sam and Jacob. The look on their faces made me laugh when they learned that the mealtime chores were now in their hands. They sputtered and began to argue over the details of the task and so I made my escape. The moment I passed the gate, I gathered up my skirt and ran.

The streets were quiet when I got there. As Pardon had predicted, there was little welcome for me there. I hallooed Mrs. Amblin, but she did not return my greeting. Mr. Van Tassel was taking his pipe on the stoop of his shop. When I waved, he actually turned his back on me. I had the misfortune of passing Tom Hazard, the surly little boy who was my regular tormentor. He sat perched on a fence and called me a gargoyle and ogre and other such things. He picked up a stone to hurl at me, but when I stared him down, he slunk off like the craven squirrel he was.

I hurried on to the inn where I found Martha sweeping broken glass and asked after her son. I was disappointed to learn that he was not there.

"Do you know where he is?"

Martha swept the glass shards into a corner. "I'm afraid not, dear. He was getting a bit boisterous with his fellows, acting the hero and all, so I chased him off."

"Oh. Well, fiddle sticks."

She looked at me suspiciously. "What do you want him for, Hester?"

"Nothing," I said too quickly. How guilty did I look? "I just wanted to thank him for saving my life."

Martha sighed. "Please, don't. The lad's puffed up on himself enough."

I thanked her and left. The stockhouse was set behind Granger's Livery, down near the creek. A formidable structure comprised of thick timbered poles, planed to points at the top end, that looked sturdy enough to withstand a cannonball. There was one entrance, a low gate of heavy oak, and posted outside of it were two guards. Peg-Leg Wilkins, who seemed sober enough, and Joseph Hendershot, son of selectman Hendershot. The two guards stood rigidly at their posts, both clutching muskets but looking much discomforted as they were being berated by a third figure on the scene. I recognized her immediately from her black dress and veil. It was the Widow Fiske, demanding to see the prisoner. They were family after all.

"I'm sorry, ma'am," Joseph said, staring over the head of the widow at the distance beyond. "Our orders are ironclad. No one is allowed."

"You can choke on your orders, little man," the widow shot back. Her blood was up. "He may be your prisoner, but he is my kin and my burden on this earth. You will open the gate!"

Joseph gripped his musket tighter. "Ma'am, you'll have to seek permission from the council. There's nothing I can do."

Peg-Leg spotted me as I came up and seemed much relieved for the distraction. "Well hello, Hester," he called out with a smile.

"Who goes there?" demanded Joseph, although he could see me clear enough.

"Don't be silly, Joe," I said. I drew up before the trio and curtsied to the woman in black. "Widow Fiske. How are you?"

"Vexed," she replied, her lips drawn back in almost a snarl. "These tree stumps won't get out of my way."

The argument went round again; the widow demanding and the guards refusing. The widow rattled off something in a language I did not know, but its intent was clear enough. For a moment, I thought she might strike poor Joseph.

"Is anyone in there with Mr. Fiske?" I asked. "Is Henry inside?"

Joseph relaxed his posture as he addressed me. "He is alone. Bidwell said he would return in the morning to check on his wound."

"I've brought something for that exactly," I said, raising the jar in my hands. "For gunshots and ax blows. It's best applied before nightfall. It won't take a minute."

Joseph was unmoved. "Sorry, Hester."

The widow stormed away, still venting in some peculiar tongue. I left the jar with Joseph, asking him to give it to the bonesetter in the morning, and then ran to catch up with the woman in black.

"May I walk with you, Mrs. Fiske?" I asked.

She grunted something but did not slow her pace.

"It's a shame they wouldn't let you see your brother-in-law," I said. "What would you have said to him?"

A peculiar smile lit beneath that veil. "I hadn't planned on saying anything. I was just going to plunge a knife into his throat."

I couldn't tell if she was jesting or not. "Will you go to the council?"

"Yes, but not to ask their permission," she said. "I had hoped that the hand that struck justice would be mine, but that is not to be. I will address the men and demand that Ephraim be hanged from the neck."

I stopped in my tracks. "You can't mean that. There must be a trial first. Charges have to be laid, a hearing tabled."

The widow leveled her gaze at me. "What is the point, Hester? The man has confessed his sins. All that remains is the swing from the gallows tree. Goodnight, Miss Stokely."

She proceeded on her way toward the marshland and the decrepit Cogburn Hall. It was already dark, and I needed to hurry home. The path through the marsh was a shorter walk than the main road and I could have accompanied the Widow on her way, but I did not. The woman's ire was fierce, and I had no want of provoking it further.

I had brought no lantern with me and had to follow the faintly visible road before me. There was no moon, but the sky was clear and prickled with stars. I stopped to gaze up in wonder at the twinkling starlight above me in all its eternal, unknowable glory. As a child, I used to think of the night as a great blanket pulled over the earth, but the material was pocked with holes through which the glory of Paradise filtered through. Now I wondered if all of those tiny lights could be the souls of those who have passed away before us. Which one was Prudence and which Faith? Which were my mother and father? Which of that multitude were the poor souls taken from Bountiful?

I crept in through the kitchen door like a cat, stealthy and without sound, only to find Hiram and Polly sitting before the fire in the parlor. Jacob was with them. All three looked distressed.

"What are you two doing up?" I said.

Polly sniffled. "It's mother."

177

Charging upstairs, I heard a commotion of violence emanating from the master bedroom. Mother Stokely was taken with some kind of fit, thrashing and churning the bedsheets while her husband and eldest son held her down. Her face was contorted into a ferocious mask and she spat a string of curses that would have made Peg-Leg Wilkins blush.

"What's happened?"

My uncle's face was strained with the effort of keeping his wife still. He was relieved to see me. "The fever's taken her. Do something!"

The tincture. I ran to fetch the blue glass bottle and returned to the bedroom. The violence of Katherine's fit would make this difficult. "You must hold her still," I said, "if I am to get this down her gullet."

Samuel was close to tears as he struggled to contain his poor mother. I reassured him Katherine would rest easy once the tincture was administered. I sat on her legs while they pinned her shoulders and kept her head still. Forcing her mouth open, I spilled a good deal of the paregoric over her chin before managing to get any down her throat. The mask of fury melted from her face. Her skin was hot and the nightgown damp with sweat. I sent Samuel downstairs to calm the little ones and put them to bed now that the crisis was over. Pardon and I changed Katherine out of her damp gown and cooled her off. Her naked flesh was distressing, waxy and thin as it was. The same way Pru and Faith looked when their time came. I said nothing of this to my uncle but the trouble in his eyes revealed our shared concerns.

We sat with her for over an hour and then I told Pardon to sleep in my bed tonight. I would watch over her. He refused at first, but I insisted.

"God bless," he said, kissing his wife's brow and then mine before leaving the room.

Katherine did not stir nor sigh. Her breathing was so shallow that I put my ear to her chest, fearing I had administered too much of the opium. She was fine, and I prayed that the morning would find her restored.

I woke in the night, sensing something was wrong. Mother Stokely was sitting up, staring at the window.

"Mother?"

"Do you hear them?" she said.

There was nothing to hear. The bullfrogs in the creek.

"Go back to sleep," I said. "It's nothing."

"Are your ears clogged? How do you not hear that?"

I tried to ease her back down, but she would not. "They are calling for me. They are scared and they are cold."

"Who?"

"The children," she said. "Prudence and Faith. And the babies. They need me."

The babies. My heart broke all over again. How much torment could the woman bear, losing so many of her children? I assured her it was just a dream. After a moment, she settled back onto the pillow.

"They won't stop," she whispered. "They need warmth and comfort and yet here I lie with you. How can they be gone and you here? You are not even my daughter."

"The fever's given you bad dreams, Katherine," I said. "Try to rest. Everything will be fine in the morning."

She became still again, her breathing steady. I thought she was asleep, but she whispered my name.

"What is it?"

"Promise me something, Hester," she said. "Watch over my family. Protect them when I am gone."

"Please don't talk like that. You will recover. I will see to it."

The bullfrogs boomed outside the window in their endless moaning. They cared not about the misery under our roof. A callous world carries on as we suffer.

Katherine whispered again. "What will become of you all when I am gone? Who will protect you then?"

"Stop this. You must sleep."

"Then promise me, Hester. Do it now."

There was no way around it. "I swear I will care for them all," I vowed. "And protect them to my dying breath."

Satisfied, she settled again. I did not know then that this would be our last coherent exchange. If I had, I would have told Katherine how much I loved her. And how grateful I was to be part of this dear family.

~

Katherine was gone when I awoke. The morning sunlight found the bed empty. I was cheered by this, not alarmed. Mother Stokely was feeling better, I thought. She was already up and downstairs in the kitchen stoking the fire. I dressed haphazardly and hurried down.

Polly and Hiram were in the kitchen, tearing chunks of bread from the loaf and dipping it into the butter pot. Children are such mice, nibbling at anything when no one was looking.

I took the butter away from them. The kitchen was cold, no fire in the hearth. "Where is mother?"

Polly's chin was shiny with grease. "Isn't she in bed?"

My nerves prickled unpleasantly. I crossed to the parlor only to find it empty. "You haven't seen her?"

Both children stood open-mouthed as I went from room to room. "Didn't you watch over her last night?" Polly asked.

She wasn't in the house. "Go and wake your father," I said as I ran outside.

Everything was quiet. Lucky lay curled up on the porch and a slight mist was rising from the damp ground as the sun hit it. In the paddock, Caesar raised his head to look at me. I ran to the barn and the woodshed and the other outbuildings. The privy. There was no sign of her. I was heading back inside when I heard the clomping of hooves on the road. A rider on a palomino hove up before our gate. It was Will Treves.

"Hester," he said. "Where is Pardon?"

"Asleep. What's wrong?"

"It's your aunt. She's at the graveyard. Hester, she's out of her mind."

The clapping of wood sounded behind me. Polly and Hiram stood on the veranda. I barked at them to tell their father to come to the graveyard immediately. I turned back to Will and reached out my hand.

"Help me up."

His boot slipped from the stirrup so I could step into it and his hand lifted me up. I had no time for propriety and didn't bother with any side-saddle nonsense. I hunkered behind him and let him have the stirrup again. "Go!" I directed.

We thundered through town and stopped at the gates of the churchyard. I plunged on ahead, leaving Will to lash the reins to the iron railing. The graveyard was unusually busy this morning with people milling about. Another funeral, perhaps two, but I had no time to wonder on it.

I knew where to look. Mother Stokely was with her children,

the four who died in infancy and the two grown to almost adult-hood. Six lost. Who among us would not lose their wits at such tragedy?

Katherine lay sprawled on the dandelion-dotted ground be-fore the graves of her children. Her hair was wet and stringy, the nightgown torn. She lay face down and her hands clutched at the earth, tearing up crusts of soil as if she meant to dig down to her offspring. A moan, strange and animal-like, rose from her.

I turned her over. "Katherine, hush now. You're all right. Come away."

Her hair was matted across her face. Her eyes seemed all wrong the way they darted and wheeled about, unable to fix on any point.

"What did I do wrong?" she wailed to me. "What sin is pun-ishable thus? Tell me!"

"Come away," I begged her. The folk around us began to stare and point. "Please, Katherine."

She clutched at me and I saw blood on her cheek, more on her hands. Her arms and legs were scratched red with welts.

"It's not fair," she seethed, turning her wrath to the sky above. "I am not Job! Why do You test me?"

Her tirade was directed at the Almighty and that frightened me more than anything. Not just the blasphemy but the bulging stares of our neighbors. I began to drag her away when Will ap-peared and together we propelled her toward the gates.

"Hurry," he said, one eye on the gawking crowd. "Before they stone her to death."

Katherine railed on, shaking a fist at the heavens. "You are cruel! I renounce—"

I slapped my palm over her mouth to silence her. She re-volted in violence and fits, but we held firm until she went limp in our arms. Passing through the cemetery gates, we lifted Kath-erine onto the back of the horse, and I climbed up after her.

"I'll lead," Will said, taking hold of the bridle. "You keep her upright."

We set off and I glanced at Will across the bobbing head of the horse.

"She's ill. She doesn't know what she's saying."

"Tell that to them," he said, looking back at the people in the graveyard.

I didn't want to think about it. "Why are there so many about? Is it another funeral?"

"The Van Tassel boy died. He's being buried this morning." Tugging the bridle, he led the palomino forward. "The Corwins are here for a different reason altogether."

The Corwin clan that Prudence was supposed to marry into. "Oh no," I said. "Don't tell me Sarah died?"

"No. But her illness has worsened. The Corwins are there to dig up their son's coffin."

"Dig it up?"

"To save the sister," he said.

I did not want to hear anymore, and we hurried on in silence.

27

SHE DIED LATER that night with her children gathered around her, praying and holding her hands. When evening came, Pardon sent everyone out and closed the bedroom door. Katherine expired some time during the night in the arms of her husband.

Grief settled over us once again, but this time it was not a visitor. It was here to stay. Katherine was dead. She was not sleeping; she was not ill. She was never coming back. We moved about like senseless things, a house of mutes. No one came to pay their respects, no neighbor dropped in to console us. We six had only each other and none looked their fellow in the eye for fear of weeping all over again. I prepared a meal, but I don't remember if anyone ate it. Mother Stokely remained in the bed behind the closed bedroom door and none of us ventured up the steps all day. We slept in the parlor, huddled around the fireplace. I even let the dog sleep indoors that night. His wagging tail and bright eyes were a distraction for us all.

The next day, life carried on. The body was brought down to the back room where it could be prepared. The task was mine alone this time. Polly offered to help, so I asked her to gather wildflowers from the meadow to make a garland. Samuel and Jacob took the wagon down to the mill on the river for more lumber. They had already used up our supply of milled timbers with the first two coffins. They returned with a wagon load of planed ash rather than the basic pine. They wanted something special for their mother to rest in.

Washing and preparing the body was difficult. Life has weight to it, heft. In death, Katherine's body seemed thirty pounds lighter. The heat of early summer was on us and the blowflies would not stop buzzing around her. When one of the filthy things crawled across Katherine's naked eyeball, I covered her face with a cloth.

We had two visitors that day and I commend each for the strength of their character in it. The first was Henry Beecham. His visit was brief but respectful, holding his hat in his hand in the parlor where the coffin lay. When Pardon asked after his father, Henry replied that his family was unwell and could not come, but he passed on their condolences. I knew Henry well enough to know that this was a story he made up to spare my uncle's feelings. I adored him all the more for it. He bowed and left after that. I had hoped to steal a moment with him but no opportunity presented itself.

Will Treves came on the third day, loyal as ever to my uncle. He helped load the coffin into the wagon and then we all made the dreary funeral march to the churchyard. Like before, there was a cluster of people in the graveyard, off to the western rim under the cherry trees. Another burial in process, I assumed. We trudged on toward the Stokely plot only to discover that no grave had been prepared. My uncle told Jacob to fetch the sexton to answer for his mistake. He had sent word the day before asking the man to dig another grave beside Faith's for his dead wife, but the order had been ignored. The sexton came and he and Pardon exchanged some harsh words and the custodian went away again.

"What did he say?" I asked when my uncle returned. "Why did he not prepare the grave?"

"He said he was too busy," Pardon replied. "And his hired man quit, leaving him as sole gravedigger."

Faith's wooden headstone stood before me. A slug had crawled onto the shadowed front and I brushed it away. "What are we to do?"

Will offered to do the job but with only one spade hand, the task would take too long. And it seemed unfair to ask Samuel and Jacob to dig their own mother's grave.

"The crypt," Pardon said. "Katherine will rest there until we can get this sorted out."

Crypt was a rather lavish term. It was more of a root cellar dug into the side of a low hill at the south end of the churchyard. The front of it was a flat wall of fieldstone with a wooden gate and latch set into it. It was used to house the dead in winter until the ground had thawed. The sexton could not be found so Pardon proceeded without him, sliding back the iron bolt on the gate. He said a prayer and then Will and the boys ferried the coffin into the dark recess. The hinges emitted an unpleasant sound as the gate was shut and the bolt slid home again.

We walked out of the churchyard without another word. Polly held her father's hand as we walked, and Hiram reached up and slipped his small hand in mine. He kept looking back over his shoulder at the crypt where his mother lay.

"Don't look back, Hiram," I said gently, echoing Katherine's own words. I did not share her peculiar belief, but I repeated it, anyway. Don't ask me why. "Let mother rest now."

He pouted. "But she'll be all alone here."

"Hush now." I hurried him along.

Passing the cluster of mourners under the cherry tree, I saw that my initial assumption had been wrong. This family, the Vaughns, were not laying a loved one to rest. They were exhuming the grave. A fire had been stoked next to it, awaiting the dead heart.

~

The house became unnaturally quiet. The children stopped bickering and Jacob spoke only in grunts. There was the creak of the floorboards, but that was all. My uncle withdrew into himself, unaware of anything around him. Samuel put on a brave face, but his coughing resumed its ragged hacking and I feared that his illness was returning. Polly clung to my waist while Hiram sat rocking back and forth the way he did as a toddler.

Jacob was angry. He snapped at me when I asked if he wished to talk and he barked at me when I asked if he was hungry. My clumsy attempts at comfort were thrown back in my face. How could I possibly know how he felt, he roared. It wasn't my mother who died, was it? His words stung and when Pardon found me sobbing, I told him why.

"Grief makes madmen of us all," he said. "Give him room to mourn. It is an awful ordeal to lose one's mother."

I was gape-mouthed at that. Had my uncle forgotten who he was talking to? Adding salt to the wound, he harangued me to feed the children and to dry their eyes. They needed comfort now, he said. Thus was my time spent caring for my cousins and facilitating their grief. None of them asked how I was holding up, but then again, it wasn't my mother who had died. The gall of it was bitter, but I pursed my lips and swallowed it.

~

The first visitors to the house after Katherine's death came at dusk the following day, but it was not Arthur Beecham, as Pardon had hoped. He was quite hurt at his friend's absence and, though he tried to conceal it, his disappointment was obvious. I too hoped that Arthur would come and bring his son with him. But that was not to be.

I opened the door to find a torso before me. Tall Ebeneezer Wickes ducked under the roof slats, his long arms trailing down like willow vines at his sides.

"How now, Hester," he said. "We've come to call on Pardon. I pray he's ready to receive callers."

My heart fluttered at the pronoun. "We?"

Ebeneezer stepped aside to reveal the figure in black behind him. The Widow Fiske. I did not mask my surprise very well.

I led them into the parlor and asked if they wanted tea. The widow touched my arm and locked her eyes on mine with an intensity that was uncomfortable.

"Hester, I am very sorry for your loss," she said. "It is a terrible thing to lose one's mother. How are you holding up?"

My tongue was thick, unable to respond. Amid all the chaos and the fog of grief, no one had asked me that simple question yet.

"I abide, madam." It was all I could think of to say before I hurried off to the kitchen.

I returned with the tray to find Pardon discussing local governance with Ebeneezer. My uncle was a cornerstone of the selectmen and the town business went on even while he grieved. Still, his consent was needed for the council to pass a motion.

"Close the churchyard?" my uncle repeated with disdain. "Whatever for?"

Ebeneezer took the teacup I offered and replied, "Because of all the damn exhumations. Half the village seems intent on digging up their dead. The place is a disgrace."

My uncle's face darkened. "They're performing the ritual?"

"Indeed. A sort of panic has set in." Ebeneezer's long-fingered hand went up in mock surrender. "And I appreciate the irony of it, since we were the ones who started the whole ghastly business. But it's gotten out of hand now."

The Widow held her teacup in her lap. "This is how it started in Bountiful. A sort of mania took hold. The graveyard became a quarry."

The widow's presence stymied me till now. Was she here to give testimony on the disruption of the graveyard? I lingered near the window on the pretense of being helpful. In truth, I was desperate for news from town. Any news, really.

Pardon swept a hand through his thinning hair. "So the solution is to lock down the cemetery?"

"For now," the tall selectman stated. "To let things cool off. We can hire on a few hands to stand guard at the gates. I know Peg-Leg is in need of duty now that the night watch has ended."

"It's a blunt remedy," my uncle said. "But can't it wait? My Katherine lies in the crypt and needs burial."

"With all due respect, Pardon, but will a few days matter? She'll rest as easy there as she will in the ground."

Pardon slumped back in his chair. "Do what you wilt, then. Why even ask me about it?"

"Because you're still on council. Your consent is needed."

My uncle looked old and very fatigued in that moment. "Is that all?"

"There is one last order of business," Ebeneezer replied. He folded his hands together to compose himself, as if reluctant to proceed. "The question of the prisoner, Ephraim Fiske. A motion has been tabled. By Mrs. Fiske herself."

Pardon frowned. "I'd forgotten all about the man. He's still alive?"

"His constitution is Olympian. The fever has made him senseless, but he endures. It is uncanny."

My uncle turned to the widow in the wingback chair. "And

what is this motion you've brought to us?"

The widow's face was stony. "That the man be executed. Immediately."

Pardon's brow shot up while Ebeneezer seemed to shrink a few inches. The widow continued in a matter-of-factly tone as if discussing the weather.

"The man is a criminal and wanton murderer. Justice has been delayed too long. Sunset tomorrow. That is enough time to construct a gibbet on the town green. I will even pay for the timber myself if that hastens the matter."

Pardon leaned forward in his chair. "Hanging is no small thing, madam. There needs to be a hearing. Charges need to be laid."

"For a confessed murderer?" the widow replied. "The man is a dangerous threat while he lives. Has he not wreaked enough damage upon you all?"

"There hasn't been a gallows in this town since the war. The punishment you seek is not what we do here."

The woman set her cup aside. "Will you give your consent?"

The muscle in my uncle's jaw stiffened. A sign he was losing patience with the widow. "I will think on it and return my answer in the morning."

The Widow Fiske stood and removed her kid gloves. For a moment I feared she would strike my uncle across the face with them, but she turned to me instead. "Hester, will you show me to a wash basin?"

I brought her through to the kitchen where a ceramic basin lay under the window, a pitcher of water next to it.

"The carbolic is there on the dish," I said. "I'll give you some privacy."

"No need." The gloves were tossed onto the table and she unpinned her hat. "Will you hold this for me?"

I held the hat and veil as she scooped water from the basin. I watched her with an uncertain fascination, those thin hands splashing water over her fine features and strong nose. I would have stared longer had not the children banged their way inside from the back porch with Jacob behind them. The three of them were so glum they barely acknowledged the guest in the kitchen. I made them sit and laid out the bread and butter on the table along with the last jar of preserves. I had seen Katherine placate her children the same way and the reminder of it seemed to give them some comfort, however small, as they tucked into it. Polly seemed especially dour, so I kissed the top of her hair and promised to read to her later. She returned a tiny smile.

The Widow remained at the basin during all this, observing the minor ruckus. When the three of them left the room, she watched me clear away the cutting board and the knife.

"They look to you for comfort now," she remarked.

"I don't know how much comfort I can give them," I said. "Providing a distraction is the best I can manage."

Her eyes followed me as I swept away the crumbs. "What a terrible thing, to lose a mother."

I agreed that it was. For a moment, I wasn't sure to whom she meant; Mother Stokely or my own lost mamma.

"You step into her shadow now," she said. "You comfort them in their grief as you feed them and dry their eyes. But who comforts you?"

I looked up at her but could find no reply. "What do you mean?"

She came around the table to where I stood. "Whose shoulder do you cry on, Hester?"

Her proximity was uncomfortable, her question unsettling. She was like a fishmonger cracking open an oyster. She wanted some pearl; a secret or a confession. I didn't know what to make of this woman. I still don't.

"I remember what it was like," she whispered. "To be the last one on their feet in a dying house."

Polly appeared in the doorway. "Sam's crying again," she said.

I excused myself and followed the girl into my uncle's study where Samuel sat looking out the window. He wasn't weeping, but his cheeks were damp, and his gaze was very far away. Of all Katherine's children, the eldest boy was the only one who seemed to have inherited his mother's habit of dark brooding. I could see he was lost to it now and there was little I could do. The brandy bottle sat on the shelf. I poured a small dram and put it in his hand, whispering him to keep it a secret. I put the bottle away and left him to it.

When I returned to the parlor, I found my uncle with a book in his lap.

"They've gone?" I asked.

"They have. But the widow invited us down to the inn to-morrow night."

"What for?"

"A small celebration, she said. She is going to give Henry his reward for capturing the fugitive." My uncle wet his index finger and turned the page in his book, adding, "She thought it might cheer us up."

28

WE SET OUT for the tavern at sunset to see Henry rewarded
for his bravery. Walking hand in hand, we may have been a tribe
diminished but we were family, nonetheless. For the first time in
weeks there was a spark of cheeriness that relieved, briefly, the
numbing mantle of grief.

Half the town jostled within the taproom, hoisting flagons
of beer and cups of cider under the greasy lamplight. The selectmen stood at the board while Arthur tapped another keg. Reverend Crane hunkered over his glass of port like a squirrel with a
nut and Peg-Leg Wilkins was already singing a ribald sea shanty.
Elizabeth Wickes was there, pressing a lilac-scented lace to her
nose against the barroom smells. Her sycophants, Mary Hazard
and Clare Finch, tittered and laughed at everything she said. The
vile Tom Hazard rattled his cup on the board, begging for another cup of punch. The man of the hour strode the floorboards
before the great hearth, regaling his friends with the telling of the
tale. Henry puffed out his chest as he narrated, spilling his tankard as he gestured. The roses in his cheeks suggested that he was
well into his cups at this early stage. On the mantel before him
glinted the gold coin nailed into the wood. Of the widow, I saw

no sign.

Pardon led the way to the counter where Martha Beecham furnished us all with cheer. I asked if I could have some wine but was told to be content with the ale.

Mrs. Beecham beamed at us. "Look at you all," she said. Her face was flush from being so busy, but her smile was a dimpled delight. "Nice to see the family out."

I chucked a thumb in Henry's direction. "You must be very proud of your son."

"He's quite taken with himself, I'll give you that. I've a mind to send him to his room if he doesn't settle down."

"It's his moment, Martha. Let him shine."

Her head shook in a discouraged fluster before she was harangued by another thirsty patron.

Peg-Leg Wilkins had acquired a fiddle and began to creak out a jaunty tune to accompany his salty songs. Boots stomped the floorboards as a jig was bounced by some of the men and I clapped my hands in time with their rhythm. For a brief but glorious span, I forgot all about the grief and tragedy and simply reveled in the hubbub of hands clasped against the darkness.

My eyes never strayed far from Henry as he danced, and my mind worked overtime to find some conceit by which I could break past his fellows to speak to him. The tankard in his hand was all but empty, most of it spilled onto the floor and I settled on a plan to bring him another. A sound tactic, I thought, but before I could execute it, a hush settled abruptly over the room.

The foot-stomping ceased. The fiddle died on a misplaced note. Every eye rose to the slender figure in black descending the stairs. The Widow Fiske must have had a number of mourning dresses on hand for this one was finely outfitted in lace and silk as if meant for a ball. Gone was the veil, revealing her regal beauty to the gathering in the tavern. The crowd parted as she made her way to the hearth where her bounty hung.

"Mister Henry Beecham," she said in a loud, clear voice. "I thank you for your bravery and gallantry in bringing down the murderer of Bountiful."

The grin on Henry's face was so comically broad that I thought his jaw would crack. He bowed to the crowd when everyone clapped and then turned to the lady before him. The widow took hold of the spike struck into the post and, without a hammer or claw, plucked it free. She caught the doubloon as it fell and placed it ceremoniously onto Henry's palm.

"Here is the gold posted," she said, "along with the balance of the bounty." At that she produced another coin, similar to the first but unmarred, and stacked it onto the first in his palm. Then she turned to address the innkeeper. "Mrs. Beecham, will you fill everyone's cup, please? And add it to my tally."

A hurrah erupted from the room and the merrymaking began anew. Men strode forward to congratulate Henry and my chance to speak to him was lost. I would have to wait for the hullabaloo to die down.

My uncle, however, had other plans. "Hester," he said to me, "it's getting late. Take Polly and Hiram home. The boys and I will be along soon."

"But we've only just got here. And the children are having a lively time."

This was true. Both Hiram and Polly were banging their feet on the boards in time with the fiddling. My uncle waved it away.

"It's time for them to be abed. Off you go, Hester."

I felt my hopes scatter like ash. My blood was up, but I kept my tone polite. "Pardon, I want to stay. Please. Let the children have fun a little longer."

My uncle's face dimpled with an impatient frown. "Don't argue with me, Hester. Take them home."

I am not sure what came over me. A rebuke spat from my tongue before my brain could choke it. "Let Sam or Jacob see to them. Or better yet, you. I am staying."

The boys stepped in. Samuel took his father's side, arguing that the little ones would only listen to me. He was respectful, I'll give him that. Jacob played peacemaker, telling his father that the younger ones could stay up a little longer. My uncle would have none of it, his face reddening at my insolence. He told me to mind my place and do as I was told.

And there, amid the singing and the merrymaking, came the undeclared, but understood, condition of my existence. I was welcome under this man's roof so long as I did as I was told. I was no more than a servant. More so now than ever, with Mother Stokely gone. The honorable Pardon Stokely would have no need to seek a new wife as was often the way for a widower with a brood. He had me; a disfigured ogre that he could not marry off.

The span of my lifetime was glimpsed in that moment; a life of toil and servitude. It tasted bitter, and I walked away, leaving them all to argue.

My heart lay snared on the far side of that busy room, bewitched in the frame of the young man brandishing two gold coins. I pushed my way through the sharp elbows and rancorous breath of the revelers. I needed to speak to Henry now before his fellows vaulted him on their shoulders and danced him out to the green. I caught only glimpses of him through the jabbering chops and jigging fools until the path opened before me. I was too late. Elizabeth Wickes and her two hens were huddled around Henry, giggling and fawning over the young hero. And judging by the sly grin on his face, Henry was lapping it up, pleased as punch with harnessing the attention of the three prettiest girls in town. Ebeneezer's daughter was considered a high catch among the young men of Wickstead. She had beauty, poise, and wealth. She even played prettily at the piano and spoke French.

I froze at the thought of breaking into their conversation with my plain clothes and cheek of melted flesh. I could already picture the disdain in the women's eyes. It withered me.

"Howdy ho!" bellowed a voice. A shudder rippled up my back at the sound of it. Tom Hazard. Hazard Tom. His eyes red, his tongue garbling his words.

"Who let you out of the barn tonight?" he barked over the tavern din. "Someone fetch me a halter and we'll lead this cow back to her pen."

If there was ever a person I loathed to see, it was Tom with his brown teeth and small pig eyes. "Go away, Tom. You're drunk." That only egged him on, like a challenge.

"Listen to the gargoyle speak!" he cried out, spilling his punch. "Do you not see the wee children about, Hester? You're going to frighten them off with that mask of yours!"

I am not a violent person. It is the last resort of the peaceable, the first resort of the brute. Henry and Elizabeth were already pivoting in my direction to see what all the clamor was about. I shoved Hazard Tom away, and not gently either. I was about to make my retreat when the cad bounced back. His boot shot one way, his elbow the other, and I went down with a wallop, face to the floorboards. Tom screeched with laughter and danced a jig around me. He emptied his punch over my head.

I'm sure every soul in the taproom must have been gawking at me but all I saw were the baleful eyes of Henry and the pale blue of Elizabeth's. Scurrying away like a mouse behind the wainscoting, I barreled through the crowd for the door, my face the hot shade of ripe apple. In my mind, I heard Henry laughing along with the others, but I was to learn later that this was not the case. According to those who saw it, Henry pounced on the Hazard boy and knocked him to the floor.

I ran across the town green with hot tears on my face and a hornet's nest in my brain. The humiliation before the object of my affections propelled me forward through the common as if I could outrace my troubles, but, of course, this was impossible. You cannot outrun your own shadow. Rather, it started a cascade of laments to spill out, one tumbling over the next in a rush to be let out. The tears over Henry collided into the grief over my sister-cousins and my aunt, my second mother.

A small bower lay on the far side of the green, next to the river. By the time I collapsed under its cone-shaped roof, I was weeping with an almost wild abandon. I don't know how long I huddled there, shedding tears onto the worn wooden boards, but when the fit passed, I lay spent and brittle.

I heard my name being called out over the green. It was Samuel's voice, searching for me. I held my tongue and waited for him to give up. Let them go home without me, I thought. I will stay out here the rest of the night. Or perhaps I'll fling myself into the river and simply be done with it all. That is how dark my thoughts had turned.

Sam's voice ceased calling me, and I lay flat on the wooden platform for a long time. The dull noise coming from the tavern ebbed away as the crowd went home and soon the only sound was that of the creek babbling nearby. I considered my fate. A sad and lonely spinster in service to my uncle. I tried to scold myself from such self-pitying indulgence. I should be grateful to have a family at all, to say nothing of shelter or the clothes on my back. I could have been eaten by flames the way my parents were or dead from consumption like Pru and Faith. Would they have dug me up if I had? Would they carve the heart out of my breast to burn it in a furnace?

My brains had become unhinged, my thoughts blown like dandelion seed. I told myself to get up, to brush myself off, and go home.

A sound in the night brought my head up. Something scuffing against the ground and getting louder. Closer.

"Who's there?"

I had meant to sound bold, but my voice cracked, no fiercer than a lamb's bleating. An invitation to the wolf.

A quarter moon hung overhead, along with a dusting of stars. The expanse of the green was a dull silver against the black night, and I saw a figure striding towards me. I called out again, demanding the stranger declare themselves.

"Hester?"

My heart clapped hard against my throat. A silly expression, but an apt one since I could not breathe. Was it really him?

"Henry?"

He shambled closer and placed a boot on the step. As weak as the moonlight was, I saw his face lit silver against the shadows. My heart clanged against my ribcage. My face was hot, and I was grateful for the dark now. He would not see my red eyes and puffy cheeks. Or the scar, for that matter.

"Why are you here?" I asked. "Did you come looking for me?"

He eased himself down on the wooden platform. "I thought you'd gone home."

I scolded myself anew for being such a ninny. "Of course."

"I reprimanded that jackass, Tom. Why does he hate you so?"

I shrugged even though he could not see that. "I wish I knew."

Henry leaned back against the railing. His words were slurry and I could smell the punch on him, but I didn't care. He was less than a foot away. I could reach out and hold his hand. In the dark, no less. I felt another hard lump in my throat. My fingers itched.

"Did you abandon your party?"

"They all went home," he said. "I wanted some air."

My palm lay flat on the wood. My fingers spider-walked a few inches closer. "Did you lose your way in the dark?"

"I like it here," he said. "No one ever comes out here to the bower. I like to sit and watch people across the green. The perspective amuses me."

I regarded the town on the other side of the common. A few stragglers were still tumbling out of the tavern. "What's so amusing about it?"

"Look at them, the way they scurry here and bustle there, all so busy and self-important. They seem like ants crawling over a hill. It's so absurd."

I did not expect this ruminative turn of mind. "Life is absurd?"

The silver cut of his face swung my way. "Doesn't it seem that way to you?"

"I'm not sure that's how I'd put it. It is arbitrary. And cruel."

My hand nudged closer until my finger brushed his wrist. It sent a spark up my flesh. I felt abruptly out of breath and light-headed.

"Cruel?" he remarked in a rum-clumsy tongue. He had certainly celebrated his victory this night. "You're too grim-minded, Hester. Tell me, sweetness, what makes it so cruel for you?"

Sweetness. The word was like honey on the tongue of a starving prisoner. I shuddered and slid my hand over his. The knuckles were bony, the hand strong. I felt bold.

"The cruelty," I said, "is wanting what we cannot hope to have."

I am not illiterate when it comes to men. Nor am I a fool. I know their wants and I knew the hazards that lay before me. Last autumn, Katherine had sat me down to discuss the topic when she caught me mooning over Henry at the meetinghouse. She was blunt in her assessment of the other sex. Give an inch, she had said, and they will take more than a mile. Prudence had told me other things. She and her beau James had stolen more than just innocent kisses behind the barn. Pru spared no detail, no romantic flourish went unmentioned. Faith had listened in on the conversation. Disgusted, she advised neither of us to ever marry, let alone be manhandled like a piece of horseflesh.

I knew all this. Forewarned, I was thus forearmed to turn away from his advance when he lifted my chin to kiss me. But I did none of that. I leaned in to mash my lips against his and inhale his scent and press myself into him. I couldn't breathe and I didn't care. I clutched at his lapel to pull him into me and we went down on the creaky boards of the bower in a knot of smacking lips and tugged lace.

This was seduction, but I did not care. Moreover, I would be hard-pressed to pinpoint exactly who was executing the seduction in that moment. All I knew was that my future lay bare as a spinster and I wanted this one instance of joy and love and, yes, lust. I needed it. This night would have to sustain me in all the nights to come as an unwed gargoyle under my uncle's roof. So I tore into him. I wanted to eat him alive.

We lay flushed and breathless on the bower floor, knotted together like wedding lace. I wished the moon had been brighter, to see his eyes. As it was, they were only shaded pits beneath his gentle brow. It is difficult to paint the colors of my heart in that moment. A shade of euphoria tinted with a hint of astonishment. A small blotch of shame and worry pushed to the edge of the canvas. But the overall hue was bliss. Sweet, sweet bliss and I will never forget it as long as I breathe.

A noise came from the darkness, sharp and distinct as a branch snapping. I sat up, reaching for my frock.

"Did you hear that?"

Henry yawned. "Hear what?"

"Is someone looking for you?"

He held his breath, listening for a sound but none came. "It's nothing. A fox, maybe."

The night began to cool our skin. We untangled our limbs, pulled our clothes back into order and he walked me to my gate. Our parting kiss was interrupted by Lucky, bounding toward us and colliding into our knees. I watched Henry's figure recede into the darkness before harrying indoors with the dog swiping my heels. I took Lucky upstairs and brought him to bed with me. I needed his rough hide against my fingers and the reassuring thump of his tail just to keep myself from exploding with bliss. I could still taste his kiss and wondered if I had consumed the wine punch from his lips. Overwhelmed and possibly drunk, I closed my eyes.

29

SLEEP DID NOT come. The flurry of thoughts spinning in my head left me dizzy. Had I dreamed it all, laying with the man I adored, or had it actually happened? The pain told its truth. My lips were swollen from the kisses and my neck was sore from where his teeth had bitten me. I am a woman now. But am I wanton? A sinner? My thought was this; How can it be a sin if I love him so? It was not the rutting of lust or licentiousness. It was the culmination of years of worship. How could true love be a sin?

The part that staggered me was that Henry loved me back. I hadn't been foolish or naive in being smitten with him all this time. Behold, my affections were returned! The only foolish thing about it was the agonizing delay in acknowledging it. Why had we waited so long? Perhaps Henry did not know his own heart. Who of us does? Read Jeremiah, chapter seventeen. *The heart is deceitful above all things and desperately wicked. Who can know it?* I know that Henry has pursued Miss Wickes but his heart must have been split all this time and now the chips have fallen and they favored me over her. Let her heart be broken now, for I have had my fill of it.

The dog stirred, his head lifting and his ears twitching at something outside. I should have known better than to bring him to bed. Now he would rouse the entire house with his barking. Tiptoeing downstairs, I let him out the back door to chase down the fox or deer that he had heard and scurried back to bed.

I had just closed my eyes when I heard a scratching sound like nails on glass. My first thought was that it was Lucky scratching at the windowpane but that was impossible since the bedroom was on the second floor. I dismissed it but the sound returned the moment I closed my eyes. A skitter-scratch against the wobbly glass, a scraping at the wooden sash. An opossum or maybe a raccoon. I pushed aside the curtain to scare it away, but I was taken aback by the drape of fog outside the window. My brows knit. I had seen no mist when I let the dog out but here it lay, thick and opaque against the glass. The scratching resumed.

A shadow loomed from the top of the glass, draping down to blotch the entire window frame. A sallow hand slithered from the pitch and scratched at the glass with fingernails chipped and blackened. It was upside down as if the figure was suspended from above.

I blinked. This is a dream, I thought. Sleep came when you weren't looking and now you are caught up in a night terror.

The nails clawed at the glass to get inside. A face emerged, bleeding from the darkness. Pallid and inverted, the ghastly image drew hard against the windowpane. And when the dark lips parted, Mother Stokely told me to unlatch the window.

The scream in my lungs would not come out. Ice sluiced through my veins. A rush of warmth ran down my leg.

Open the latch, she whispered.

"No."

I am cold. Open it.

My fingers fell on the latch piece. I do not know how they got there. I did not want to open the window, but my hand disobeyed me.

"Go away," I stammered. My molars gritted hard. My fingers withdrew from the latch.

The inverted face hardened. *This is my house*, she said. *Let me in.*

"You are dead."

Mother Stokely's lips curled back over strangely sharp teeth, like that of a serpent. *You have always been a burden. We were happy until you brought misery to our door. And now you have stained it with sin.*

The scream that was corkscrewing inside my lungs finally erupted. "You are dead! Dead!"

The specter withdrew, leaving only the fog pressed against the pane. A sudden dizziness brought me to my knees. The last thing I recall is the sound of the dog barking outside.

~

The floor was cold against my cheek. The window above me framed the bluish gray of pre-dawn. Sitting up, I tried to pull my brains from the haze when the horror of the previous night came up sharp and curt. A nightmare was the only conclusion. I must have fallen out of bed after suffering the convulsions of a bad dream.

The ghastly vision of Mother Stokely outside the window, hanging upside down like a loathsome lizard, rattled my nerves and would not leave no matter how hard I tried to flush it from my mind. It only receded when I forced my thoughts to Henry and our sweet liaison on the bower. That too now seemed like a dream in the harsh rays of sunup and for a moment, I wondered if the entire night had been a phantasm brought on by too much punch at the tavern.

No, the union had been real, the kisses true and pure. Had he whispered his love into my ear or was that my panting confession into his? I could not recall the specifics. How cruel that such a tender moment should be followed by a horrific vision of my dead aunt in the window. My thought was this: the former was the cause of the latter. The guilt at having lain with a man had conjured up this ghostly specter to reprimand me. How feckless our minds are.

The day was on me and the fire needed starting in the kitchen. Padding out to the stairs, I heard a whimper from the children's room. Both Polly and Hiram were prone to night terrors, and it was not unusual to find them crying under their quilts. Polly was huddled in a corner with her arms clasped around her shins and her face buried in her knees.

"Polly, what is it?" I said, flattening my palm over her hair.

The poor thing flinched. Her whole frame was trembling.

"Polly, what's wrong? Speak to me."

All she did was point at the bed near the window. And the

small frame that lay there with an ashen face.

"Hiram!"

He was sprawled half off the bed with his head slung over the side. His breathing was labored and there was blood on his chin and hands. I barked at Polly to get her father as I swung the boy's head to the pillow and pressed my ear to his chest. His lungs rattled with a wet sucking sound so shallow that I feared he was dying. His skin was cold and far too white. The telltale signs of the consumptive.

I rubbed him down to bring his color back and cradled him across my knee to thump on his back to clear his lungs. Pardon and the two boys rushed in and chaos held as we worked to rouse the boy. His small frame jerked with a spasm and he coughed up a bloodied mass of phlegm onto the bed sheet. His breathing steadied, and we fussed to make him comfortable before each of us snapped questions as to what had happened to him. How had he succumbed overnight to the wasting plague? Our queries turned to Polly. How long had he been like this? Had something brought the coughing on?

The poor girl's face was riven with terror. "It was mother," she said.

My mouth went dry. Pardon scolded her to make sense, but Samuel was gentler, asking his sister to explain.

"Mother came back," she gibbered. "She was holding Hiram and rocking him in her arms like he was a baby."

"Polly, please!" my uncle spat. He stomped the boards, pulling at his hair. For a moment, I thought he might strike the girl. "Speak some sense, child."

Samuel drew his sister close. "Mother's passed, sweetheart. Remember? Did you dream about her?"

The girl was resolute, shaking her head at the suggestion. "It was her! She came through the window and gathered him up and kissed him. Too hard. He was bleeding. I told her to stop, but she wouldn't."

Pardon turned to the window in disgust. The pane was unlatched, letting in the morning breeze.

My knees went slack at her words. "Polly, what did mother say?"

Her small fists clutched her brother's shirt. "She said I was to be patient. That she had kisses for me too."

"That's enough!" Pardon spun on his heel, bellowing orders. "Samuel, take her downstairs and get some food into her. Hester, see to Hiram. Make him better."

With that, Pardon marched from the room. Sam carried his little sister down to the kitchen. I asked Jacob for a wet cloth and he went to the basin to wring a compress. He watched me drape it over his brother's brow.

"Is it consumption?"

The crack in Jacob's voice broke my heart, but I kept my steel. "I don't know." It was a lie, but what else was there to say?

He asked me to pray with him. Kneeling on opposite sides of the bed, we clasped hands over the wheezing child and recited the Pater Noster through our tears.

~

Hiram's condition improved as the morning unfolded. His breathing eased and some of his color returned as the sun filled the window. As I rinsed the blood from his scratched flesh, a sickening thought possessed me: last night's vision had been no bad dream. Mother Stokely had risen from the grave and returned to her family. She had embraced her young son, her favored one, and stolen a portion of his life. His blood. And this was connected to the awful business in the graveyard that we had been forced to participate in. It was true.

Samuel and Jacob were in the kitchen, huddled around their little sister, trying to get the poor thing to eat. I found my uncle outside, leaning against the paddock fence, feeding unripe apples to his favorite horse. I racked my feeble brains for some way to say the unspeakable, but nothing came. I joined him at the railing and watched my uncle stroke Caesar's nose. The poor man. Losing two children and a wife in such a short span. What I had to say might break him.

The horse blew and shied from my presence. Pardon held another spring apple out to the horse to coax him back. He did not look at me when he spoke.

"How is Hiram?"

"Resting."

"Is he consumptive?"

I dithered. Given the revelation last night, it was clear that the illness was not solely consumption, but something much worse. "I am not sure."

No reaction passed over my uncle's face. He ran a brush down the flickering muscles of the horse. "Look at these burs," he said, tugging at the nasty tangles in the mane. "His grooming has been neglected. I'll have to speak to Samuel about that."

"He won't let Sam groom him," I said. "Caesar prefers you to do it."

Pardon nuzzled his face against the horse's cheek. "Stubborn animal."

I brushed a fly away and then I took a deep breath and let it spill. "Polly was speaking the truth about what she saw."

"The child had a nightmare," he responded dismissively.

There was no going back now. "I saw her, too. She scratched at my window, wanting inside."

The brush stopped. "Stop. That is my wife you are talking about. The woman who cared for you like a mother."

I kept my tone as dispassionate as I could manage, "I saw her. Katherine came back last night. When I refused to let her in, she must have scratched at the children's window and—"

I did not see the blow coming, nor had I expected it. I simply felt its sting across my scarred cheek and the force that knocked me down.

"Shut your mouth! I will not hear this. Not about her. How dare you, Hester!"

I sat there in the grass, more flummoxed than hurt. My uncle rarely raised his hand against me, or his children. The tears welling up were more from embarrassment than anything, but I could not say which of us I was more ashamed for.

"I know what I saw. My aunt is not dead. Not truly dead—"

He flattened his palms against his ears. "Be quiet!"

"She attacked Hiram. And she will be back come nightfall. What are we going to do?"

The horse whinnied and shied again. Pardon nickered at him to come but Caesar would not. His eyes were red. "See what you've done," he said, blaming me for his pet's skittishness.

I got up off the ground. "That business in the graveyard, I thought that was just more strange superstition, but it's not, is it? It ended Pru's suffering. The same must be done for Katherine now."

"Hasn't the woman suffered enough? You expect me to

carve her up and burn her heart? I will never inflict that horror on her!"

"Then what are we to do?" My voice was shrill, and it spooked the horse again.

My uncle snatched my arm and dragged me back to the house. "Damn your insolence, Hester! Will you never know your place? Get back inside!" He threw me to the veranda steps. "No more talk of this. None! Mind your duties to this family or get out."

We were not alone. Polly and her brothers came running to the veranda to see what the ruckus was about. They stood slack-jawed before us. Jacob said something to his father but was told to be quiet. Pardon stormed past them on his way inside.

Samuel glared at me. "What did you say to him?"

"Leave it alone, Sam," Jacob said. He reached out for my hand. "Hester, come inside."

I could not bear to look at any of them. Even Polly. So I ran.

30

TRUTH, LIKE SECRETS, will sting when flushed into the daylight, but the result is a clarification. One knows where they stand. I was tolerated so long as I was useful. I was loved, after a fashion, for my servitude to the family. Take that away and all that remained were empty gestures and propriety. False love, false family.

I ran from the homestead with no destination in mind, just the need to get away. My feet led me into town. Pushing me along was the urge to see Henry. I could endure the awful truth of my adopted family if I could see his face again. It was like I was starving and only his presence would nourish me.

I stopped at a watering trough to cool my face and compose myself. My first stop was the tavern, but his mother said Henry was not there. I went to the merchant's, the barber shop and the stable but my quarry was not at any of those haunts. I remembered something Will once mentioned, about an illicit games room in the back of Wicke's print shop where the men played at Faro. I went there, skirting around to the dusty yard behind Ebeneezer's shop. A rumble of voices spilled from an open door. Stepping through, I found a dimly lit room where young men sat at green baize tables, turning cards as they played the "game of the Pharaohs." Joseph Hendershot sat playing at one of the tables and hovering at his shoulder was Henry.

I touched his arm. "Henry?"

His face blanched and his eyes darted around to the other patrons of the Faro house. Women were not welcome at this gambling den. "Hester, what are you doing here?"

It was not my intention to put him on the spot. I tugged him toward the exit. "I need to speak to you."

The man doling out the fanciful cards glared at me for my intrusion. The two men wagering against the dealer did not look up, oblivious to anything outside the throw of the cards.

"I'm busy," Henry said.

"Please. It's important."

He withdrew to save face. Someone at another table made a crude remark about consulting with lepers. I ignored the comment. This was not my element, and I was ignorant of its etiquette.

Henry led me out to the dusty laneway. His tone was impatient. "What is it?"

"I wanted to see you."

His eyes darted around the lane as if looking for something. "Whatever for?"

"Are you upset with me?"

"Hester, please!" He seemed desperate to get away. "Let me go back to my game."

It seemed there were more harsh truths for me to learn. This one no less brutal than the last. "Are you ashamed to be seen with me? After last night?"

His face altered then. The impatience dropped away, and in its place came a cool wariness. "What are you on about?"

Was he still drunk? Or fevered from all the gambling? "Henry, last night. Under the bower on the green, we kissed. We were lovers—"

He took a step back. "No such thing happened. I found you weeping on the bower. You were tippled from the punch and I brought you home."

Something clanged loudly inside my chest. The iron bars of a prison locking up my heart.

"How can you say that? There's no need to be ashamed of

it, Henry. Not to me. I love you."

"You must have dreamed it, Hester. Mother's punch is known to bring on delusions." He walked away from me, hurrying from the laneway to the main street. "I shouldn't go around repeating that story if I were you," he called back to me. "People will think you wanton."

The iron lock turned, and my heart was trapped. I couldn't move, frozen in salt like Lot's wife. Stupidly, I ran after him. I should have ran in a different direction. If I had, I would not have seen Henry walking along the thoroughfare with young Elizabeth Wickes on his arm.

Everything looked abruptly strange to me. What was once familiar, the shop fronts and faces of passing citizens, now seemed foreign and ugly. I was crushed, and yet the sun continued to shine, and people went about their stupid business as if nothing had changed. Did they not know that the world had just ended? I had been spurned and rejected. A pathetic puppet in a very old stage play.

I staggered away with a hundred questions buzzing at me like angry bees. Why had Henry spurned me? Because he does not love you. Because he is ashamed of our tryst. Then why had he seduced me in the first place?

Because he could. Because he knew how compliant I would be to his overture.

I must have looked like some madwoman careening through town. Was I talking to myself? Perhaps. I found myself on the common when I heard the sound of hammers knocking away. The racket lifted my eyes to the sight of two carpenters building a scaffold out of raw pine boards. I recognized one of the builders, Franklin Brown, a carpenter. He touched his cap as I approached.

"How now, Hester," he said, his face glowing from his exertion. "What brings you into town?"

"Foolishness."

"Beg your pardon?"

"Nothing." I squinted up at the framework of uprights and crossbeam. "What are you building there, Franklin?"

The cheer in his eyes fell away. "Gallows."

The prisoner in the stockhouse. I had forgotten all about him. "But they can't. My uncle has not sanctioned their motion."

"They passed it without his consent," the carpenter replied. "He's to swing at sundown tonight."

"Tonight? But you mustn't. It's not right."

Franklin took up his hammer again. "I'm only building the gibbet. I have no say in its application."

Retreating from that ghastly execution machine, I wondered if my uncle knew of this. It seemed unlikely. He hadn't attended a meeting of the selectmen since Faith passed away. I considered running home to tell him, but I was still angry and did not want to see his face.

I marched back across the common to the old stockhouse near the creek. I needed to speak to Ephraim Fiske, although I wasn't sure how I would persuade the guard to let me see him. I had no pockets nor purse, let alone any coins to bribe the guard with. I am not adept at guile so tricking the man was out of the question. With any luck, Peg-Leg Wilkins would be on duty and probably slumped asleep at his post. Barring that, I would beg if I had to.

Fortune, for once, was with me this day. Will Treves stood guarding the makeshift prison, a musket tucked into the crook of his arm.

"Have you hired on as permanent watchman, Will?"

His face lit up when he saw me. I imagine guard duty was lonely, and he seemed grateful for company. "Just my turn in the rotation. But at least there's a day's wages in it."

"How's Mr. Fiske?"

"A bit improved actually. He's mending up, just in time to be hung." His eyes studied me. "Are you all right, Hester? You look a little piqued."

"Just a bad night," I said. I sidled closer to him and lowered my voice. "Will, I need to speak to Mr. Fiske. Will you let me in?"

"I can't. And you shouldn't ask, either."

"I know, but it is urgent. Especially now." I have never liked the way some women will bat their lashes and make their voices sing-songy to get their way. Prudence was a master at playing the coquette, as was Elizabeth Wilkes. I considered aping that act now, but I could not bring myself to flutter my eyes. It seemed ridiculous to try, so I stuck with simple manners. Please, I said.

He surveyed the road east and west and then slid back the wooden block on the door. "Keep it quiet. If anyone finds out I let you in, they'll swing me alongside him."

I slipped inside and the gate banged closed behind me. The interior of the stockhouse was gloomy and without windows. The only light came from the broken masonry between the upright poles of the palisade walls. When my eyes adjusted, I spotted the prisoner sitting on the cot with his head resting on his knees.

"Mister Fiske," I said. "Are you in pain?"

He sat up, squinting curiously until he recognized me. "You. Why are you here?"

"I needed to speak to you."

"I have nothing to say." He put his head down again.

A small stool was near the gate. I carried it toward the cot and sat down facing him. "I need to know what happened to you in Bountiful. The truth, this time."

He stared at the floor as if deaf. Was he beyond help?

I smoothed my skirt over my knees. "My aunt Katherine died three days ago. Last night she returned, scratching at my window."

The change was instant. His back straightened and his eyes bore into mine. "Did you let her in?"

"No. She made her way to another entry and attacked her own son. Now he is gravely ill."

At this, he made the sign of the cross, which I thought unusual. Ephraim Fiske did not strike me as a follower of the Roman church.

"Make me understand this, Mr. Fiske," I pleaded. "How could she slip from her coffin and return to us? How could she injure her own flesh and blood like that? The boy is only eight years old."

His shoulder slumped as if weighed under by some force. "She wanted to go home. They all do."

"I prepared her for burial myself. And yet I saw Katherine outside my window."

"Show me your hands," he said.

"What?"

"Your palms. Let me see them."

I did not want to go any closer, but he grew agitated at my reluctance. He gripped both wrists and turned my palms up to study them. What he sought there, I did not know. Was he a gypsy reading my fortune?

"What are you looking for?"

"The mark of the devil." He released me, satisfied at his divination. "It is not there."

"Why would I bear the mark of the devil in my palm?"

The man scrutinized his own palms for a moment and then folded his hands together. "There is an evil at play here, Hester Stokely. A spirit that preys on the unwary the way a viper will lull its victim before devouring it."

"Mister Fiske," I said, "please speak plainly to me."

He seemed to laugh. "This evil animates the dead. It drives them from their graves to seek out the blood of the living. The place they turn to is home. Where else would they go? They feed and their victim wastes away, much like the way consumption will eat the living. And one by one, a family will go under, each following the next into the grave."

I struggled to parse his meaning. "Like Prudence," I said. "And Faith and now Mother Stokely. That was the purpose behind digging up their graves and burning Prudence's heart?"

"That is how it happened in Bountiful," he replied. "Slowly at first, with one family taken ill with consumption. Then another and another until the panic set in. People stormed the churchyard gates to dig up their dead and burn their hearts, to destroy this evil spirit. But they failed to stop it."

I thought back to the rifled graves I had seen in Bountiful, the coffins left strewn about like rubbish. A thought occurred to me. "Is that why you killed your own brother? Because he had this evil in him?"

"No. His death was not my doing. But he was the one who brought the misery down on us." He shook slightly with a strange laugh. "And to think we welcomed it at the time."

I became exasperated with his oblique speeches. "Ephraim, no more riddles. Tell me what happened."

"I am sorry," he sighed. "I am sorry for a great many things. One of them being responsible for the misery on your house."

That was unexpected. "Are you saying you caused this horror?"

"No. But I led it straight to your door, Hester. You took me in, and I repaid your kindness with tragedy. It followed me, you see, from Bountiful. Hunting me down. And I led it to your doorstep. That is why yours was the first family afflicted."

"What followed you?"

"The evil spirit," he said. "The woman who put a bounty on my head."

There was a humming in my ear. My fists tight, molars clenched. "The Widow?"

"The Lady Szabina Constantin Fiske, wife to my brother. She is not what she appears to be."

Was he mad, as had been claimed by the woman he spoke of? Or was there truth, no matter how outrageous, to his claim?

"Then," I said, "what is she?"

"I don't know. She appears human, but that is a ruse. Perhaps she was, at one time." He rubbed his temples as if trying to concentrate. "The troubles started after her arrival. My brother, Nathaniel, was proud of his new bride, this 'princess' he claimed to have rescued from a remote corner of Europe. I was happy for him, but I never held much affection for my new sister. She was strange and aloof. Given to dark moods and brooding. And bizarre calamities seem to follow her. Her maid hung herself in a barn. A fire consumed the home of some new friend she had made. And then the consumption came. Slowly at first, one family and then another. After a while, almost every household was laid low with one stricken member or another and nothing could be done to stop it. Then the whispering came; that the dead were not truly dead and were somehow causing their kin to fall ill. That they were feeding on their blood. This was followed by the ritual you observed in your own family. Digging up the grave and burning the heart. The graveyard was overrun by people exhuming their dead. It got so bad that the selectmen of Bountiful closed the churchyard to quell the panic. But the people would have none of it. They cudgeled the guards and pushed down the gates.

"The townsfolk believed that the Devil himself had come to roost in our village and they were not wrong. The population, which was small to begin with, was devastated by then, the village in ruins. Those that could manage packed up and left. The rest wasted away. Some took to sleeping in the church, convinced that the Devil would slip through the window to carry them off in their sleep.

"My brother was stricken with a kind of malady at this time. Not the consumption, but a sort of brain fever that left Nathaniel listless and confused. It was a sad transformation of character.

Nathaniel had always been bright and joyful, mad for adventures to far-flung places. But now he was like a changeling, a different person altogether. When he returned from Europe, he was happy and very much in love with his new bride, but now he grew obsessive over her. And highly jealous. He fretted that she had taken a lover and would leave him. He swore he saw her smirk and bat her eyes at every man around. Even some of the women. He would not listen to reason and I feared for his safety as much as his poor health. After a while he became a recluse, refusing visitors and never leaving the house. He tried to lock Szabina up in the house, but she laughed at him and did as she pleased.

"I went round to knock at his door. My sister-in-law said that her husband was ill and was not to be disturbed. When I became insistent, she bolted the door against me.

"Alarmed, I withdrew to a distance and waited for the lady of the house to leave. She kept strange hours. She left at dusk, and I went around the back and found an unlocked window. Nathaniel I found in an upstairs bedroom, curled up in a corner in a distressed state. I barely recognized him he was so pale and wild-eyed. When I asked him what he was doing there, he said his wife ordered him to stay up here until she returned, and he dared not disobey her. Then he began to cry, saying he was sick and wanted to die. His mind was simply gone, but his tears were what distressed me the most, for they were not normal. He was weeping tears of blood.

"I dragged him out of there, intent on getting him out of that prison, but he would not go. Szabina would never allow it, he said. It vexed me to no end seeing him in mortal terror of his own wife, but nothing would shake him out of it. When I demanded to know what spell she had over him, he could not explain. But, he said he could show me. So he led me down into the cellar.

"I will never forget the stench wafting up from those stairs; it was worse than a charnel house. Nathaniel led me down into that dank cellar and raised the lantern high to illuminate the floor. There reflected a small pool of blood and within that mess was a small slipper, like one belonging to a child. I turned away, feeling sick.

"There's more, my brother whispered to me. Look, he said. The light cast upon a large object before us. It was made of stone and several feet long and I blinked at it until I realized it was a stone sarcophagus. Very old and fashioned with the figure of a reposing woman carved onto the lid, like the tombs of saints and kings. The lid was heavy, and it took both of us to slide it open. There was no occupant inside, but the bottom of the sandstone coffin was filled with red blood, two fingers of it, like some ghastly bath.

"My brother was giggling now, his eyes fiendish. This, he said, is where she sleeps. See there, the face on the relief. He moved the lantern over the figure chiseled on the lid. The carved face was a fair rendering of his beloved Szabina.

"I ran from the cellar, dragging my poor brother with me. It was like a nightmare from which I could not awaken. When we reached the parlor, I took the lantern from him and hurled it against the bookcase. The oil ignited fast, blazing up the wall. I found another lantern and broke its contents across the furniture and the drapes and flung a cinder at it. The whole house rippled up with flames and poor Nathaniel just giggled like some ape, entranced by the fire. I pulled him away to escape the blaze but when I flung open the front door, Szabina was there. And the fury on her face was unlike anything I had ever seen. Her rage made her taller, a giant. She flung me across the room, shrieking at me in a foreign tongue. Her power was incredible, her rage like that of a wild animal as she struck me down with blow after blow. Nathaniel was forgotten in the melee, standing there chittering away. The house gave out a thunderous crack and the roof, blazing, collapsed onto him. His wife rushed to save him, but the fire was too much. The inferno raged around us and more walls tumbled in and I fled. A powerful gale had struck, the wind changing direction and when I glanced back, the fire had already spread to the houses on both sides.

"The fire moved quickly through the village, buffeted by the strong winds. People were running skelter in the street. I ran home and bolted the door. My fervent prayer was that the creature that was my brother's wife had been consumed in the flames, but I scrambled for my pistol and poured the gunpowder and packed the ball down with trembling hands. The door burst open, and she was there. I shot her in the chest, ejecting her back out into the night. She simply got up again, the wound smoking on her chest. I grabbed a knife and my Bible and ran out back to get my horse. I loaded the pistol again before saddling the horse and when Szabina struck, I shot her again and rode off. I tore through the countryside with that fiend pursuing me all the while and she did not relent until the dawn broke. I pressed on for three days, never stopping until I stumbled into your fair town. The rest, you know."

Drained from the narrative, Ephraim Fiske lowered his head again. It was only then that I noticed the pain in my hand. My fingernails had left red welts in my palm. I stared at it for a long time, unable to get my head right after this strange tale. Ephraim had begun to sob.

The gate scraped open, startling me. Will poked his head inside.

"Hester, come away. Someone is coming!"

I do not remember if I said goodbye to Mr. Fiske. I hope that I had.

31

THE LAST NAIL was hammered into the gallows structure by late afternoon, the swing trap set and tested. When the sun began to dip toward the western tree line, the citizens of Wickstead gathered on the green to witness the first public execution in more than a decade.

I had managed to slip out of the prison unseen thanks to Will's warning, and I ran home with Ephraim Fiske's horrific tale ringing through my brain. The thought of the dead rising from their graves seemed the highest flight of fantasy, but had I not witnessed it with my own eyes? And if that were true, what then to make of the Widow Fiske? What was she?

My earlier trials were forgotten. The argument with Pardon and the heartbreak of Henry's shunning, what did these matter now? I rushed into the house and found Pardon in his study. With panting breath I told him that the selectmen had acted without his consent and condemned Ephraim to hang this day. He didn't believe me at first, but when I reported that the gallows were being constructed, he took his hat from the peg in the hall and marched for town, declaring he would get to the bottom of this. I checked on Hiram and found him resting. Polly was with her brothers in the barn, helping them with their chores. We went about our usual duties and no one mentioned the earlier clash with their father.

My uncle returned a few hours later, looking ashen-faced. His demand to halt the execution was rebuffed. He learned that he had been removed from the council of selectmen. Temporarily, they had said, to relieve him during his time of grief. Horse shit, Pardon had spat. He said he was removed for not going along with the others, for giving into a blatant need to punish someone for their collective ills. It was the first, and only, time that I had ever heard my uncle utter sailor's language.

The day crept on. I kept looking up at the sky to determine the arc of the sun. Samuel asked if we would go to witness the hanging. My uncle said he had no interest in seeing the barbaric act played out. Samuel wanted to go. He asked if it wasn't our civic duty, but Pardon rejected that notion. It was no duty of ours to bear witness to an unjust act. Sam still wanted to go. So did Jacob. And myself. My uncle dismissed the three of us to do as we pleased. Lifting Polly into his arms, he went upstairs to watch over his youngest son. So the three of us set off for town.

Every soul was there on the common, crowded before the wooden frame of the hangman's engine. The people murmured one to another, all jostling for a better view. There was a carnival atmosphere to the whole thing that struck me as perverse and cruel. When I mentioned this to Jacob, he only shrugged and noted that we three were here also. My nose caught a strong whiff of lilacs and I found Elizabeth Wickes on my left, tittering with her hens. Elizabeth wore a lilac perfume that she claimed was French but was far too pungent for my liking. Of Henry I saw no sign.

At the peel of the church bell, the assembled flesh grew quiet. Ebeneezer Wickes and Halton Hazard ascended the platform, both bedecked in their powdered wigs and red sashes, the marks of their offices. A third man was present but his face was hidden beneath the executioner's hood. The prisoner was led up the steps of the gallows deck. Ebeneezer addressed the crowd, but I could not make out what he said over the noise. Halton Hazard, bible in hand, read from the good book as the hangman pulled a burlap sack over the head of Ephraim Fiske. The noose was slid down and cinched tight over the prisoner's neck. The black-masked executioner took hold of the switch and watched the selectmen for his cue.

There was a quick nod, and the lever was pulled. The trap fell under his feet and Ephraim Fiske dropped and popped when the cord went taut. The crowd had gone silent, holding their breath so the sharp crack of the neck was heard clearly across the green. The limp figure swayed on the rope as lifeless as a stone.

~

The sound of that awful snap stayed with me as we left the common, the abruptness of it startling my ears over and over. But the ending of Ephraim Fiske's life left me with more than an awful memory; I now had a predicament and the only soul who could help me was dead. Night was coming on fast and with it came the prospect of Katherine's return.

What was I to do? Pardon would not hear any more of my talk. Would the boys be any more receptive? How could I tell them that their dead mother would slip from her grave and come back to the house? That she intended to harm her own children?

I stood as the townsfolk passed around me, paralyzed by this wretched dilemma. This was my thought on the matter: there is no one to turn to, so you alone must defend the family. You will keep watch and prevent the Devil from entering.

The crowd thinned and there, standing among them, emerged an ally. Will Treves was watching the crowd disburse from the ghastly spectacle. With the execution of the prisoner, he had been relieved of his gaol house duty. Samuel hollered at me to hurry along, but I told him to go on without me and ran to where the one-handed man stood. Hadn't Will always been there to help? Wasn't he loyal to Pardon?

"Will," I said in a huff. "I'm glad to see you."

His eyes were on the far side of the green where the hanged man was being cut down. "I can't believe they went through with it," he said. "I heard someone cheer when his neck broke. I don't recognize these people anymore."

I looked back to the gallows tree in the distance. I hadn't noticed till now how close the hanging engine was to the old bower, the site of my misguided passion. I turned away. "I agree. Something strange has taken hold here."

"It's a good thing no one saw you speaking to that poor man. They might have strung you up alongside him."

"They might yet," I said.

"What does that mean?"

"Nothing." I took a breath to collect my thoughts. "Will, I need help with something. I know you've helped us so many times as it is, but this is important. Will you help me?"

He turned to me. "I would do anything for you, Hester." Something in his voice unsettled me. I don't know why. "Say the word."

What words indeed? What was I to tell him without sounding like a lunatic? I have always considered myself a forthright person who was uneasy with lies, but this too was a lie. Under pressure, a lie came effortlessly.

"I'm worried that we might be in danger. Some of the families have turned their backs on us, believing that we caused the consumption to spread. I believe someone will come to harm us tonight."

"Harm you? How so? Who?"

"I don't know," I lied again. "They might hurl rocks through a window or shoot the horses. Maybe even set fire to the barn. I am going to stay up tonight and keep watch. We have a pistol. Would you help me watch over the family? Please?"

Will was taken aback at this news. "Surely your uncle will stand guard? Or Sam and Jacob?"

"They don't believe me," I said. At least that was not an untruth. "Please, Will. I don't know who else to turn to."

His good hand reached out to touch my elbow. "You truly are scared, aren't you?"

"I am." Nothing could be truer.

He looked at the ground. "I'm afraid I can't. I'm on watch duty tonight. I'm sorry."

"Watch duty? But Fiske was caught. Why do they still want a night watch?"

"It's at the churchyard. To keep people from defiling anymore graves. What about Henry? I'm sure he'd help you."

The very name galled me. "Henry can go to Hell."

Will blanched at the strong language. I apologized.

"I wish I could help, Hester," he said. "Keep a light on in a window. Vandals might have second thoughts if they think someone is awake." He tipped his cap and set off. "If everything is quiet tonight, I'll try and slip away to come check on you."

I thanked him and turned toward home, dreading the night to come.

~

In the parlor, I sat watching the embers glow in the hearth. Everyone had gone to bed, and I was alone. Waiting.

I had done what I could to prepare. The personal effects confiscated from Ephraim Fiske remained in our home, stored in a cupboard in my uncle's study. When my uncle went for his after-dinner constitutional, I went to claim them. The knife with its large blade was still there, along with the pistol and its kit. There was also the religious talismans Ephraim had on his person. The rosary bead wrapped around his fist and the pages of the Bible stuffed into his pockets. These I took to the kitchen to contemplate how best to use them. The knife was obvious, but the flintlock was another matter. Unaccustomed to firearms and how they worked, I asked Samuel to come into the kitchen and showed him the piece with its various components laid out on the table.

He looked at the lot. "This is the fugitive's property, isn't it?" When I confirmed that it was, he said, "Are you laying claim to it now that he's dead?"

I held the pistol out to him. "Show me how to load this."

He hesitated. "Do you aim to shoot someone with it?"

"I'm just curious. Please."

Samuel shrugged and stood the pistol upright and poured a measure of gunpowder from the flask down the muzzle. Then he nestled the metal ball in a cloth wad into the bore and rammed it home with the rod, packing it hard into the bottom. Leveling the weapon, he added a bit of powder to the pan and showed me how to lower the metal tongue called the frizzen. Next he drew back the hammer, which held a small rock of flint.

"All that's left," he said, "is to pull the trigger piece here."

I pursed my lips. "It's a lot of steps."

"Have you ever fired one?"

He already knew the answer, so he led me outside and thrust the loaded weapon into my hands. "Aim at the shed there. Draw your eye down the barrel and squeeze the trigger. But grip the piece steady."

The pistol erupted in a thunderclap of noise and smoke. The force of the kick surprised me. The fingers of my right hand were mired with gunblack.

He let out a whoop at my expression. "The recoil is shocking, isn't it?"

Jacob and Polly came rushing out onto the back veranda. When they saw what had caused the racket, Jacob wanted to try it. I shooed them away and returned to the kitchen table. Samuel wiped the burn residue from the pan and frizzen on the pistol and handed it back to me. I asked him to guide me as I cleaned and reloaded the piece. He offered a few words of advice but when I was done, he declared it to be loaded and ready to fire.

"You'll be a steady shot with a bit of practice," he said. "But what made you want to try your hand at shooting?"

"A fox has been skulking round the chicken coop," I replied. "I hope to put it down."

The evening resumed its usual routine after that. When Pardon returned, he sat before the fire with a book in his lap while Jacob and Polly played checkers. I brought Hiram down to nestle in my lap while Samuel read an article from the latest broadsheet. The fire crackled as Sam read to us and soon Pardon was snoring in his chair. The moment was brief, but we were content amongst ourselves, despite our losses. This ragtag family. I remembered the vow I had made to Katherine to keep her family safe no matter what. When my uncle stirred and harried everyone off to bed, I bolted the doors and the windows and fetched the pistol. The weapon lay on the table before me as I waited.

Was I fearful as the hours ticked on? Of course, but my lungs were strong, and I knew that a good shriek would bring my uncle and his sons running. In fact, this was my plan. If my aunt returned to haunt our home, I would rouse the men and they would see with their own eyes the horror that stalked us. The creature would be repulsed, if not destroyed outright. At the very least, I would know that I had not dreamed the whole gruesome thing and the matter would be dealt with one way or another.

I waited.

The wind rustled outside the door. Above me a joist would creak, below a floorboard ticked, the usual rheumatic groans of any house but each had me flinching and reaching for the flintlock. I scolded myself for my jumpy nerves. It wouldn't do to carelessly fire the gun inside the house and wake everyone. Not yet, anyway.

I waited.

I reflected on what Ephraim Fiske had told me about his mad brother and the woman he knew as his sister-in-law. Nathaniel Fiske had traveled to the continent and met a beguiling woman in the mountains of far Europe. A princess trapped in a lonely castle. Wasn't that how he had described the Lady Szabina? He married this woman, and they crossed the Atlantic to begin a new life on the Fiske homestead in Bountiful. And the consumptive deaths had begun after that. What year had that been? I should have asked Ephraim when I had the chance. Was it before my parent's death? Was I living in Bountiful at the time when Nathaniel arrived with his new bride? For all I knew, my mother and father may have even met Lady Szabina. The thought was unsettling.

So. What then was this widow, the Lady Szabina? Some devil in human form, come to wreak havoc on an unsuspecting populace? Was she some kind of ghost like I suspected Katherine Stokely to be? It seemed absurd. I had met the woman, spoken to her. Her hand was as solid as any other I had shaken. She was no phantom.

I waited still. Perhaps the apparition would not appear tonight. It was late, and I was so very tired. The thought of sprawling on my little cot seemed suddenly delicious, and that was when I heard a rattling sound at the door. I was instantly alive with a tingle of nerves down to my fingertips. I took up the pistol and crept down the hall. The glass in the door was black with night but no face leered there. No unseen hand jiggled the knob on the other side. The wind. Still, I stood there for some time with the heavy pistol in my hand. If some unlucky neighbor were to knock at that moment, I would have shot them through the glass. The wind blew and blew but nothing disturbed the entrance.

Withdrawing from the doorway, I caught movement in the corner of my eye. The spinning wheel near the window was turning round and round, pedaled by a figure at the stool. It was her. The shroud lay draped over her like a shawl. The thing that was once my aunt did not react to my presence. Hunched at the stool she simply pushed the pedal that turned the wheel as if mesmerized by its rotations. An unfinished strip of yarn hung limp from the bobbin.

My hands went cold. It would not raise the pistol no matter

how hard I tried. The wheel kept spinning and the dark figure hunched over it was rocking back and forth in a sort of trance much like Katherine did in life.

The pedal stopped, and the wheel slowed. The filthy shroud rustled. The thing turned to look at me. It resembled my aunt in an oblique way, but it was not her. This face was dead and lifeless, the cloudy eyes lit from within by some unnatural spark. The jaw moved, the dark lips stretching to form words. I did not want to hear what it had to say.

Panic brought my hand to life. The pistol came up, and I leveled the barrel directly at that gaunt face and pulled the trigger. The powder fizzled and smoked but did not fire.

The thing moved like quicksilver, slamming me against the wall. Its cold hand snatched my hair and yanked my head back. The breath from that black maw was poison.

Filthy orphan, it whispered to me. *Why do you stay? No heart cherishes you here.*

I thrust the knife up, plunging the blade up under the jaw to shut its mouth. Its foul blood spewed over me as it shrieked. I was hurled aside, crashing into the sideboard. I rolled onto my back with the blade up, but the room was empty.

I screamed my uncle's name as I ran for the stairs. I screamed for Samuel and I screamed for Jacob. I didn't want to face this alone anymore. They would see now, they would believe. Why had they not come running already?

When I burst into the master bedroom, my uncle lay still on the bed.

"Pardon, wake up! Wake up now!"

He didn't move. His eyes were open, staring vacantly at the ceiling, but no amount of shaking would rouse him. I ran bellowing to the boy's room only to find them in the same catatonic state; eyes open but no intelligence in them. A cry rang out from the hallway.

Good God, the children.

I threw open their door. Polly was upright. It was she who had screamed. Hiram was out of bed, tottering sleepily across the room to the dark thing crouched under the dormer. Its pale arms wide, waiting to embrace the boy.

"No!" I snatched Hiram away and pulled him behind me. The light was dim, and I could not see its face under the shade of the shroud. But I heard it hiss.

"Katherine," I said to it. Could it hear me? Was anything of the woman I knew still within this ghoul? "You mustn't harm him anymore."

The thing rose to its feet, a column of inky darkness towering to the ceiling.

"Polly!" I hollered. "Take Hiram downstairs to the kitchen. Hurry!"

The girl sprang from the bed and dragged her brother from the room. I heard their feet hammering the steps. Brave child. I backed toward the door, never taking my eyes from the dead woman before me. When I saw it coil up to pounce, I slammed the door shut and tumbled down the stairs after the little ones.

They were hiding under the table, gesturing at me to join them. The misfired pistol was still in my hand, the kit on the table where I had left it. With trembling hands, I took the flask and shook powder down the muzzle. I managed to seat the wadding and the ball, and I was packing it home when the figure rose up at the doorway. The children clung to my skirt as I spilled more powder onto the pan. The dead woman skirted the end of the table, passing before the window, just as I hauled back on the hammer mechanism. This time the shot was true. The clap of gunfire was followed by the crash of breaking glass as the fiend was blown through the window. Smoke filled the air.

I was not prepared to go out and meet the damned thing, so I raked the frizzen clean of spent powder and reloaded the pistol. The children were crying and clutching at me as I packed the load and drew the hammer back. I pushed them away and told them to go back under the table.

I eased the door open with the pistol high before me. The dead woman lay sprawled against the railing of the veranda. Smoke rose from the blast wound to her chest. Her jaw chopped and chopped as if biting the air. Her expression was now altered, the hissing fury replaced with fear. The strange light in her eyes had dimmed, and she looked more like the woman I knew.

God in Heaven, what have I done?

I knelt before her but stayed out of striking distance. "Katherine?"

Her eyes locked on the weapon in my hand. *Use it. Don't miss.*

The gun had suddenly doubled its weight in my grip. I brought it up, steadied with both hands, and drew aim at her face.

"Turn away," I pleaded.

Her neck swiveled to one side with a clicking sound. Her left temple now exposed to my aim.

"Hester?" called a voice from the darkness.

Will Treves, coming round the house, panting. He must have been on his way to check on us when he heard the gunfire. His eyes rotated from me to the dead woman against the railing, his face draining as he saw hers.

I fired.

Her head snapped back violently and lolled loose on her neck. Gore spewed from the catastrophe that had been her left ear. It hadn't been enough. Her arms snaked and her frame jerked in a fit. The rage returned to her face, and the hissing started anew. I backed away from it. Poor Will was like a petrified stump, blinking at the horror he witnessed.

The thing that was Mother Stokely rose up and glared at me. Never in my life had I seen such berserk hatred on a human face. I expected her to lash out again, but she did not. Her form seemed to melt through the railing until she was swallowed by the night.

32

"WHAT'S WRONG WITH them?"

"I don't know," I said. "I can't wake them."

We stood before Samuel's bed, Will and I, looking down at his vacant eyes. "Jacob and Pardon are in the same state. It's like they're under some spell."

Will laid his palm flat against Samuel's chest. "He's breathing." He snapped his fingers before my cousin's bald eyes. "I don't know what to make of it, Hester. Any of it. Not the least that thing you fired at."

"Let's go back downstairs," I replied. "I don't want to leave the children alone."

Polly and Hiram refused to leave the safety of the kitchen. They had gone back to hiding under the table while I showed Will the strange sleep malady that gripped my uncle and cousins. His questions had come stuttering out in fits and starts, unable to apply words to what he had witnessed. I wasn't much better. I asked him to start the fire in the parlor while I coaxed the children out from under the table. They were like frightened rabbits, trembling with wide eyes.

They refused to go back to their room, so I gathered the

two of them up in a quilt and nestled them before the fire. They insisted I not leave the room again, and I promised them that Will and I would watch over them. The poor things shivered for a time under the quilt, and I cooed to them that this had all been a bad dream but it was over now and it was time to sleep. The clock ticked on. After a while, they slept.

Will sat in one of the tall chairs before the hearth. My uncle's preferred chair. The flintlock sat on the side table next to him. He had cleaned the pistol and reloaded the shot. He gazed at the fire with a peculiar expression.

"Are you all right?" I asked.

"I keep thinking that this is all just a nightmare," he said. "But I can't seem to wake from it."

I took a deep breath and unpacked it all as best as I was able. I told him about my aunt returning from the grave and attacking Hiram. About Ephraim's claims that the widow was the true reason why Bountiful had burnt to the ground. Will's jaw fell lower at each revelation. By the time I finished, his mouth hung open in muted bafflement.

I reached out to touch his hand. I don't know why. To reassure him, I suppose. Or to snap him back to the here and now.

He flinched. "The widow is the source of this evil?"

I nodded. "According to Ephraim."

"But now he's dead, so there is no way to question his story."

"There's the widow," I said. "We could ask her to confirm the tale."

He was not amused. I have never been good at poking fun. He said, "I saw you fire a pistol ball into that thing's head. And it just walked away."

"It's not a thing. It is Katherine."

His face hardened. "That was not your aunt, Hester. That was some wraith plucked out of Hell itself."

I had no mind to debate the issue. "But there is something of Katherine still there. Her mind or soul, I can't say. She became lucid for a moment, aware of herself. And she was horrified."

The quiet of the house settled heavily around us. I noticed a black mark on my hand and tried to scrub it away.

"This thing," he said. "Will it come back?"

"Tomorrow night. And the night after that and anon."

"What do we do?"

I sighed. "I promised Katherine that I would protect her family. Even from herself. So that it was what I will do."

"How? Putting a ball into its skull didn't sway it to die."

The answer was obvious, but I kept circling around it, unwilling to land the bull's eye. "The ritual performed on Pru and Faith. The same must be done to Mother Stokely."

Will grimaced, but he did not look surprised. He must have come to the same silent conclusion. "That will be difficult for Pardon. And the boys."

"I won't involve them. I won't even tell them."

"Why on earth not?"

"I said I would protect them, didn't I?" I said. "Besides, Pardon wouldn't believe me. I already tried and he all but ejected me from his home. So, I won't burden them with it."

He looked at me expectantly.

"What?"

"You are going to ask me to help you," he said.

Annoyed, I said, "You have done enough for this family as it is, Will. I can't ask for anything more."

A grin appeared. "If you think I would let you do this alone, Hester, then you don't know me very well."

I suppose I did know that he would help. I don't know why I tried to be stoic about it. I don't know why I say things I don't mean.

He turned to the dark window. "Perhaps we should do this now."

"What, go to the graveyard?"

The grin returned. "I know for a fact that the watchman has abandoned his post. If we go now, before sunup, no one will catch us."

I shook my head. "I am not setting foot in that place until the sun is up. Besides, I can't leave the family in the state they're in."

"That's going to be a stickier problem. There'll be a different watchman posted at the churchyard tomorrow. He won't let us in."

I knelt on the floor before the children. The two of them looked absurdly innocent as they slept. "But it has to be during the day. Nighttime is when it roams, and I am not ready for another confrontation like tonight. Are you on duty tomorrow night?"

"I am." He snapped his fingers. "That's how we'll do it. I'll start my watch early while the sun is still up. I'm sure the guard on day watch will be happy to be relieved."

"Then it's settled," I replied, rubbing at the stain on my hand. It would not wipe clean.

Will watched me. "What's wrong with your hand?"

"This soot from the pistol. It won't come clean."

Kneeling beside me, he took my hand and turned it to the light of the fire. "The gunblack. It's burnt its way under the skin. You'll have that mark for a while yet."

Lovely, I thought. Another mark on my flesh, to accompany the scar.

~

Will left to return to his neglected post at the churchyard gates. I huddled beside the children on the floor and tried to sleep but could not. When I closed my eyes, I saw that last vision of Mother Stokely when her true spirit emerged briefly before the demoniac returned. What torments was she suffering in her current state? Was she aware of what she had become? I tried to cool my own misery by knowing that tomorrow Will and I would end her suffering.

By morning, my uncle and his sons had improved slightly. They remained unconscious but their eyes had at last closed and they appeared to be simply asleep. I did what I could to make them comfortable, praying they would recover. The children were their usual selves; chatty, bickering, and hungry. Hiram, in fact, seemed to have regained much of the color he had lost. I could only assume that was because Katherine's unholy torment on the boy had been denied.

Mercifully, Hiram had no memory of the incident. Polly was a different story. She knew what she had seen, but it confused her. She asked me why mother came back. Why had she hurt her brother?

My first instinct was to dismiss it as a bad dream but that would be unfair to the child. She had seen the truth, even if she couldn't understand it. Instead, I tried to hammer a round peg of truth into a square hole. Mother's spirit had visited us, I told her, because she didn't want to leave her family. But soon, I reassured

Polly, Mother's spirit would wing its way to the Almighty and would find peace. She seemed unsure of my conclusion but did not bring it up again.

We kept busy as best we could, cleaning up the mess from last night. The children helped sweep away the broken glass from the veranda and then we looked over our depleted stock of lumber to cover the shattered window. The coffin-making had left us with only scrap ends of timber, but we took what we had and nailed them up over the gaping window. The result was an unsightly patch job, but it would have to do until the glass could be replaced.

Mid-afternoon saw the men wake from their sleep. All three were weak and shivering from a chill so I made them huddle before the fire with a bowl of soup in their laps. Neither Pardon nor the two boys had any knowledge of what had happened, but all spoke of bad dreams. They were listless and irritable for the rest of the day. When I told my uncle that I would be out later, he did not have the strength to question it. I prepared dinner beforehand and told the children it was their job to feed the others. They were quite pleased when they learned they were to be left in charge of the household.

The pistol I cleaned and slid into a satchel, along with the powder flask and supply of shot. In went the big knife, two jars of lamp oil, candles, matches, and a few other incidentals. As an afterthought, I stuffed the Bible inside, although I wasn't sure what good it would do us. Perhaps for kindling. Will came at five of the afternoon with a spade in his hand. He spoke to Pardon briefly, glad to see him awake again, and then we quit the house. Two visitors were coming up the walk as we left. It was Pardon's fellow selectman, Halton Hazard, and his odious son, Tom. Both wore pinched, impatient expressions.

I hallooed them from the veranda. Neither returned my smile.

"Is your uncle home?" Halton asked stiffly.

"He is, but I'm afraid he's not well. Could you call tomorrow?"

He came up the steps anyway. "I must speak to him. It's very important."

I stood blocking the door. "Please, Mr. Halton. He's really doing poorly at the moment. He's just not up to receiving visitors now."

Tom Hazard, my eternal tormentor, stood behind his father. He glared at me with an ugly smirk on his stupid face. He even giggled as if remembering some joke he had heard.

His father remained cold. "This cannot wait."

There was no time for this, but I could not refuse him. I opened the door to show him in. "Very well. Can I take your hat?"

This was a simple gesture of common hospitality, one that I performed hundreds of times before when Mr. Hazard called on us. But this time, he recoiled from me as if I were a leper.

"Keep your hands to yourself, thank you." He stormed past me. "I can see myself in. Come along, Thomas."

Tom Hazard just grinned at me as he followed his father inside. I had a sudden urge to slap the smugness from his freckled face.

Will observed the brief exchange. "What was that all about?"

"I wish I knew." I took up my satchel. "Are you ready to go?"

He made a buffoonish display of doffing his cap to me. "Lead on, captain."

~

The lighthearted moment faded as we approached the gates of the churchyard. The heavy iron railing was closed and sitting before it was Peg-Leg Wilkins. With his back against the gate and his legs stretched out before him, he dozed peacefully. I stepped into the thicket where I wouldn't be seen as Will went up to the napping guard and kicked his boot. I watched them exchange a few words, Peg-Leg yawned and scratched his belly until he finally rose, clapped the younger man on the shoulder and walked away. Once he was out of sight, Will waved at me to join him.

"Did he give you any trouble," I asked.

"No, he just seemed confused was all." Will looked up at the heavens and marked the sun's progress toward the hills in the west. "We'd best get on with it."

He slid the iron bolt back, and we slipped through and he closed the gates behind us. We marched up the path through the tilted headstones to the mound of earth that served as the crypt. The vault was little more than a dug-out carved into the side of a low hill. The facade was mortared fieldstone topped with a decorative finial ball with a heavy wooden door braced under it. Anchored just below the finial was a rusty bell with a cord that snaked into the interior of the crypt. This was a cautionary alarm for any unfortunate soul who, mistakenly declared dead, awoke inside the vault. Although I have heard spook stories told round a fire of this happening, I cannot confirm any of these as true. Still, the threat of being buried alive was enough to ensure that the bell and cord were properly maintained.

I studied the weathered surface of the door and the heavy latch that kept it closed. The thought of opening it made me shudder. "This is going to be harder than I'd anticipated," I said to Will. "Silly of me, isn't it?"

"None of this is going to be easy," he said. "Let's get the fire started first. Then we'll face that door."

Taking up his spade, Will dug a small pit for the fire while I gathered all the dry wood I could find. Will said he wanted the fire low to avoid it being seen from the road. The smoke, he hoped, would be masked under the overcast sky. We took turns with the spade, as it was difficult for Will to dig with one hand. With the pit dug, we soon had a fire going. Will braced a few logs over it to keep it burning and then we turned to the crypt. The latch was stubborn with rust and had to be hammered up. The door swung open to reveal only darkness within. I lit the candles I had brought, and we ducked under the lintel. The inside of the crypt resembled a root cellar with its bare earthen walls and floor of packed dirt. The smell of rot and death was so thick it made my eyes water.

"Damn," Will said, holding his candle high.

The tallow light wafted over three plain coffins inside the vault. I had not anticipated this. Stupid of me, really. Of course other people had died. With the closing of the graveyard, the coffins had been stored here.

Will knelt and swept the dust from the lid of the nearest coffin. "Do you know which one is hers?"

"They all look the same," I said. All three were plainly built with no gaudy ornamentation. Ostentation in death was as reviled among our kind as much as it was in life. I moved my candle over the coffin next to me, looking for anything on the wood. "They must have marked these in some way. How are they going to know which is which?"

"I guess they were in a rush to shut these up and get out of here."

The thought of opening one after the other to find my aunt had my stomach churning. I could tell by Will's expression that he had reached the same conclusion. There was nothing to be done about it and time was wasting.

Will dug into his sack and brought out a hammer. He looked at me and nodded at the three boxes before us. "Pick one."

You would think I would remember the coffin that I had placed my aunt inside of, but I could not. I pointed, randomly, at the one nearest him and he began hammering up the lid. The wood split as he hammered the seam open. We pried off the lid and recoiled at the miasma blowing up at us. The body of a man lay there with pennies over the eyes and his hands clasped peacefully over his chest. A black scarf was draped over his brow.

"Edwin Barrow," Will declared. "He died last week."

"Consumption?"

He shook his head. "Kicked in the head by his own horse."

We fitted the lid back as best we could, and Will hammered the nails back down.

"You pick the next one," I said. "I clearly have no talent for it."

Will bit his lip for a moment and then moved deeper into the vault. He ignored the coffin closest to the door and chose the casket at the far end of the crypt. Where it was darkest. I wished he hadn't.

Again with the hammer and the heaving and the squeak of nails being pried up. The stench was even worse this time. The occupant of this coffin was hidden beneath a shroud of unbleached cotton and the material was seeped through with blood. Will gasped, and I almost ran from the vault. He tugged at the shroud and the gaunt face of my aunt emerged.

"Help me," he said.

Gripping the rough handles, we dragged the coffin out of the crypt and into the light of day. I took a deep breath and turned to face the dead woman. There was a ghastly wound on her chest and a dark hole where her left ear should have been. The marks left by the two pistol shots fired into her. As unsightly as these wounds were, more appalling was the sight of her red lips and the blood smeared over her chin. Good God, I thought. Were those stained lips smiling?

"Don't look at her," Will said. He removed his cap, wiped his forearm over his brow and squared the cap back on. "Did you bring that big butcher's blade?"

I removed the knife from my satchel along with the heavy apron I had brought. I put this on and rolled up my sleeves. Will did the same, and we knelt on each side of the coffin. Using the sharpened blade, I cut away first the bodice and then slit the knife up the lace of the dress and pulled it away to expose the belly. Like before, my plan was to go in under the ribcage rather than to cut through the breastplate. I placed the tip of the blade just below the sternum and whispered a small prayer. Then I plunged in and sawed down to the navel.

"Oh God," Will gasped.

Mother Stokely's eyelids rolled back. Her lips parted and one hand rose and splayed open to stop the trauma. Will scrambled to push it down. The awful sight of those eyes withered my resolve. Lit with that terrible, profane light, the eyes dipped to behold me and my hands went numb.

"For Christ's sakes, Hester," Will barked. "Don't stop now!"

The shrill of his voice broke the spell. I bore down on the knife with both hands. Dark blood and offal erupted from the belly. I slashed open a second cut, across the stomach to widen the breach. Then I held my breath and pulled out her insides, piling the steaming mess aside. When I plunged my hand under her ribs, she began to twist and jerk.

"Hold her down, Will!"

"I'm trying!"

Pressing her shoulders flat, he had all but climbed into the coffin with her. She gnashed her teeth, chopping them hard and the sound made me queasy. Nausea rippled through me as I dug into the putrescent gore, feeling my way blind until at last my fingers wrapped around the heart. It was cold and slippery, but it pulsed fast in my hand.

Will cried out. The thing that was Katherine had bit down onto the stump of his right arm. Her strangely sharp teeth clamped down like a leech, spilling his blood. He tugged and jerked but the thing would not relent. The rage in her weird eyes was white hot.

I hauled on the heart, ripping it free from its stringy roots. The sound of it was terrible, a wet pop and a gurgling snap. Katherine shrieked with an obscene cry and her face twisted in agony. It was like some unholy birthing scene, with me midwifing this horrible thing into the light.

"I have it!"

I held it up in my hand. It beat against my palm. The thing in the coffin ceased its flailing. Katherine's hand clawed at nothing but air now.

Will scrambled away from the casket. "Throw it into the fire!"

The elation I felt evaporated. I doubled over, retching onto the grass and Katherine's severed heart tumbled to the dirt. Choking and spitting, I caught my breath and a new sound, strange and bright, caught my attention.

A bell peeled. The rusty bell over the crypt door was tinkling softly, disturbed by some movement within.

33

A SHAPE SLITHERED in the dark square of the crypt opening as the bell over it rang in gentle peels.

"Will, the door!" I sputtered. "Close it!"

He hesitated as if unsure what to do, blood trickling from the wound in his scarred wrist. When I screamed at him again, he bolted to the crypt and threw his shoulder against the wooden door. A moment too late as a cadaverous hand emerged to grip the edge of it. The door bashed it hard, but the hand stayed, preventing Will from throwing the bolt. All he could do was lean into it to keep the thing from slipping out.

"The heart," he cried. "Burn it!"

The darkened muscle lay on the ground, grit clinging to it like a dusting of flour. I scooped it up, ready to fling it into the fire, when I heard Katherine's voice.

Mine. Give it to me.

I held it aloft, just out of reach of her clawing hands.

"Katherine, who did this to you?"

Mine!

"Tell me!"

The hatred in her eyes was pure. Her lips peeled back against the teeth. *The widow*.

I dropped the heart into the fire and listened to it sizzle and pop against the hot embers. Flesh is difficult to burn and I had with me two flasks of lamp oil to aid in the cremation. I took one from my satchel and poured it into the fire pit. The flames roiled up, emitting a greasy black smoke.

I turned to the coffin. The flailing hands slowed to an eerie pantomime. The clawing fingers atrophied. The chomping jaw became still. Whatever animated Katherine's dead body was fading as the heart burned up in the pit. I had expected some change to come over her face, a stillness or look of peaceful rest. This did not occur. Her features remained set in a rictus of unholy fury. The skin began to blister and pop as if melting. I looked away.

I had neglected Will. His boots skidded against the ground as he fought to keep the door shut. But the thing inside was gaining ground as the wooden gate yawned open.

"Get the knife!" he barked at me.

I did as he asked, throwing myself against the door. It rattled and banged with a sudden fury. He took the knife from me and slashed and stabbed at the pale hand trapped against the jam. Like a man possessed, he butchered it until the severed fingers fell to the ground and the door clanged shut in its casement. The thick bar was slammed home, sealing it.

We crawled away from the vault. The door banged and thudded but remained closed, trapping the thing inside. I couldn't help but wonder if it was Mr. Barrow or the occupant of the third, unopened coffin. One of the severed fingers lay in the dirt, curling up like a worm exposed to sunlight. I kicked it away.

We watched the fire blaze and listened to it pop and hiss. I took the spade and stirred the embers, looking for Katherine's heart. All that remained of it was a shriveled coal of charred flesh.

"Should we toss more fuel on it?" he said.

"No. It's gone."

He sat down in the grass. "Praise be."

The memory of that face in the coffin was fixed in my mind's eye like a butterfly to a corkboard. I did not want that to be the lasting memory of my poor aunt, so I dug for other memories of her. I thought of her kindness when I was hurt, and I remembered her gentleness with me when she took me in. A kiss to a scraped elbow, a warm squeeze when the night terrors had me. I began to cry, caught up in all that remembrance.

To his credit, Will offered no cheap words of solace. He simply put his ruined arm around my shoulders and held me while I sobbed. It was a good while before I could speak again. I reached out for his good hand and squeezed it.

"I don't know how to thank you, Will."

"There's no need."

"You risked your neck to help me."

He looked at me and shrugged and then looked away. "I will always help you, Hester. No matter what the task."

The candor made me feel strangely vulnerable, but before I could make sense of it, the bell over the crypt door peeled again. The thing trapped inside it was still moving.

We got to our feet and looked down at the remains of Katherine Stokely in the coffin. I arranged her arms over her chest and drew the shroud over her. Will fit the lid into place and hammered the nails back down.

The door of the vault thudded. Will looked up at me. "We can't put her back in the crypt."

"Then she'll stay out here," I replied. The bell peeled again. "What do we about the one inside?"

"I'm not opening that door now, I'll tell you that much. We can deal with it tomorrow, in the sunlight."

The fire had diminished to a low bed of coals. Will took the spade and plowed the dirt atop it, snuffing the embers with a hiss until it was silenced under the backfilled earth. Dusk was on us and the shadows of the trees stretched long over the tombstones.

"We should get you home," he said.

I did not tell him that there was one more duty to perform.

~

We took the wagon track that skirted the marsh on the southern end of town. Halfway across, I stopped and looked out over the festering wetland. Rising from the swaying reeds and bulrushes were the worn gables of Cogburn Hall.

Will clutched my elbow. "Why are we stopping?"

"This is where she resides."

"The widow?"

"The widow."

I watched his eyes roam over the moss-covered veranda and

rotting clapboards. The old house glared down at us with an unnatural menace. Cogburn Hall had always looked forlorn in its lichen-encrusted decay, but now it exhaled something like malice. I can only assume it had taken on the character of its occupant.

"We are not going in there."

"I am not asking you to."

Confusion ran riot in his eyes. "Are you mad? That woman is in there."

"This will only take a minute. Wait here."

"What are you going to do?"

I slipped the satchel from my shoulder and produced the second flask of lamp oil. "I am going to burn it to the ground."

He would not let go of my arm. "You mustn't. I don't claim to know what we're dealing with, Hester, or whatever that woman may be, but I know she's dangerous."

I yanked my arm free. "She killed Katherine. And Pru and Faith. I won't have her skulking back for the rest of them."

I turned and marched up the mossy steps of the house. I expected Will to follow me. In fact, I hoped he would, but I did not hear his footsteps behind me. The tall doors hung tilted from the rusty hinges and would only open when I shouldered them aside. The foyer and staircase looked as it had before; black with mold and dusty from neglect. The dry bones of small animals crunched under my boots. Situated so close to the swamp, the house was mildewed with damp rot, and I wished I had more lamp oil to fling about. Damp wood would be difficult to set ablaze and I wanted to burn this horrid nest to the ground. I needed to move quickly. I did not want to spend one unnecessary minute in this decrepit tomb.

There was a racket at the doorway, and I was much relieved to find Will following me after all. I was even more relieved to see the loaded flintlock in his good hand.

He was cross with me. "You go too far, Hester. One of these days, it is going to bite you."

"Then help me."

His eyes darted about at the staircase and the lofty ceiling, alert to any danger. "How?"

I pulled the stopper on the flask and flung the oil over the heavy drapes. "There's a lamp there on the mantel. Splash the fuel over anything that will burn quickly."

"Careful," he said, nodding at the floor before me. The boards had rotted away, revealing a dark gutted hole at my feet. God only knew what lay below. "Watch where you step."

I emptied the flask and searched for more fuel but all I found were a few rocks of coal in the dry hearth. These I flung onto the tattered divan under the window. I looked to Will on the far side of the room, splashing oil across the moth-eaten drapes. Emptying it, he hurled the glass receptacle against the drooping wallpaper.

The box of matches rattled in my hand, but I managed to strike one and fling it at the oil-slicked curtains. The fire rippled fast up the drapery. The fuel burned hot and bright before me and I turned to see Will ignite his side of the room. Inside the span of a few heartbeats, the grand foyer of Cogburn Hall was an inferno.

I retreated toward the entrance and called to him. "Hurry, Will! It is finished!"

His face beamed with victory and, with a cry of hurrah, he ran to join me. But he had forgotten his own admonition to watch where one stepped. An awful snap broke over the sound of the fire and Will plunged through the floor, vanishing from sight.

I ran to the edge of the broken floorboards and looked down. There was darkness and nothing else.

"Will!"

No reply came, then or on the tenth time I called his name. The fire roared up around me, roasting across the vaulted ceiling. I dashed around the grand staircase where I found a discrete door and threw it open. Dusty stairs led down into the darkness of the cellar. The third step snapped under my heel, causing me to tumble but the handrail came away as I latched onto it for support. Rump over teakettle I fell to the flagstone floor.

A small patch of light fell on the rotten stairs but beyond that, the darkness was as thick and cloying as mud. I called out to Will but heard no reply. Scrambling for the matches and a candle from my satchel, I lit the tallow and ventured into the dark. The cellar of Cogburn Hall was more like a dungeon than a root cellar, with its limestone walls and arched doorways. Old furniture was stacked here and there, the pathway blocked with splintered chairs and moldy wardrobes. The further I ventured, the more I feared finding my way out. The darkness was so suffocating that I lost my bearings. Overhead I could hear the rumble of the fire but beyond that were snatches of sound all around me, like something scuttling through the dark. Rats were my first thought, causing me to shake even more. This was pushed aside by another fear of what might be skulking in the darkness. A woman draped in night.

I screamed Will's name. At the very least, I hoped the noise would keep the rats away. I almost fainted when I heard him reply. I plunged further into the cellar, ducking under a low arch and worming past the battered furniture. With relief I saw a glow of light and found myself in a clearing illuminated by the flames from the hole in the floor above. Will was on his knees, steadying himself against a pillar.

"Are you all right?"

"I'm dizzy," he said, eyes wheeling crazily. His fingertips were dotted with blood. I held the candle up to see where he was injured but could not find a mark. It wasn't until I prodded his scalp that I felt the wet warmth on the back of his skull. He stumbled just then, leaning against me.

"Can you walk?"

"Of course," he replied, but he was unsteady and had to brace my shoulder to stay upright. He looked up at the gap of floor he had fallen through. Flames rippled hot in the room above. "How stupid of me,"

"Where's the pistol?"

Looking at his empty hand, he seemed surprised to find it empty. "I must have dropped it."

We scanned the gritty floor but there was no sign of it. "Leave it," I said. "We must go."

We stumbled back through the dark and the wax from the candle stung my fingers. A light appeared through the maze, but my heart sank when we drew close. The staircase was engulfed in flames.

"There has to be another way out," he said.

I agreed, but where? The thought of groping blind through the dark was not inviting but a blazing timber crashed down on the stairs, sending a flurry of sparks over us. We retreated back into the labyrinth of the cellar, rounding a pillar and ducking under a low doorway, but we found no other staircase or even a window to the outside. All was deep night.

Will flattened his palm against the bare stone wall. "It's damp down here," he said. "Maybe the fire won't touch us."

His injury was worse than I had feared, rendering his judgment as wobbly as his knees. "The smoke will find us," I said. "And that we won't survive."

We pressed on, squeezing past the rubble of old crates and ancient barrels, until we emerged into a new chamber. I lit a fresh candle off the old one and gave it to Will to expand the glow and gain our bearings. Something loomed before us in the guttering candlelight. At first, I mistook it for more broken furniture, but this was like nothing else in that house.

It was solid stone and very old. On the top of it was a figure carved in the stone, a woman reposed as if in sleep. The sandstone hands were clasped together in prayer below the serene face.

"What is that?" asked Will.

"Nothing," I said. This was a lie. Before us lay the massive sarcophagus that Ephraim had spoken of.

Will drew his candle over the stone face. "My God. It's her."

He spoke truthfully. The resemblance was startling, but I looked away from it.

The great lid of the stone coffin was tilted out of its casement and my heart iced up at what might lie within. I could not help myself, nor could Will. We inched forward, compelled to see what lay within that dreadful object.

The winking candlelight crawled down the stone walls to the bottom. No horrid face greeted us; no gibbering demon gnashed it teeth. The sarcophagus was flooded with some dark liquid that reflected the light of the candle. It was blood, two hands deep of the stuff like some unholy bath.

Will's voice broke in a gasp. "Christ in heaven. Does the witch bathe in the stuff? Where did it all come from?"

Katherine, I thought. The blood pooled here had belonged to my aunt. And Prudence and Faith and every other victim in our settlement.

The surface of the blood was smooth like glass, reflecting the candlelight. Then a ripple disturbed the silken sheen. Something in its depth was rising to the surface.

Will pulled me away, backing us hard against the far wall.

We were without weapons, having lost both the pistol and the knife. Above us came the thunder of falling beams and roaring fire as the decrepit house tumbled in on itself. Cornered in this dark maze, we were trapped without a means of escape. And something inside the sarcophagus was stirring.

Fingers emerged from the stone box. A red-drenched hand gripped the side of the sarcophagus lid and slid it back with a terrible grating sound of stone against stone.

I did not want to see the thing rising from the blood. Neither did Will. Trembling hard against me, he whispered one word over and over. No, no, no.

She rose from the ancient tomb, naked and terrible. Red from crown to toe with the blood of her victims. Will flattened against the wall in terror. I screamed.

The Widow loomed over us, blood dripping from every limb. Her eyes, hot and sharp, fixed on me. And when she spoke, her voice was all wrong.

"Hester, you sound just like your mother when you scream."

My mind snapped at that moment, like a turtle clapping its beak shut, unable to take any more horror.

Then an abrupt noise sounded above us. I feared was the floor collapsing, but I was wrong. Glass rained down on us from a shattered window overhead. The waning daylight cut through the primordial darkness of the cellar like a bolt, exposing the red woman to its purifying rays. Her flesh blistered and erupted into flames. She fled into the darkness, shrieking.

"Hester, look!" Will exclaimed. "A window."

I could see now that the window had been draped with a black cloth to blot out the sunlight. An arm reached inside to knock the shards of glass from the pane, and then a face appeared. I thought I was dreaming.

It was Henry Beecham, reaching down to us.

"Hester, what the devil are you doing in there? Quick, the house is on fire!"

We were rescued, but, in that moment, I thought Will and I would die, attacked by the blood-drenched woman behind us. It was not to be. She was gone.

"Hurry!" Henry barked at us.

I told Will to climb up first because he was injured, but he would have none of that. The casement was a good four feet above our stretched hands, so he boosted me up on one shoulder and launched me to where Henry caught my wrists. I scraped over the fangs of broken glass and tumbled onto the lawn. With the heat of the fire roasting our backs, Henry and I reached down to drag Will out of the window. The three of us scrambled to get away from the inferno.

Collapsing into the reeds, we watched the tilted frame of Cogburn Hall go up in flames. Timbers split and the gabled roof caved in and foul smoke billowed from the wreckage. I watched through watering eyes for a figure to run screaming from the blaze, but none appeared.

My thoughts were this and only this: Burn, you monster. Roast all the way back to Hell.

Henry sat breathing hard. "What the devil were you doing in there?"

Will waited to hear how I would answer. I said, "Looking for the widow."

Henry rose up. I swear to God, he was ready to run back in to save her also. "She's still in there?"

"She's gone," Will said, clutching Henry's arm to hold him.

"How did you find us?" I asked.

"I saw the house burning from the road. When I got close, I heard screaming inside."

Will sighed, deflating with a profound gratitude. He reached out for Henry's hand. "Thank you, Henry. You saved us from roasting."

Henry beamed. He was becoming accustomed to his role as the fearless hero. Turning to me, he asked, "Do you know how the fire started?"

I scrambled for another lie. Will beat me to it.

"God knows," he replied. "A house that old, anything could have started it."

Henry scoffed. "Houses don't just combust. Something had to have set it off."

By now, a small clutch of townsfolk stood by the road watching the fire. No one moved to put it out and there was no concern over it spreading as the old house sat at the edge of the marsh. They just watched it burn as if glad to see it go.

Wisps of smoke rose from my smoldering hem. Brushing at

it, I said, "Will is hurt."

"The bleeding's stopped." Will tested his scalp and his fingers came away dry.

Henry helped us to our feet. "Come along. I've got the wagon with me."

The wagon waited at the road with a dray horse in the traces. The words 'Beecham's Landing' had been whimsically rendered in red and white script on the side of the wagonbox. It seemed to me the most cheerful sight in the world.

Will's home was closer, so we rolled there first. It was little more than a raw shack with a tin flue for a chimney. A white cat sat on the front step and a dirty-faced little boy was in the yard, bashing a stick against the trunk of a yew tree.

Will eased himself slowly to the ground. I stepped down and wrapped my arms around him. "Have your mother clean that wound. If you vomit from it, send for me."

He was reluctant to let go. Just before he did, he whispered into my ear. "Tell no one of what we did."

I promised him, although I thought it might be a lie. I could not think any further ahead than falling into bed.

Henry helped me back up into the wagon and we watched Will Treves limp to his sad little home. Henry nickered the horse back into motion, and I watched the dirty-faced boy dropped his stick and follow his older brother inside.

We trundled on to my house. My uncle's house, I should say. I did not know how I would be received. My plan was to slip quietly up to my bed without bothering anyone and deal with them later.

Henry came around to help me down, but he held onto my hand for a moment. "Hester," he said quietly, "I'm sorry for the way I treated you. It was callous of me."

I felt sorry for him in that moment. I don't know why. My own emotions are a mystery to me at exactly the wrong moments. I should have been furious with him, but I could not rally.

"Thank you for saying so," I said. "It surprised me. But then I had let my imagination run wild after our indiscretion under the bower."

His cheeks reddened. "I am sorry for that, too. I am not some rake looking to ruin lives. It was a heady night for me, and I went too far. Can you forgive me?"

It meant nothing to him, that much was obvious. Why would I cling to nothing? I absolved him. "We shall speak no more of it and it will be like it never happened. Does that suit you?"

"You are kind, Hester."

"But," I said, raising a finger like a school teacher, "we are to remain friends. I won't have you shun me after this."

"Agreed." He nodded in the direction of the gate. "Do you need help getting indoors?"

I told him I could manage and said goodbye. Doffing his cap, he climbed back into the wagon and rolled away. I turned to the house but made no move to go inside. The woodpile had been left haphazardly lying in the yard and there was an upright log on the grass. I sat down on it and started to cry. The dog came running from around the house and sat on my foot.

I don't know how long I sat sobbing, but I did not hear the others come out of the house. Polly was the first to find me, then Hiram. The two of them rubbed my back and told me not to cry. Looking up with bleary eyes I saw Samuel and Jacob come out and surround me. Pardon came last and together they huddled me inside, cooing at me tenderly and wondering where I had been or how I came to be in such a sooty, disheveled state.

New tears came. I could not remember feeling more loved.

34

I SPENT THE next day in bed recovering. Polly and Hiram never left my side. They read to me and brought me tea when I was awake, and they curled up with me when I rested. Jacob cleaned and dressed my wounds and Samuel prepared soup for me. It was over-salted and bitter, but I didn't care. The fuss they showed overwhelmed me at times. Samuel told me later that they had all been worried sick when they couldn't find me, fretting that something terrible had happened. Pardon especially. The dog snuck into the room later and curled up next to me in the cot.

My uncle came to check on me before dinner that day, telling the little ones to go help their brothers with the meal. He pulled the chair close to the cot and laid his palm over my brow.

"How are you feeling?"

"Much better," I said. "I'll be fine tomorrow, I'm sure of it. I don't mean to cause such a fuss."

"Pish-posh. Rest up properly." He leaned back in the chair and studied me. "We were all quite concerned about you, you know."

"I am sorry for that. It wasn't my intention. I was just

upset."

Pardon nodded in agreement. "I'm the one who needs to show contrition. I spoke cruelly to you, Hester. Forgive me."

His lip quivered, and I feared he would cry. I was grateful when he composed himself because his tears would have sparked my own.

"We've all been through a trying time. Nerves fray."

He leaned forward and set his gaze squarely on mine. "Where did you go? We thought you had run away."

What was I to tell him? That I had desecrated his wife's corpse and burnt her heart? That Katherine had been transformed into a monster? I spun more lies.

"I just needed to be alone," I said. "I'll admit I thought of running away. I felt like I was not wanted here."

"That lies on me. But it's not true. You must believe that."

"I do." It felt good to utter truth now.

He rubbed his eyes. "I was in a state when I thought you'd run off. I couldn't bear the thought of losing another daughter. Not after all this."

If his intent was to bring tears, then he succeeded. Unable to speak, I simply reached for his hand and he clasped it tight.

Composing himself a second time, he patted my hand and said, "Dinner is almost ready. I shall bring you up a plate of whatever dreadful dish Sam has concocted."

I laughed. "Don't be mean. He's trying."

He stood up and as he did so, the cheer fell from his face. I asked him what was wrong.

"There's some business we need to address," he said. "But that's for tomorrow. So rest up. I'll be back in a moment with Sam's gruel."

His evasion left me unsettled. "What business do you mean?"

"Tomorrow," he said. "For now, get better."

He left the room. I leaned back against the pillow, wondering what had troubled him. Did he have questions about the razing of Cogburn Hall? Its destruction would mean a capital loss to him. I suppose he'd want to know why Will and I were there in the first place. More lies would be needed. I was not looking forward to it.

~

I was much restored the next day and grateful to get out of bed. Washed and dressed, I hurried down to the kitchen to stoke the fire and prepare breakfast. I was eager to get back to normal now that the darkness had passed. Although my mind kept drifting back to the nightmare at Cogburn Hall, and the Widow's last words, I resolved to push it aside. There would be time later to ponder what it all meant, but for now I wanted to correct our course back to its normal routine. We all needed it now.

And so the day unraveled much as it used to. Hiram, who I kept a close eye on, showed no signs of the trauma that had been inflicted on him. If Polly remembered what had happened, she did not mention it. Samuel, whose health was like a tide, rising and ebbing for so long, had recovered significantly, although his hacking cough crept up on him now and again. I would have to monitor that.

My uncle seemed content to have his family clanging around him at the breakfast table, but he was unusually quiet, and I could see distraction kept tugging his attention from us. The "business" he mentioned the night before began to trouble my stomach. Mid-morning, he went to fetch his cap and walking stick and handed my bonnet to me. We were going for a walk into town, he told me, but said nothing more when I inquired the purpose behind it.

The sun was warm on my face and I was glad to be in the fresh air after a day cooped up in bed. Gaining the high street, I had hoped to run across Henry or Will, even if it were to simply wave hello. Will especially. I was worried about the gash to his skull and whether it was being looked after. Although Will rarely spoke of his mother, I had heard gossip that the woman was quite odd and feeble. Some claimed she was even a drunkard who would have perished long ago if not for the care from her own children. I do not know if this was true and should refrain from repeating gossip. I was simply worried about him.

We encountered neither young man on our walk. In fact, there seemed to be fewer people about at all. The thoroughfare was often bustling with wagons and horses and citizenry side-stepping the road apples left in the dusty street. When Pardon led the way to Beecham's Landing, my heart lit up. I just might see Henry after all.

He was there, but he was not glad to see me. He looked

positively cowed as if he had received some terrible news. My first thought was that the consumption had touched their house, but this was not the case as both his parents were there, along with his sister Agnes. Other than these three, the taproom was empty. When we entered, the girl was sent from the room.

Arthur Beecham was grim-faced, his wife, Martha, ramrod straight with a hard set to her features. My stomach began to churn. When Pardon asked me to go stand at the hearth where Henry was, I began to feel sick. The three parents stood facing us like an inquisition.

Arthur spoke first. "We know what you did. You have shamed both of our families with your indiscretions."

My knees wobbled. This can't be happening.

"I cannot speak for you, Pardon," said Martha Beecham. "But I blame myself. I tried my best to bring Henry up right in a moral and God-fearing way, but it is clear that I have failed."

My uncle cleared his throat. He was not angry like the other two, but he was painfully disappointed and that cut worse than any anger he could have displayed. "I must also shoulder the blame," he said, "for this lack of moral guidance."

I was drowning, unable to catch my breath. On the other side of the hearth, Henry was like stone, his glare fixed on some knotty spot on the floor. The only emotion I could parse from his red face was that of shame.

My voice, when it came, cracked in my throat. "Please, let me explain—"

"What is there to explain?" demanded Arthur. "It is not complicated to understand. It is as simple as two rutting dogs in heat."

Henry spoke. His voice was seething. "How did you know?"

"Why?" asked his mother. "So you can deny it?"

Henry kept his mouth shut. There was nothing either of us could say. Any response would only condemn us further.

"You were seen," said Pardon. "By the Hazard boy. And the three of us had the displeasure of being informed by his father. Can you imagine our mortification?"

Tom Hazard. That pinch-faced little bastard. He must have followed us out to the bower the night Henry was celebrating. He spied on us and ran tattling to his father. I vowed to bash his brains in the next time I saw him.

"The fault is mine," I blurted out. I don't know why I was scooping up all the blame, but I couldn't bear to see Henry shamed like this. My shoulders were broad enough to bear it. "I was upset and not thinking clearly that night. And I—"

"Stop!" Martha snapped at me. "We will not discuss the sordid details. Have you no shame, Hester Stokely?"

I shut my mouth. I wished that this were an actual firing squad we faced. At least it would be over quickly.

Pardon and Martha and Arthur turned away for a moment to talk out of our earshot. They seemed to debate some points between them. Our punishment, I suppose. I risked a side glance at Henry, but he would not look at me. My thought was this; we have destroyed our future. Mine was already closed, a spinster in my uncle's house, but Henry's was bright and full of promise. I had ruined it.

Our inquisitors adjourned their debate and turned to face us again.

"There is only one way to save all of us from ruin," Martha declared. "The two of you are to be wed. Immediately and without fuss."

My jaw fell with an audible pop. I must have misheard her. Beside me, Henry sputtered like there was a fish bone caught in his craw.

"Married?" he spat back at his mother. "You must be joking!"

"Quiet!" his father bellowed at him. His tone was so imperious that it rattled the dishes on the shelf. "The marriage shall take place tonight in this room. There will be only our two families. Reverend Crane will officiate and Ebeneezer will notarize the union. We will disregard reading the banns and all other formalities."

I don't recall what was said after that. My head was spinning, and my balance was off. I felt Pardon take my arm and lead me out of the inn. He spoke quietly as we walked home but not a word of it registered with me. Only one thought bounced around inside my skull, like a caged bird: Henry and I were going to be wed!

~

It was by no means a lavish affair. For a wedding dress, my uncle let me pilfer his late wife's wardrobe. My own clothes were drab

and shabby, even my church clothes, and would not do. I chose
the teal dress that Mother Stokely wore for the rare cotillion balls
with a darker petticoat underneath. The jacket was a dark brocade
with a high collar. The veil was also Katherine's, saved from her
own wedding day, and I was proud to drape it over my face.

After outfitting the children into their Sunday best and helping Jacob with his tie, our small party piled into the wagon and
trotted off into town. Even old Caesar was trumped up, as Pardon had adorned his mane with a few garlands. I did not have
time to brush out the dog, but Lucky didn't seem to care, ambling
after the wagon with his tongue lolling.

The taproom at the inn was cheery with a bouquet of wildflowers near the door and a gentle fire in the hearth. The Stokelys,
all five of them, assembled on one side as the Beechams took up
positions on the opposite end. Alongside Mr. And Mrs. Beecham
were Henry's sister, Agnes, and his aunt Madeline. Ebeneezer
Wickes took a seat near the back with his registry balanced on his
lanky knees and Reverend Crane stood before the fireplace with
the Bible in his hand.

Henry was a sight in his starched shirt and ivory cravat under a prim tailcoat. He looked so dashing and handsome that I
could not stop grinning like a fool beneath my veil. His demeanor
was difficult to parse. He bowed politely and a small smile fluttered his lips, but that was all. We hadn't spoken since this morning and here we were, walking down the makeshift aisle to be cast
into the volcano of matrimony. A pagan sacrifice, I mused, to
redeem the moral honor of our collective families. Although neither of us were pure anymore. That was an omen I chose not to
heed.

Of the ceremony itself, I remember very little. I was light-
headed and not myself, gaping in disbelief at what was taking
place. I recited some words about honor and duty and fealty, but
little of it made sense in that moment. Then Henry lifted the veil,
and I was surprised to see the stern cut of his jaw. The kiss was
brief, the stroke of a butterfly wing, followed by a polite clapping
from the assembled guests.

A late supper was served of mushroom broth and blood
pudding, followed by a fricassee of quail with beetroot salad and
an unpleasant barley-and-raisin dish that I did not care for. There
was a heavy fruitcake that Henry sawed into, along with a serving

of Bishop's fingers. The wine was lovely, although I have had little experience of it. I'll admit I was a little squiffy by the time coffee was served. Henry certainly imbibed his own weight of the stuff and more than once I caught his father firing a scolding glance at his son. Ebeneezer Wickes laid his registry before us and each of us signed our names to it. I noted with some surprise that Henry scribed an X in place of his signature. Could my groom not sign his own name?

Dusting the wet ink, Ebeneezer declared the union official and complete. Peg-Leg Wilkins had been hired to arrive at the end of the dinner to rattle out a tune on his fiddle, but he did not show. Presumably he was snoring away against the side of a barn with a bottle in his hand. No one danced.

When the supper was concluded, Pardon approached us alongside Henry's parents to grant us a wedding gift. It was a cottage to call our very own. They had purchased it together that very morning.

I couldn't believe my ears. A cottage for Henry and me to make into a home. How could such good fortune shine down on two people, I wondered? I had done nothing to deserve such bounty and an exquisite guilt gnawed at my belly.

This is a dream. Surely I will wake in my own miserable cot. Or worse, I will find myself in a coffin inside the ghastly vault, unable to find the bell string to call for help. My thoughts turned to such dark places now. Perhaps it was just the wine.

The feast over, we climbed into our wagon and the Beecham's climbed into theirs, the handsome one with the cheery sign on the box. We rattled across town, past the common and the meetinghouse and down a lane behind the tannery. Situated behind a scrabbly spruce hedge rose a small shack of dingy lime mortar with a roof of moss-covered shingles. The veranda was tiny, and the tilting post gave the impression that the whole thing would cave in. A ginger cat dozed on the front step. It scampered when it spotted Lucky.

Henry jumped down out of the carriage. "I know this place," he said. "This is Mr. Barrow's cottage."

"It was," replied Pardon. "But he died with no heirs, so your father and I purchased it."

"At a goodly price, too," added Arthur.

Henry looked over the old shack. "I can see why."

I don't know what I was expecting. A quaint cottage with a rosebush under the window, I suppose. The late Mr. Barrow, whom I had last seen in the crypt, had not kept his home in good condition. I was reluctant to see inside of it.

"It will need some work, obviously," Pardon said. "But it will give you a chance to reshape it to suit the two of you. The boys and I will help with the repairs."

Martha sat stiffly in the wagon. "We've provided a few essentials. There on the table. Enough to get you started, at least."

"Enjoy," hollered Arthur.

With that, they climbed back into the wagons and trundled off, leaving Henry and I stranded before this forlorn little abode. I suppose we must have seemed like lost children in a storybook, staring up at a witch's cottage. It leered down at us, eager to swallow us both.

"Shall we?" Henry said, tugging the front door open. The hinges squealed.

The inside was dreary and quite small. One room comprised both kitchen and parlor, with a small bedroom and a pantry set behind it. There was a table and two battered chairs, a massive butcher's block near the washstand and a sooty fireplace with a dingy mantel. The only nice piece of furniture was the ottoman before the hearth. The embroidered seat was of a Turkish pattern and the scrollwork detailed with leaves and acorns. It stood apart from everything as if pilfered from a rich home and set oddly within this ramshackle hut.

There was a basket on the table. I lifted out some bed sheets, clean but not new, along with a teapot and a few dishes and two mugs. Henry recognized them as belonging to the taproom. There was cheese wrapped in cloth and some bread, a small vial of salt and a greenglass bottle of cider.

Henry uncorked the bottle as soon as I had the fire going. We stood before the glow of the hearth with cups in our hands, but few words on our tongues.

"Well," he said, staring into the flames. "How did we end up here?"

His eyes were glazed and shining. We were both a little bubbly from the drink.

"It's been quite a storm in a teacup, I suppose." My head was full of vapors. Idle chitchat seemed impossible.

He grunted a laugh and then pulled the ottoman over and sat.

I said, "I know this is unexpected, but I hope you are not unhappy. I don't wish to make you miserable, Henry."

"Nor I you. I am sure this is not how you imagined your wedding day, is it?" He raised his glass to me. "We shall make the best of it."

"Agreed." I was truly content in that moment, smiling at my husband across the fire. My husband, I thought.

We chatted for a while, joking over the state of our crumbling little cottage. And then it was time for bed. My belly flipped and flopped inside me, dreading and anticipating this moment. It was confusing to say the least.

We lit candles and looked down at the bed. It was not very big. There was a headboard, but it was chipped in many places and Henry joked that old Barrow had made notches in it to mark his conquests. We laid the clean sheets over it and Henry kicked off his boots and threw his jacket onto the broken chair in the corner. He sat back against that scarred headboard and told me to undress.

I did as I was told, but the wine had left me less graceful than I had wished. The laces and the buttons and the folds, it all took time to unravel. I stood before him, vulnerable and thrilled and my skin prickled in gooseflesh. I plucked the bones from my hair and let it fall, draping it self-consciously down to hide the scar on my jaw line. That was the part of myself that I was shy about.

Henry smiled then and I went to him. The candles burned all the way down, and in the morning, there was a puddle of hard wax on the windowsill.

35

I AWOKE WITH a start at the unfamiliar lumps in the bed and the foreign damp stain on the ceiling above me. Then my eyes fell on Henry, balanced on the broken chair and reality had me upright. I was married and lying in the conjugal bed. The man pulling his boots on, the man I had been smitten with for as long as I could remember, was my husband. I would have pinched myself but there was no need as a needle of hay poking from the mattress under me was sharp enough.

"Good morning," I said. I pulled the sheet up to my chin. The boldness of our wedding night had vanished with the sunlight streaming through the grimy window.

Henry grunted, stamping his heel against the floor to get the boot on. His eyes were bloodshot, and his temper seemed short. Wine vapors will do that to you.

"Where are you going?"

He stood, tucking his shirt tails under his belt. "I have to go see Mr. Hendershot about his beef cattle. He's being stingy about his prices since his latest child was born. No doubt his wife is pressuring him to fleece his loyal buyers."

"Oh," I said. "Will you be home by noon?"

He ran his hand through his tangled hair, annoyed at my questions. "I have a lot to do today, Hester. I'll be back this evening."

I wanted to ask for a kiss, but his patience was clearly thin, so I let him go. I did not know if it was the wine vapors that made him testy or if he was simply crabby in the morning. There was so much about him that I didn't know, in fact. How does one meld two lives together? I suppose I was about to learn.

I reclined in bed for a while longer, luxuriating in the unfamiliar delicacy of an empty house. There was no one clanging the table for their breakfast or wanting help with pressing a shirt or feeding the animals. After living cheek-by-jowl in a busy household, the sheer indulgence of solitude was as heady as wedding wine.

I got dressed, started the fire and looked over the shabby abode of the late Mr. Barrow that was now to be the nest for Henry and me. The drab walls and crumbling ceiling left me with no good feelings. I set about scrubbing every surface in sight. The ceramic inlay of the washstand was stained yellow and would not relent no matter how much I scoured it. The horsehair plaster crumbled under my rag where I tried to scrub the mold away. Sweeping the floor, one of the boards tipped under my heel and popped loose. There I found a curious thing scratched into the underside of the board. A witch mark burnt into the raw wood. It was meant to ward off evil coming from below and I could only assume that Mr. Barrow had put it there himself. Since he was dead, the protective symbol, a crude star, was now toothless. I found an awl among the clattering junk in a drawer and set about scribing my own hex sign into the raw side of the loose floorboard. The configuration I chose was a daisy head circled with a ring. As the new occupants, this mark would ward off any evil spirits from below. Slotting the board back into place, I realized I needed to address the other points of entry in our home to protect them properly.

The door at the back of the house opened onto an unkempt yard where the outbuildings sank in tall grass. Using the awl, I scratched the same daisy symbol into the brittle mortar over the door. Crossing to the front of the cottage, I found the veneer over the main entrance to be clean and without fracture and was reluctant to scratch it up. I found a scrap of paper and a piece of lead and drew the same symbol there. Below it I scrawled out my name and Henry's, followed by three crosses. The paper was rolled tight and, standing on a chair, I slipped it into the seam of the lintel beam. This way my talisman would be fitted into the bones of the house, ensuring our protection. More than the cleaning or even the lovemaking, this made the cottage our home, safe from harm and things that skulked in the darkness.

All the scrubbing and sweeping made little difference as the small house seemed as drab as before. Frustrated, I closed it up and walked back home. Or the Stokely homestead, I should say. It wasn't my home now. Lucky came bounding out of the gate to greet me and bounced around my shins as I cooed to him. I decided I would take him home with me. If anything could bring cheer to our grubby little cottage, a dog was it.

The kitchen was in a disastrous state as the two older boys had prepared their noontime meal, but the family seemed contented and happy to see me. Much of the gloom had diminished and the house was noisy with chatter and the crabbing of one sibling against another. Now and then, someone would mention Prudence or Faith or Mother Stokely as if the person was in the other room and the remembrance of them would quiet the chatter. But that was not a bad thing for it meant that they were very much in our thoughts and in our hearts. We all were still adjusting to the fact that they were really gone.

My uncle asked how Henry and I were getting along in our new home and I, without sounding ungrateful, told him of the repairs it would need and the lack of furniture.

I happily spent most of the day with them and the warmth I felt struck me as wryly funny. Now that I felt truly a part of this odd, lovely family, I had been removed from it. This was not a complaint or grousing but simply an observation.

Towards evening, I gathered up some of my clothes and personal effects and left for home with the dog trotting at my heels. He looked up at me with such devotion in his big eyes as we made our way through town that I stopped every once in a while to nuzzle his ears in gratitude. I wondered if Henry would come to adore the poor mutt as much as I did. How could he not?

A few people greeted me on my way and others seemed to shun me. Mrs. Amblin wished me well and Peg-Leg doffed his hat to me in his oafish manner. Mrs. Van Tassel looked the other way when I waved to her and stiff-lipped Halton Hazard glared at me as I passed. I kept an eye peeled for any sign of his loathsome son for I wanted to box Tom Hazard's ears, but the little troll was nowhere to be seen. Passing the printer's shop, I did see Elizabeth Wickes. She was without her hens and seemed less glamorous than usual. She froze when she saw me and then burst into tears and ran. It must have been a shock to learn of Henry's abrupt nuptials and the poor thing was now left brokenhearted. And I was struck with the odd sensation of having pity for my former rival. Nothing is simple, is it?

I decided to take a rambling path home, off the high road to the back end of town where the houses were smaller and not so grand. I came to the Treves home and saw Will in the front yard stacking wood.

I called out his name and he looked up from his labor, his face lit wide. "Hester!"

Crossing the yard to meet me, he was greeted by the dog colliding into his shins and circling his knees. He thumped Lucky's ribs to settle him. "Easy, boy."

"I'm not sure which of us is happier to see you," I said. "You look well, Will."

"That's a lie, but thank you anyway," he replied. "You look lovely today. But then you always do."

I was momentarily taken aback until I realized he was having sport with me. "Very funny, Mr. Treves."

His broad smile wilted, his tone became formal. "I hear congratulations are in order."

"Oh yes, thank you," I stammered, my cheeks warming. "It's all very sudden."

"Shocking, more like. I wasn't aware that Henry was courting you."

"Yes, well, we kept it quiet." My stomach clenched tight. Not more lies, not to Will. But what choice did I have? Did he know the reason behind the quick marriage? I prayed he didn't. "You know me. I don't like fuss or extravagance. Besides, I've been smitten with Henry for a long time."

"I know."

His expression was difficult to read. Was he disappointed in me or ashamed? Saddened, even? Either way, the cast stung at me and I looked at my feet. I was eager to change the subject.

"You've recovered from our ordeal?" I asked him. "No lingering injuries?"

Shaking off his diffident expression, he raised his right arm. Sneaking from the empty sleeve came the severed stump bound with linen. "My arm swelled up where the teeth got me. Left me a little feverish, like a snake bite, but it's healing."

"I hope it's nothing serious." I held his arm still to inspect the bandage. It was damp and grimy. "You should change this dressing."

He withdrew his arm. "Have you heard any news about the widow?"

"No. Have you?"

"No one's seen her," he said. "Either she was killed in the blaze or she fled."

"I pray it was the fire." A shudder rippled from my shoulders to the small of my back. I wanted to forget the whole ordeal, but it was always there, skulking in the shadows of my memory.

"It's all a bit blurry to me. The way nightmares are." His brow creased and his focus narrowed. "That stone coffin. You saw it, too, didn't you? I didn't imagine that part of it?"

"How could I forget it? Why do you ask?"

He scratched his head as if unsure how to proceed. "I went back there with Ebenezer and Mr. Corwin. They wanted to know what started the fire. I wanted to make sure there was nothing left."

My belly flipped. "Did you tell them the fire was deliberate?"

He shook his head. "I told them we saw the smoke from the road and rushed inside to find the tenant. Which is a partial truth, I suppose." His voice softened although there was no one around to overhear us. "There was nothing but ash. I found no stone coffin there, nor any bones."

"Perhaps it was buried under the rubble?"

"I kicked through all of that ashy mess. It's not there."

I didn't want to think about it. "Maybe it was all pulverized when the house collapsed. It was clearly very old."

"Perhaps," he said. Another shrug. "I hope so."

The dog yapped at the scraggly chicken in the yard, and Will called him back. He bent to scratch the dog's ear and Lucky's tail wagged furiously in response. Will looked up at me, squinting against the daylight. "I can't decide if we should tell the selectmen what we saw."

The shrug this time was mine. "What would be the point? Would they believe us? Or blame us somehow? The way they blamed Ephraim?"

The dog bolted again, darting for the road after something only he could see. I called to him, but Lucky paid me no heed.

"I should go," I said. "Before he murders someone's poultry."

"Of course." Will offered a small bow to me. "Congratulations again, Hester. I hope Henry knows what a fortunate man he is."

Again I was taken aback by something in his tone. The rawness of it dug under my skin and demanded a reply of commensurate weight. So I took hold of his hand.

"Thank you, Will, for helping me. I know your loyalty to my uncle makes you amenable, but I can't tell you how much it means to me."

Lucky was barking in the distance and Will wagged his chin in his direction. "You better catch that dog."

I ran off, but I heard him call out to me. "It's not Pardon that I'm loyal to!"

In my haste to catch the silly dog, I did not stop to puzzle out his parting shot.

~

Henry was not home when I returned to the dusty cottage behind the tannery. No matter, I thought. I had pilfered my uncle's larder for some provisions and set about making a hearty meal for my new husband. The dog spent the good part of an hour sniffing around the house and the yard outside, inspecting every nook and cranny and marking the perimeter of the drooping fence. By the time the stew bubbled to perfection in the cauldron over the fire, Lucky was fast asleep on the fancy ottoman.

A moment later, his head lifted from the cushion with his ears up. The door banged open and Henry swept into our little home, surveying the small quarters that comprised both kitchen and parlor. The rough-milled table held place settings for two with candles aglow and three daisies in a small glass. Humble yes, but appropriate to our means as the newly betrothed.

He looked me over like he was surprised to see me. "Hello."

I returned his greeting. We stood at opposite ends of the room and an awkward stiffness filled the small cottage. I brushed it aside and went to kiss him and help him out of his coat. His breath smelled a little of brandy and something else that I couldn't place. Lilacs?

"Come sit," I said. "You must be hungry."

"I am," he declared. Sniffing the air, he said, "That smells good. What is it?"

"Rabbit and hominy."

He dropped into a chair with the grace of a rag doll.

"You've been imbibing," I said.

"Celebrating," he corrected me. "The lads insisted on toasting my rise in society. Isn't that a laugh?"

"Very." I hadn't meant to sound so cutting.

"Is there any of the cider left?"

"It's all gone," I replied. Of the glassware that we owned, there were two receptacles, both mismatched. I held up his. The water inside was cloudy. "We have this. Something is amiss with the well."

"Wonderful," was his droll response.

I set out the bowls of stew and Henry tucked into it noisily. He stopped when the dog emerged from under the table and hopped onto the ottoman. Henry looked at me, one eyebrow arched high.

"Hester, did you know there is a stray dog in our house?"

"Yes. That's Lucky. Didn't I tell you about him?"

"The mutt from Bountiful?" He shrugged and resumed scooping up the stew. "He'll be a good guard dog, I suppose."

"If we are ever besieged by yard fowl, yes."

Henry leaned back in his chair, contented. I cleared the dishes away quickly. It wasn't very late, but I wondered if we should retire. The anticipation of it was making my face hot.

"Are you tired, my dear?" I asked him. Employing the endearment gave me a little thrill.

"Let's sit by the fire." He rose and chased the dog from his roost. The embroidered ottoman was not only the nicest piece of furniture, but it was the only piece in the parlor. He pulled it closer to the fire and said, "Come sit here."

"Where will you sit?"

He stretched out on the floor with his boots toward the

hearth. "This will do." Brushing a palm against the rough floor-boards, he added, "We'll need to get a good rug for this."

I felt the warmth of the fire and wished there were something to serve after dinner. We had no port or sherry, or even any tea. Our destitute pantry held only a cracked jar of salt and a few dried cloves.

I set another piece of wood onto the fire and resumed my seat. The dog came to me and lay across my toes.

"Why the long face?" Henry asked. "Do you brood?"

"I'm still pinching myself," I said. "But I'm not brooding. I'm happy. I'm just not sure I deserve to be."

He sat up, folding his hands in his lap. "What do you mean?"

"This." I gestured to the house around us. "The hearth. The husband. Even the dog. This was not to be my destiny. Prudence was the one who was to be married. But she's gone, as is her man, James. But here I sit."

A spark popped from the fire and landed on his knee. He brushed it away. "I'm not sure if deserve has anything to do with it. God's will can be fickle. And arbitrary. It is useless to demand some meaning out of it all."

I didn't have an answer to that, so I watched the fire. The dog sighed. I turned to my husband.

"Shall we go to bed?"

"Will you read to me?"

"Read to you?"

"Yes," he said. "Letters do not come easily for me. But I like to be read to. Indulge me."

Here now was another detail that I was ignorant of. "Of course," I said and rose to fetch one of the books standing upright on the windowsill. Four volumes made up the totality of the late Mr. Barrow's library. Two were almanacs dated long ago, and another was a ledger of some kind. The last book was the Lives of the Saints, which made me smile as it reminded me of Faith.

"Our library is quite selective," I told him as I set the volume on my knees. "Is there any particular saint you would like to hear about?"

"Saints?" he repeated skeptically. "Sounds thrilling."

"Some of these hagiographies are quite strange." I flipped through the pages and stopped at one that I recognized. "Here.

Saint Barbara had an unusual life. We'll try this."

I swiveled on my perch to face him directly and catch the light of the fire and began to read the story of this noblewoman from the fourth century. Henry crossed his boots one over the other and watched me. When I glanced up at him, he sported a small frown.

"Is the story boring?" I asked.

"The story's fine," he said. "Turn your position to the left a little."

I pivoted a few degrees, presenting a third-quarter profile of my good side. "This is better?"

"It is."

"How so?" I asked. I knew the answer.

"The light favors you this way."

I read on.

Acknowledgements

Books can be messy beasts, but luckily there are friends and allies along the way to help wrangle them into shape. I want to thank Brian Francis for his encouragement, helpful bitch 'n beer sessions, and notes on fugly first drafts. Thanks also to Jeff McFarlane, because you are missed. Your influence is in here somewhere. A tip of the hat to scholar, Michael E. Bell, whose work on New England vampires lit a fire of inspiration. Huge thanks to Samantha Kolesnik and Off Limits Press for giving this little book a home. Many thanks to editor Karmen Wells for tightening all the bolts. Existential thanks goes to author/podcaster Joanna Penn for her enthusiasm, and life-saving advice on "comparisonitis." A metric ton of thanks to my wife, who makes everything possible, every single day. I also want to thank my mom, a supporter since day one.

Tim McGregor is the author of the *Spookshow* series and the *Bad Wolf* trilogy, along with a handful of standalone novels. Tim is the screenwriter behind three feature films, and a member of the Horror Writers Association. He lives in Toronto with his wife, children, and the spiteful ghost of an old Irish lady.

9 780578 840512